THE MEMORIES WE HIDE

JODI GIBSON

VERB PUBLISHING

First published in Australia in 2019
By Jodi Gibson
https://jfgibson.com.au/

Copyright © Jodi Gibson 2019

Print ISBN 978-0-6485512-0-1
Epub ISBN 978-0-6485512-1-8

Cover design Stuart Bache

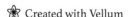 Created with Vellum

DEDICATION

For my girls. Dreams do come true.

1

Autumn 2018

LAURA ZIPPED UP the suitcase on her bed and exhaled as the deep ache inside her intensified. This ache was one she had experienced constantly for the past nine years. One she'd learned to live with. An ache of loss. An ache of guilt. And now the ache was so much more complicated. It wasn't every day that her mum rang to tell her she had advanced stage cancer. That she didn't have long *to go*. It wasn't every day that Laura resigned from her job at the beauty salon in order to spend every moment possible with her dying mother.

Laura sucked in a shaky breath as she pulled the suitcase off the bed and glanced around the room. She wondered why she felt such a finality at packing her suitcase and leaving her Melbourne apartment, as if it were for the last time.

The bedroom door swung open, and Laura jumped, her nerves

on edge. Luke, her fiancé, came in and placed his hand on her shoulder. 'You okay?' he asked.

Laura nodded, afraid that if she spoke her voice would give away the fact that she was far from okay.

'Babe,' he continued, 'I know I said I'd be able to come up on weekends to visit you and your mum, but I'm not sure how often it'll be. You know, with work and everything.'

Laura frowned. 'What do you mean?'

'I've put my hand up for the promotion.'

'Now? And?'

'Well, I can't just up and leave on a Friday night and be three hundred odd kilometers away in the middle of nowhere. Do they even have internet there?'

'Of course we have internet! It may be a small country town, but it's not the Dark Ages.'

Luke ran his hands through his slicked-back hair. 'It's just there'll be more meetings, more trips to Sydney. It's bad timing.'

Laura's hackles rose. 'Well I'm sorry my mother's cancer is inconvenient for you.'

Luke dropped his hands to his hips. 'Come on. You know I don't mean that. I'm simply saying I may not be able to get there every weekend, that's all.'

Laura swallowed back a lump of realization in her throat.

'I'm sorry, babe, but you know how important this promotion is. It will set us up for life. We could finally get married, buy a house, start a family.'

Laura shook her head. 'I can't think about things like that right now. My mother is dying!'

'I know, it's awful. But, we have to think about our future too,' Luke said, reaching toward her.

Laura batted his hand away. 'This is so typical of you, Luke.

Work always comes first. I thought you'd have my back on this and be there for me.'

'I am, babe, but—'

'And stop calling me babe. You know I hate it.'

Luke cocked his head to the side and slumped his shoulders. 'Look, I know you're hurting, and believe me, if I could do anything to change things, I would, but ...'

With a clenched her jaw and her body shaking with adrenaline Laura reached for her suitcase and turned toward the door.

'Laura, hey, come on. Don't leave things this way. Let's talk it through.'

Laura paused in the doorway and looked back at Luke, wondering what she ever saw in him. Sure, he'd charmed her with his Brad Pitt smile and Chris Hemsworth biceps, and his promises of the world as he climbed the advertising ladder. But, when it came down to it, when it really mattered, he never had her back. This wasn't the first time, and she knew it wouldn't be the last. Work always took priority for Luke. Money and status were his first loves—probably his only loves. Why had it taken so goddamn long for her to realize that?

'I'm not one of your clients who will *talk it through*. I'm not doing this anymore. It's over, Luke. Goodbye,' she said coolly.

It wasn't until she stepped into the elevator that she let the tears flow. She expected Luke to chase after her. Apologize. She even paused in the car for a moment, but he didn't follow, and in fact, Laura realized she didn't care. Instead, she felt a sense of relief. Pleased she'd found a strength within herself she hadn't realized she possessed. She started the engine, her emotions still high.

· · ·

HALF AN HOUR LATER, Laura found herself backed up in the afternoon traffic trying to navigate the exit to the Hume Freeway. She was stuck between a garbage truck and a semi, crawling along slower than a Melbourne winter. She tapped her fingers on the steering wheel and chewed the inside of her cheek. 'Come on!' she whispered under her breath, not sure if she was more frustrated with her thoughts that wouldn't shut up or the crawl of traffic and insistent rumble of the garbage truck in front of her.

The traffic ground to a halt, and Laura stretched her neck to relieve the tension, the glint of the diamond on her left ring finger catching her eye. She slipped it from her finger and dropped it into the center console. Out of sight, out of mind. If only she could rewind her life back to happier times. Simpler times. But when? She was only twenty-seven, and yet, the only time she remembered being truly happy was during her childhood, when it was just her and her mum in small-town Banyula. She shook her head. Things had changed dramatically since then in ways she didn't want to remember. Laura felt the tears begin to form and bit her lip to stop them. *Was that really the last time I was happy?*

The sharp sound of a car horn jolted her back to the present, and she pushed down on the accelerator, realizing the traffic had begun to move again. Time to shut away useless thoughts like that and focus on getting back safely to her mum.

AFTER SHE HAD FINALLY ESCAPED the city traffic, Laura found herself focusing on the broken white lines of the country highway. The last time she was on this stretch of road, she was traveling in the opposite direction, away from her mother's weatherboard cottage on the tree-lined street near the railway line. The railway line. That was always the memory that caused her thoughts to snag. Nostalgia was mixed with the harsh truth of why Laura had left almost ten years earlier and had never been able to return. But, like a shadow, her past was always right behind her. She had come one hundred eighty degrees, the city an almost nonexistent speck in the rearview mirror. Every kilometer brought her closer, brought her back to her childhood home.

She chastised herself for the selfish emotions consuming her energy. She should be thinking of her mum right now. Nothing else should matter. But it was too late. Well-hidden memories once pushed purposely into the back of her mind had come forward again. She knew it was inevitable. That going back wouldn't be just about looking after her mum in her last days. Everything she'd run from all those years ago would resurface. She'd have to face Tom. And what about Rachel? She'd have to cross that railway line every single day.

She switched on the radio to take her mind off things, the sultry voice of Whitney Houston's 'Saving All My Love' filtered through the speakers. She smiled. Her mum loved Whitney.

The large green sign ahead indicated 320km to Banyula, and all of a sudden Laura felt an overwhelming sense of nausea wash over her, the saltiness rising to the back of her throat. She pulled the car to a halt on the gravel at the side of the road and opened the door. She made it to the grass just in time.

2

Banyula was a typical country town, big enough to be more than a speck on the map, but small enough that it felt more like a community than a town. At least, that's how Laura remembered it. Her mum had told her about the changing weather patterns and the effects on the local farmers, and there was growing concern about the lack of jobs in the area to keep people around, especially with the relocation of the textile mill to a more viable location. And there was, of course, the other mill that kept small towns running, and running hot: the gossip mill. Everyone knew everyone's business, or at least they thought they did. That was something Laura liked about the big city. No one cared. Everyone was too wrapped up in their own lives to worry about anyone else's, which Laura knew wasn't a great thing either, but it had suited her, especially when she'd first moved to Melbourne. No one really asked where she was from. She was able to get away with brushing over details and waving things off, always turning the conversation back to the other person. You couldn't do that in a place like Banyula.

The sun hung low in the western sky as Laura hit the outskirts of the township. A mass of clouds with undertones of dark gray gathered along the distant ranges. The gas station, which had once been a bright welcoming beacon with its large golden shell sign, was now boarded up, the sign faded and dull. There was a new electronics store a bit farther along, its hot pink façade almost insulting to the ranges and slopes on the horizon. Laura indicated, taking a left turn to avoid the main street. She wasn't ready to be seen by anyone just yet, though she wondered how long she could remain unnoticed, then scoffed at the thought. No more than five minutes, probably.

Laura saw the railway line up ahead, jutting as always through the quiet streets, separating one side of town from the other. There was no way around it, only over. She gripped the steering wheel, her knuckles turning white and her chest feeling like it held a flock of panicked birds within, their wings beating at her ribs trying to escape. She almost closed her eyes as her Mazda 3 bumped over the lines and then onto the smooth asphalt of the other side. She pulled to the curb a hundred meters up the road and exhaled.

Laura's heart calmed after a minute, and she looked at her childhood home. The weatherboards were not as white as she remembered, now tinged cream with age. The purple clematis bush had overtaken the front corner of the garden, stringy and overgrown, a willy wagtail dancing from side to side upon one of the vines without a care in the world. The pale, blue-front picket fence that Laura had helped her mum paint when she was eight was peeling and weather beaten, and the red tin roof was faded from too many relentless, hot summers that this part of the country knew all too well.

After grabbing her bags, Laura followed the concrete path to the front door, avoiding the cracks like she used to when she was younger. She glanced over her shoulder, feeling as if someone was watching her, and noticed Mrs. Hatfield peeking out from behind her curtains in the red brick bungalow across the street. She had to be at least ninety now. She gave Laura a nod from her worn face and disappeared behind the lace.

'Mum?' Laura called softly as she opened the front door, pausing before stepping across the scratched wooden threshold. She placed her bags against the wall and walked slowly down the hallway. Her old bedroom was to her left, the living room to her right, and at the end of the hall, the kitchen. Tears pricked at her eyes as she pictured herself running down the hallway, the floorboards creaking under her feet, as her mum called her for dinner. 'Stop running down the hall! You sound like an elephant!' her mother would call out.

The kitchen was just as she remembered. The old-style kettle, pale blue with a white dove on the end of the spout that whistled when it came to a boil, sat in its usual place at the center of the stovetop. Matching blue-and-white tea towels hung from the door of the wood-burning stove. The iconic blue-and-white willow-patterned dinner set was still proudly displayed on the wooden shelves. Below on the counter, Judy's favorite teacup—the Wedgwood 'Daisy' blue—sat lonely on its matching saucer. Laura picked up the cup and ran her finger around the gold rim, which had faded due to accidental meetings with the dishwasher over time. 'This teacup does not go in the dishwasher, Laura,' her mum's voice echoed in her head. 'See! The gold is wearing away.'

A warm tear ran down Laura's cheek. She placed the cup back on the saucer and walked through the back sitting room and toward her mum's bedroom. She could smell a hint of White Diamonds—her mum's favorite perfume—the subtle scent of rose, jasmine, and sandalwood ingrained in the walls.

'Mum?' Laura pushed open the door slowly to see her mother

lying peacefully under the rose-patterned quilt. Although the room was dim thanks to the blinds, Laura's breath caught in her throat as she saw Judy. Her face was soft, but the fleshy cheeks Laura used to love kissing were now sunken into her angled cheekbones. And her mum's hair, once thick and shiny, fell limp and dull beside her head. Laura was torn between wanting to hold her mother and sob or running away. She looked away, blinking back the tears.

'Laura? Is that you?'

'Yes, Mum. It's me.' Laura turned back, smiled, and then fell onto the bed embracing her mother, the tears falling freely.

'Oh, darling. I've missed you.'

'Me too, Mum. Me too.'

THAT EVENING LAURA fell into her old bed and pulled the covers to her chin. Seeing her mother like this had caught her more off guard than she'd expected. Guilt weighed heavily on her heart, regret cutting into her chest for being so selfish the past ten years. For letting her self-centered problems come between her and her mother, rendering Laura paralyzed and unable to return home all these years. Judy had made the effort to visit Laura in the city a couple of times each year, including every Christmas—except the last one. Now Laura had to make up for all those years. She had to cram a lifetime of memories into whatever time they had left.

Laura swallowed her emotions. She'd be strong for her mother. She'd put aside her past and focus solely on Judy. She'd make sure of it.

LAURA WOKE EARLY the next morning, the quiet surroundings both familiar and strange after being in the city for so long. She looked at her phone. It was only 7:30 a.m., but Laura decided to get up and get a head start on the day. While preparing some pancakes, Laura looked up to see her mum appear in the doorway of the kitchen.

'Mum, should you be up and about?'

'Oh, Laura. Stop fussing. But I could use a nice hot cup of tea.'

Laura helped her mum into a chair at the table and poured her tea from the pot she'd just made.

'It's so good to have you here,' Judy said, reaching her hand across to Laura's.

'It's good to be here.'

'Now, I don't want you fussing over me, okay? Just having you here is enough for now. There will be a time ...,' Judy sighed and stared into her tea, 'soon, when, well ...'

'Mum. It's okay. I'm here, and that's all that matters for now.'

Judy looked up at Laura and smiled. 'You're right. That's all that matters.'

LAURA SPENT the next few days reminiscing with her mum, recalling times of both joy and heartbreak, but most of all just being with each other. Laura hadn't ventured out, apart from sneaking down to the supermarket first thing yesterday morning in her baseball cap and sunglasses, like some sort of celebrity wanting to slip under the radar. And it had worked. She hadn't run into anyone who had recognized her. But she also knew that wouldn't last long.

'Mum?' Laura said, poking her head around into the living room, which smelled like a fresh spring day thanks to the late autumn roses Laura had picked from the back garden and arranged into a vase on the mantle.

Judy opened her eyes from her chair by the window. The dated

Jason recliner, with soft pink velvet fabric that was now faded and worn, had a reclining action that would cause a screech louder than car tires when it reclined.. It had always been Judy's favorite. To Laura, the chair was as much a part of the family as anything.

'Just resting my eyes,' Judy said as she slowly edged herself up. 'It's lovely here by the window in the morning, even though there's not much sun.'

'This came for you,' Laura said, handing her mum an envelope with a beachscape printed across the bottom. 'I think it's a post-card inside.'

Judy took the letter. 'Can you pass my glasses, honey?' Judy motioned toward the floral glasses case on the side table. Laura opened the case, pulled out the bright purple frames and handed them to her mum.

Judy slid them onto her face, twitched her nose to adjust them, and ran her finger underneath the seal of the envelope. As she pulled out the postcard, Laura saw a line of camels parading across sand in front of a burnt orange sunset, the words *Broome – The Pearl of the North* emblazoned on the front in bold block letters. Judy flipped the postcard over, and Laura watched her eyes scan the short message.

'Who's in Broome?' Laura asked, puzzled.

'Janet and Mac Gordon.'

Laura shifted on the couch, smoothing down a frayed piece of fabric. Tom's parents. Guilt crawled down Laura's spine like a spider as she thought of Tom. Of how, after what happened to Ryan, she left so suddenly, cutting off all ties with Tom, her closest and oldest friend.

'It's wonderful, isn't it?'

Laura stood up. 'What's wonderful?' she said, adjusting the roses.

'That Tom's taken over the farm and Jan and Mac are off traveling. They always wanted to. As much as ol' Mac poo-hooed the idea for so long. And now, they're having the time of their lives, at least according to Janet. I'm sure Mac's still pulling on his grumpy pants now and then, though.' Judy chuckled warmly.

'How is Tom doing?' she asked, attempting to make her voice light.

'Tom? Busy on the farm, of course, but that's what he's always loved. He calls in once a week or so to say hi.'

Laura turned to face her mother. 'To see you? You never told me that,' she said, frowning.

'Really? I'm sure I did.' Judy sighed as she leaned the postcard against the windowsill. 'I'm sure he'll call around any day now.'

Laura stiffened.

'You know, you should call him or send him a Chatsnap or whatever it is you do these days,' she said. 'He's always asking after you.'

'He is?'

'Whenever I see him, yes.'

'He's just being polite.'

'You know very well it's more than that, Laura. You and Tom were such good friends. He's a nice boy, well, man now. I've always liked him.'

Laura shrugged the weight off her shoulders.

'It hit him badly too,' Judy said with a quiet voice, as if preempting Laura's reaction.

'I know, Mum. Please, just leave it.' Laura leaned against the wall, wishing she didn't have to take this trip down memory lane again. But it was hard. Everything, everyone, in Banyula screamed her past.

'Anyway,' Judy continued. 'Like I said, I'm sure he'll be around soon enough.'

Laura recognized the resignation with a touch of distaste in her mother's voice, and again the tingle of guilt pulsed through Laura's nerves. 'Yeah,' was all she could muster, preferring to cross that bridge when she came to it.

LATER THAT AFTERNOON, as the breeze picked up outside and the trees rustled against the roof, Laura stirred a pot of chicken soup on the stove while Judy rested in her bedroom. Laura had spent the day making a list of what needed to be done around the house. The backyard and front garden needed tending to, the laundry tap was leaking—probably just a washer—and a few of the kitchen cabinet doors needed readjusting. There was, of course, cleaning and packing to be done, but Laura wasn't ready to tackle any of that. That could wait.

A sharp rap on the glass beside the front door jolted Laura from her thoughts. She turned the gas down on the pot and wiped her hands on a tea towel, glancing at her watch—almost four p.m.

When Laura opened the door, she saw Tom, and it felt like she was transported back in time. Although it had been nearly ten years since she'd seen him, he didn't look a day older, save for some manly stubble and a few crow's-feet bordering his sky-blue eyes.

The look on his face also told her he wasn't expecting Laura to answer the door, as much as she wasn't expecting to see his face on the other side of it.

'Tom!' Laura gasped almost breathlessly.

'Wow. Laura. I ... I didn't realize you were ... I mean ...' Tom fumbled over his words as he turned his Akubra hat in his hands in front of him.

'Ah, yeah. I'm back. I'm here to look after Mum.' Laura swallowed.

'Of course. Yeah. Um ...' Tom ran his hand through his dark curls, his eyes darting from Laura to the ground.

'You here to see Mum?'

'Yeah. I usually call around when I'm in town. You know, just to see how she's doing.'

Laura nodded, opening the door a little wider. 'Um, come in. She's just resting.'

'Oh, no. Don't wake her. I'll come back another time.'

Laura's heart began to settle. 'You sure?' She wanted to add something more, like, 'I'll make you a cuppa' or 'We can catch up while we wait for her to wake.' But her tongue was caught on the roof of her mouth, something in her tightening chest preventing her from offering.

'Yeah. I'm in town again in a few days. I'll call back then.' Tom put his hat back on his head and nodded.

Laura forced a thin smile. 'Okay then.'

The air was thick with unspoken words as Tom stepped down the porch before turning back to Laura. 'It's good to see you, Laura. Really good.' And without waiting for a response, he turned and walked down the path.

Laura closed the door and leaned on it, listening as his Ute pulled away from the curb and disappeared into the neighborhood. Her heart thumped, and her eyes spilled fat tears down her cheeks. This was going to be harder than she'd thought.

3

OVER THE NEXT few days, Laura busied herself at home with her mum. They played Monopoly as the rain tinkled on the tin roof, watched old favorite TV shows like *Everybody Loves Raymond* and *McLeod's Daughters*, and sat together on the back porch each morning. Laura had run into a few people she knew during her trips to the grocery store and bakery but had managed to avoid stirring any memories that didn't need stirring.

Friday afternoon as Laura and Judy sat quietly in the living room, Judy resting her eyes and Laura scrolling through Facebook, Laura's messenger flashed on the screen. It was a message from Luke.

Hey, I'm sorry. I was an insensitive arse. As usual. Anyway, can we talk?

Laura stared at the message and at Luke's profile picture. It was a picture of them both, beanies pulled over their heads as they huddled on Brighton Beach on a freezing Melbourne day about four years ago. The memory should have brought a smile to Laura's face. It had been a sunny day and they'd decided to drive to the beach and take a walk, yet as soon as they arrived, Melbourne's 'four seasons in one day' kicked in, and the sky turned a dark gray as storm clouds gathered and a southerly wind blew off the bay. Shortly after the photo was taken, they'd found refuge in a café by a gas log fire and sipped coffee to warm up. But all the memory did was remind Laura how much she had been playing a role for the last ten years. The role of the heartbroken girl who had toughened up and moved on with her life, always looking forward, never back. She'd posted Instagram quotes like 'Life is tough, but so am I' and 'Difficult roads lead to beautiful destinations.' She had thrown herself into a life with Luke without really thinking about it. She was moving on. Moving forward. But now, as she sat here soaking in every piece of her mother that she could, she knew it had all been a lie. She wasn't moving forward at all. She was as stuck in the past as always.

Her fingers hovered over her phone, and then she typed,

I'm sorry, Luke. Right now I have to focus on my mum. I know you'll understand.

She hit reply and logged out of Facebook as the front door opened.

'Yoo-hoo! Jude? Laura? It's only me.'

Laura rose to her feet, a wave of happiness overcoming her as she met Stella in the hallway, her arms full of plastic bags.

'Oh, Laura! Sweetie. Give me a hand?'

'What on earth ...' Laura began grabbing a couple of bags and taking them into the kitchen.

'Well, I didn't know what you needed, so I thought I'd just bring a few things. Just basics, you know. Milk, butter, bread ...'

'Chocolate brownies?' Laura said, pulling out a Tupperware container, the contents still warm.

'Oh yes. Well, they're mine, of course.'

Laura lifted the lid and a warm waft of chocolate took her

straight back to Stella's kitchen. Stella was Judy's best friend, almost like a second mother to Laura. She'd spent many a day baking with Stella in the kitchen, or sorting the millions of buttons from Stella's button collection on the living-room floor. 'Wow! I missed these,' Laura said, inhaling the aroma.

'Well, hang on there,' Stella said, grabbing Laura's shoulders. 'Let me look at you.' Stella's eyes began to well. 'What a beautiful young woman you are! Come here.' She pulled Laura into her arms, Laura managing to sniff back her own tears.

'Right,' Stella said, letting her go. 'Now you can have a brownie. Where's my Judy?'

Laura took a bite of the fudgy chocolate brownie and nodded to the living room. 'Just resting.'

'Good. How is she?'

'She's okay. Getting more tired with each day. The pain isn't good some days. The district nurse is visiting every morning to check on her and monitor her medication.'

Stella clicked her tongue. 'Oh, Laura. Life's not fair, is it? But, you're here now. That's all she wanted, you know?'

'I know.' Laura nodded, avoiding Stella's eye contact, the guilt resting under her skin.

'And how are you?' Stella patted Laura's hand.

'I'm okay. Really. It's all about Mum now. We've had fun going through the photo albums.'

Stella threw her head back with a chuckle. 'Oh, I bet you have! I can only imagine what lurks in those albums—bad fashion and even worse hair!'

Laura laughed. 'And some!'

'But beautiful memories.'

'I'd know that voice anywhere!'

Laura and Stella turned to see Judy standing in the doorway, holding on to the frame.

'Jude, darling! What are you doing sneaking up on us like that?'

'Just wanting to join in the fun.' She managed a smile. 'And maybe a brownie!'

THE THREE OF them enjoyed afternoon tea and a trip down memory lane, until Judy tired and Laura settled her in bed while Stella cleaned up the kitchen.

'Thanks, Stella,' Laura said, entering the kitchen after she'd finished with her mum.

'Not at all. Now, if you need anything, call out. I'll try and pop around as much as I can. But for now, I must get home to Gemma.'

'Oh,' Laura said, feeling horrible for not asking after Stella's daughter sooner. 'How is Gemma?'

Stella's lips twitched. 'She's okay. You know. Typical teenager. Angsty, moody, and all that. I can't do a thing right, of course.'

Laura smiled. 'I was once there. I'm sure she'll grow out of it. She must be almost eighteen now?'

'Yes, in a few months.'

'I'll have to call round and see her.'

Stella stopped fussing with her handbag and caught Laura's eyes. 'Oh, would you, Laura? She's in a bit of a dark place at the moment. I know she'd love that. She used to love hanging around you when you were younger.'

'She was like my shadow at your place!' Laura smiled. 'Sure. I'll try and get round.'

'Just if you can. It would mean the world to me—to her.'

Something in Stella's eyes told Laura that there was more to the situation than Stella was letting on, but before Laura could ask more, Stella had pulled her in for a hug and hurried out the door, waving goodbye.

. . .

THE NEXT FEW weeks passed with the days drawing in, the air cooler, the leaves yellowing on the trees, and Judy's health deteriorating. Laura woke early, as she did each morning, wanting to make the most of every day, pushing the thoughts of the inevitable aside. She sat at the kitchen table and checked her email and sipped on her tea. Her boss had emailed, asking if she would reconsider her decision to resign, saying she'd gladly have her back at any time. She was finding it hard to replace Laura. The work-experience girl had also quit, and they were terribly understaffed. Laura thanked her for the offer and said she'd think about it. But her job at the beautician was something she hadn't missed since being home at Banyula. She'd fallen into the job by chance not long after moving to the city, answering an ad on their window for a trainee, and hadn't looked back. She enjoyed it, but it certainly hadn't been her career goal. Not that anything had quite turned out like she had planned. At least the discount on beauty products was good.

Laura closed her laptop and switched on the radio to distract her from the eerie quiet inside the house. The DJ announced it was eight o'clock and that more rain was in the forecast for the afternoon. Laura went to check if her mum was awake. The nurse was due to arrive any minute to check on her.

She peeked her head around the bedroom door. Her mum lay peacefully, eyes closed.

'Mum?' Laura whispered. 'You awake?'

Judy's eyes flickered open, and the corners of her lips turned upward slightly. She motioned for Laura with her hand.

Laura sat on the edge of the bed and lifted her mum's hand into hers. Judy's hands were always cold these days, but they were colder than usual today. Laura gently rubbed the paper-thin skin to try and circulate some warmth.

Her mother's eyes drifted closed again, and Laura looked at

her. Her hair was spread over the pillow like a halo. Laura had loved playing with her mum's hair when she was younger, practicing her braiding skills. She'd inherited her mother's hair. Although not as dark, the thickness and the slight curl—which she always tried to straighten out—were the spitting image of her mother's. Laura's eyes stung. Now, she wanted more than ever to have that curl in her hair.

'Thank you, honey,' Judy whispered through dry lips.

'Thank you for what?'

'For looking after me,' Judy said, opening her eyes again.

Tears immediately sprung to Laura's own, and she squeezed them back. 'You don't have to thank me.'

'I know I don't. But,' she paused, 'I know it's an imposition, that's all.'

'Mum, don't be silly. Of course it's not an imposition. I wouldn't want to be anywhere else.' Laura inhaled the shame. 'I'm sorry, Mum,' she said, the tears escaping down her cheeks.

Judy's brow furrowed. 'You don't have anything to be sorry about.'

'But I do. I've been so selfish. Not coming home all those years. Making you have to come to me.'

'Oh, Laura. I don't ever want you to feel bad about that. I understand,' she said, shifting her position in bed. Laura nodded, continuing to rub her hand.

Judy cleared her throat. A small, exhausted cough erupted from her lungs. 'But,' she said slowly, 'I do think you need to face things.'

Laura nodded.

'Oh, Laura, you put on such a brave face. You always have. Remember that time you fell off the monkey bars at school, and I had to take you to the emergency room? You swore you didn't break your wrist. You wanted to stay at school to finish reading the class book that afternoon. Oh gosh, what was it?'

'*Charlotte's Web.*' Laura smiled, remembering how she was desperate to find out what happened to Charlotte's eggs.

'Of course! You didn't even cry when the doctor had to set your arm in plaster. You were a tough little cookie.' Judy paused. 'But you don't always have to be so tough. I knew you were crying inside back then, just like I see it now.'

Laura shot her mother a look of panic. Of realization. She should have known better than to try and hide anything from her mother. She was all-knowing.

'Why didn't you tell me you broke things off with Luke?'

'What? How did you...?' Laura smiled. 'Ah, Stella.'

'She's worried about you too. What happened?'

'I don't know. We just ... want different things.' Laura swallowed, wishing she didn't have to have this conversation.

'Or are you just unsure about committing to Luke?'

Laura couldn't look her mother in the eye. Instead, she began fiddling with the sleeves of her jumper, pulling them over her hands.

'You don't have to answer,' Judy continued.

Laura felt like she was breaking from the inside out. Her heart crumbled like pastry, into tiny flakes of helplessness. She knew Luke wasn't the right one for her, but she also knew she was holding back. And deep down, although she'd never admit it, she was scared of letting anyone in after Ryan. She inhaled sharply, surprised at how certain she was in her thoughts.

'I know, Mum,' she said. 'But, I ... I just keep waiting and hoping I'd know what I want out of life, but ....' Laura's words choked up like a traffic jam in her throat.

Judy squeezed her hand. 'You still think of Ryan?'

Laura flinched at the sound of his name, memories of his

shocking death flickering to life in her mind like a buffering video.

'I can't. I have to move forward from that.'

'Do you remember anything more?'

'What do you mean?'

'About that night?'

Laura averted her gaze to hide the pain. She hadn't revisited that night for years. She'd blocked everything out, the ache too hard to deal with. She'd locked it deep in her memory and thrown away the key. There may be certain things she'd have to confront from her past, but that night was one she had no intention of revisiting. Ever.

'Mum, I can't look back. You know that. I've got to move forward.'

'I do know that, sweetie. But I think it's affecting you in ways you don't realize. I've kept quiet, supporting you for so long, but I won't be here much longer, and I ... I only ever wanted you to find happiness.'

'Mum,' Laura began.

'No, let me finish. I'm no psychologist, but I think you need to say goodbye to Ryan,' she said, as if inside Laura's head. 'Properly.'

Laura's eyes swam with tears that she unsuccessfully tried to swallow back. Judy squeezed her hand.

'Please, Laura, I want you to promise me you will.'

Laura considered her mother's eyes. They were so tired, so sucked of the vibrancy and life they used to hold. But they were still so full of love—a sticky, warm toffee love that coated Laura completely. She caved. 'Okay,' Laura said, leaning down to rest her head gently on her mother's chest. 'I promise.'

'That's my girl.'

Tears spilled out of Laura's eyes, soaking into her mother's quilt as she squeezed her eyes tight.

'You need to forgive. To move on. For you. For Rachel. Tom.'

Her mum paused to inhale a short breath. 'I don't want you to hurt anymore, sweetie,' Judy said, smoothing Laura's hair. 'I should have been there for you.'

Laura sat up and looked at her mum's glassy eyes. 'No, Mum. You were there. I ... I just didn't want any help. I wanted to forget everything.'

'I know, sweetie. But you can't. I did that when your dad died. I wanted to push everyone away, but I had you. I had to make myself say goodbye and move on. And you do too, Laura. You have your whole life ahead of you. You can't go on like this.'

Laura nodded, wiping the tears of truth from her cheek. She knew Judy was right.

'Promise me you'll say goodbye to Ryan. Make amends with Tom. Maybe even Rachel if you can. Please, darling.'

'I will. I promise.'

Judy patted her hand and smiled. 'Good. Now, where's my smoothie? You know how much I love those horrible, green things you make me for breakfast.'

4

THE PALLIATIVE CARE nurse visited morning and night now, but Judy wilted with each day. Her laugh mellowed to a smile and then to a nod. Laura sat by the bed as the nurse finished checking Judy on her morning visit. Laura held her mother's hand. Her skin was soft and loose as it hung slackly off her bones. The hand that was once so firm and strong. The hand that had rubbed her back when she was sick. The hand that had caressed her face when she cried. The hand that once tickled her ribs, tying them both in ribbons of laughter.

The nurse packed up her things, put her hand on Laura's shoulder, and leaned to whisper in her ear. 'She's as comfortable as can be.'

Laura looked at the nurse. They didn't need words. They both knew it was time. The doctor had been by yesterday, offering for Judy to come into the hospital where they could administer some morphine to make her more comfortable, but Judy had refused. 'It is time,' Judy had whispered to Laura.

The nurse patted Laura's hand. 'I'll put the kettle on for you,' she whispered.

Laura watched as her mother's eyes wandered around the room and then focused on Laura, seemingly tracing the outline of her face, before the corner of her mouth twitched into a half smile and she gently closed her eyes.

Laura felt the grip on her hand tighten, as if her mother was communicating the words she couldn't speak. She watched her chest rise and fall, taking in a final breath before it sank gently and remained perfectly calm and still. A warm feeling came over Laura, like a fluffy blanket. A hug. A goodbye. Laura laid her head next to her mum's hand and sobbed. Her heart felt like it was being choked, her lungs searching for air. Emotions enveloped her thoughts. Guilt. Loss. Heartbreak. Loneliness. Despair. Helplessness.

She moved closer and pushed the hair from her mother's pale face. She touched her sunken cheeks and ran her fingers over her mother's cracked lips, thinking of the kisses her mother used to smother her with every bedtime. Judy would tuck the sheets up close to Laura's chin and then cover her cheeks and forehead with a flourish of what felt like a thousand kisses that would leave Laura in fits of giggles. Laura remembered when she was about ten, asking her mum why it was her ritual every night. She replied, 'Because you should always go to sleep happy and knowing you are loved. Every single night.' She'd smiled before adding, 'I love you more than ice cream'–something Laura first declared at the age of four–something that had stuck and become their sign-off every night since.

Laura wiped the tears with the back of her hand and whispered in her mum's ear, 'I love you more than ice cream.'

.   .   .

THE NEXT FEW hours passed in a blur with Laura dealing robotically with the formalities that needed her attention. Finally, she found herself sitting at the kitchen table, the quietness of the house descending upon her. She picked up her phone and dialed Stella's number.

'Laura, you just caught me. How are you, sweetie? How's Jude?'

Laura swallowed, the tears rolling down her cheeks. 'She's gone, Stel.' There was no easy way to push those words out.

Stella gasped, and then Laura heard her begin to cry.

'Oh, darling. I'm so sorry.' She paused to sniffle. 'Oh, Jude.'

Laura's shoulders shook. All she wanted to do was sink into Stella's warm arms and be comforted by her peony scent of familiarity.

'I'll be right there,' Stella whispered.

'HAVE you thought about the funeral, honey?' Stella said as they sat at the kitchen table after their initial grief had subsided.

'I was thinking Thursday. I don't want to drag it out. I have to ring the minister yet, and hopefully the CWA hall will be free, and—'

'Laura, stop. Leave it all to me. I will handle it all.'

'Stella, it's okay...'

'No. I insist.'

Laura didn't think she had any more tears to cry, but they still escaped her eyes.

'Oh, darling. I'm so sorry. She loved you more than—'

'More than ice cream. I know.'

Stella chuckled through her sobs. 'Oh, Laura. I'm here for you. Always know that, right?'

'I know, Stella. Thank you.'

5

'I'M SORRY ABOUT your mum.'

Laura's shoulders flinched as the deep voice echoed around her. Her legs were numb, the blood flow constricted after sitting on the white plastic chair overlooking the grave for so long. She vaguely remembered people nodding their condolences as they headed off to the hall across the road for the wake. Stella had told her she would wait, but Laura insisted she wanted to spend these last few moments alone. Since then, time had become irrelevant. She didn't know how long she'd been sitting staring at the grave.

Laura glanced up toward the imposing figure silhouetted by the dark clouds overhead. Gradually, Tom came into focus.

He bent down at the other side of the grave, removed his Akubra and dropped a pink carnation on top of the mahogany coffin. 'Carnations, right? Her favorite?'

Laura smiled. 'How do you remember that?'

'Memories are all we got, aren't they?'

Laura swallowed as her throat tightened. He was right. Memories were all she had. She sucked on her bottom lip to stop it from shaking.

Tom rounded the grave and put his arm around Laura's hunched shoulders. She breathed out, relaxing under the familiar weight. 'Come on, you'd better make an appearance at the wake. Don't want to give the small-town gossip mill anything to talk about, do you?' Tom stood up, offering her a bent elbow.

Laura wiped the tears from her cheeks and rose off the chair. 'How do I look?' she asked.

Tom reached over and tucked a strand of her hair behind her ear. 'You'll do.' He smiled.

THE COUNTRY WOMEN'S ASSOCIATION hall was packed to the rafters with a monochrome pattern of people clustered in various small groups, some spilling out the open doors onto the grassed area. It appeared the whole township of Banyula was there.

'Lucky with the weather,' Tom stated as they neared the doors. 'They're forecasting rain. A lot apparently.'

Tom's hand was warm on her lower back as he ushered Laura through the door. Her heart became loud in her ears, and Laura wished she could skip the wake and head straight home, but it was too late for that. Immediately people drew closer to her, offering her warm smiles and embraces of sympathy. Laura smiled and nodded politely. There were old faces that she remembered. Some hadn't changed a bit, and others had weathered more unkindly due to the passage of time. The hall smelled of lavender and scones, and the myriad voices gathered in the void between the rafters and the high, timber-lined ceiling.

Laura glanced around the room. There were a few groups of people mingling around the tea and coffee table, sipping their drinks and nodding their heads as they talked. Others were gathered around the food table, taking bites out of cucumber sandwiches or scones spread with lashings of homemade jams—Stella's, no doubt. And there was Stella, busily arranging trays with an air of control and order. Laura smiled. Stella was a marvel. She did it all—cooked, baked, sewed, all while teaching at the public high school. Laura wondered how she and her mum would have ever survived without her. She'd been there for all Laura's big occasions: birthdays, first communion, her debutante ball. Stella glanced up from her fussing to catch Laura's eye and made a beeline toward her with outstretched arms.

'Oh, darling,' Stella said, embracing Laura. 'Come on. You need to have something to eat.' She led Laura to a trestle table covered in a fancy floral tablecloth. 'Here, have my date slice. I know it's your favorite,' she said, passing it to Laura on a paper plate.

The last thing Laura felt like doing was eating, even though she couldn't remember the last time she ate. Her stomach grumbled despite herself as she bit into the sticky slice. Stella was right. It was her favorite. Memories of a hot date slice from the oven in Stella's kitchen flooded back to her. Her mum and Stella laughed over the latest gossip Mrs. Hatfield was up in arms about while Laura licked the bowl, waiting patiently for the slice to be ready.

'How are you doing, honey?' Stella asked, rubbing Laura's arm. 'Are you sure you don't want to stay at my place tonight? I hate to think of you alone around there.'

'It's okay. I'll be fine. Might even get a start on packing things up.'

Stella shook her head and tutted. 'You haven't changed a bit, have you? Always taking care of things. But it's okay to take your time, you know? And of course, I'll be around to help you tomorrow. Just tell me a time, and I'll be there.'

Laura swallowed the last mouthful of slice, running her tongue over her teeth before speaking. 'Stella, you don't have to.'

'I know, sweetheart, but I want to.'

Laura stiffened slightly. Stella meant well, but Laura wanted—needed—to be alone. The emotion of the past few weeks had started to wear her down. All she wanted was to be left alone, do what she needed to do, and get back to the city. Leave Banyula for good. 'I ... I just think I need to do it ... you know, by myself,' Laura whispered. 'Just for the next day or so.'

Stella put her hands on Laura's shoulders, tears in her eyes. 'It's okay, love. I understand. Just promise me you'll call if you need anything. Anything at all.'

In the distance, someone beckoned Stella. The coffee urn had run out of water. 'Hang on, Marge, I'm coming!' she called out before turning back to Laura. 'Promise me?'

Laura nodded. As Stella hurried off through the crowd, Tom reappeared at Laura's side.

'Did you see Mr. Tate over there?'

'Oh no,' Laura mumbled under her breath.

Tom pointed to a balding man who looked like he had a bowling ball or three stuffed under his shirt, the buttons straining at the seams. He hadn't changed a bit. Mr. Tate had been their year twelve English teacher and had given all of them a year to remember. He was constantly on their backs, keeping them in for detention—even Laura, and she was the star student. Laura cringed. 'Oh god, he's spotted us.' Sure enough, Mr. Tate was waddling his way through the crowd, waving his hand in the air at Laura.

'Hello, Mr. Tate. So nice to see you.' Laura smiled, glancing at a grinning Tom out of the corner of her eye.

'Ms. Murphy. Laura. I'm so sorry about your mum. Bloody cancer. Mind my French, of course.'

Laura smiled. 'Thank you.'

'Ah, and Mr. Gordon. How's the farm going? I hear you have some big plans?'

Tom nodded, swallowing a mouthful of scone. 'Yeah, I'm setting up for the breeding program with my star Angus.'

'Very good. Very good. Please say hi to your folks when you speak to them next. Are they still away?'

'Yep, they're up near Broome at the moment. Loving the gray nomad life.'

Mr. Tate nodded, his beady eyes turning to Laura. 'And Laura, what about you? What are you doing with yourself these days? It's been so long. You're still in the city, right? No doubt followed the law path, yes?'

Laura swallowed. 'Well, no. Not exactly.'

Mr. Tate cocked his head, waiting for more, as Laura glanced sideways for an escape before lowering her voice. 'I'm ... um ... in the beauty industry.'

Mr. Tate raised his bushy, overgrown eyebrows. If eyebrows could talk, they'd tell her just how disappointed he was. Laura Murphy, star student, the one most likely to succeed at the year twelve awards, a *beautician*? 'Oh, I thought when you went to the city it was to study law?'

'Well, that was my plan.' It had been her plan. But after Ryan's death ...

'Mm-hmm, I see.'

Laura wanted the ground to open and swallow her whole as her cheeks burned with shame. She thought about adding in how she had started a counseling course a couple of years ago, but that was only another plan she hadn't had the drive to follow through with.

'Excuse us, Mr. Tate, there's someone Laura needs to see over there,' Tom said, grabbing Laura's arm and pulling her toward the double doors on the side of the hall in quick fashion. Laura felt herself relax as they stepped out into the fresh air.

'Thanks,' Laura said once they were standing under the dappled shade of a young magnolia tree. 'I felt like he was going to order me to detention or something!' Laura rolled her eyes. She accidently knocked elbows with the person behind her and looked around. 'I'm sorry,' Laura said quickly before realizing who it was. 'Oh, Gemma, hi!'

The last time Laura had seen her, she was a scraggly girl of eight, with a wide smile and pale aqua eyes full of cheek. Now, she had grown into her lanky legs and filled out her once boyish figure. Her brown hair was pulled back into a messy ponytail, and her eyes were flanked with dark shadows and rimmed with thick black eyeliner. Gemma quickly butted out the cigarette she'd been smoking, stamping it under her Doc Martens.

'Um, hi,' Gemma said, her eyes darting from Laura to Tom.

'Hi, Gemma,' Tom said. 'Hey, Lauz, I'm just going to grab something else to eat. Want anything?'

Laura shook her head, and Tom headed back into the hall.

'Wow. It's been ages,' said Laura. Gemma nodded, not offering anything in return. 'How's your story writing going?' Gemma was always telling Laura about the latest story she was writing. 'You still writing?'

Laura watched as Gemma's cheeks flushed a deep pink. 'Ah, no. Um, look, I'd better go.' And without so much as a goodbye, Gemma disappeared around the other side of the tree and into the crowd of hats.

Laura instantly thought back to the conversation she'd had with Stella. Gemma had changed. Laura always knew her to be such a bubbly girl. In fact, Laura found she was a bit annoying to have around sometimes because she never stopped talking, following her around like a puppy dog. How things changed. But, it had been a long time, and Gemma was now on the verge of adulthood, just as Laura had been when her life fell apart. Laura forced herself to concentrate on the clouds overhead to keep from waking her memories. The clouds were moving fast, gathering as if called to attention by mother nature. A storm was brewing.

Tom returned with a cream bun, half in his hand, half stuffed in his mouth.

Laura raised her eyebrows and smiled.

'Shush-ten-ance,' Tom mumbled through a mouthful, cream covering his top lip.

'Right.' Laura smiled and then let out a deep sigh, louder than she intended.

'You look like you've had enough of people for one day. You want a lift home?' Tom asked.

Was it really that obvious? Although, Tom could always read her like a book. Laura nodded, pushing a stray hair behind her ear. She'd come to the funeral with Stella, but no doubt Stella would be here for a few more hours yet chatting and then cleaning up. Exhaustion knocked at Laura's bones. 'That'd be nice. Thanks. I just need to say goodbye to Stella.'

'No worries. My Ute's over there,' Tom said, motioning to the parking lot. 'I'll meet you there in five.'

Head down, Laura walked with purpose back inside, trying not to make eye contact. She spotted Stella carrying a fresh batch of homemade sausage rolls from the kitchen and placing them on the food table where hungry hands snapped them up like lions at feeding time. Laura felt her chest tighten with emotion. All these people had come to say goodbye to her mother. These were many of the same people who would have been at Ryan's funeral. If she'd been there, she would have known for sure. But she hadn't been.

Unable to face both the grief that overwhelmed her and the

pity of the townsfolk, Laura took a moment to breathe as her lip trembled. Thankfully Stella saw her and pulled her into her generous bosom. 'Oh, darling, why don't I take you home. I know it's all a bit much,' she said, patting her back gently.

Laura cleared her throat. 'It's okay. Tom's offered to drive me. I was just coming to say goodbye. And to thank you.'

'Oh, love, you don't have to thank me,' Stella said as she broke the embrace to look Laura in the eyes.

'But I do. You organized practically everything. And you've always been there, Stella. Even when ...' Her voice began to break.

'Shh, come on. Enough of that. Not today. You go home. Rest. Do whatever you have to and take as long as you need. And as I said, if you need anything, you know where to find me. I'll give you a tinkle tonight to make sure you're okay, right?'

Laura nodded as she wiped her eyes for the umpteenth time. 'Thanks.'

'Wow. It's immaculate,' Laura said as she opened the door of Tom's HQ Ute. The blue was as vibrant as when he'd first shown her years ago, the night of the Easter party before he turned eighteen. His dad was still working on getting it going for him as his eighteenth birthday present.

She slid inside; the black vinyl interior was so shiny she could almost see her own reflection.

'She's my baby,' Tom said, smiling, as he shifted the Ute into gear, giving the engine a little rev until it began to purr like a contented kitten.

They rumbled out of the parking lot, and Tom made small talk on their way to Laura's. Laura stared through the window, memories of the place she once called home pounding in her head. The patchy roads and worn footpaths. The same tired shop façades she remembered, some now clearly vacant, some replaced with new stores she didn't recognize. The biggest change had been the renovation of the local supermarket, but apart from that, Banyula was much the same as it had been ten years earlier.

As Tom drove the Ute toward the railway line, Laura noticed him glance at her out of the corner of his eye. An understanding passed between them, and no words were necessary as they slowly bumped over the tracks.

Moments later, Tom pulled up to the curb. 'Do you want me to come in?' he asked as he screeched the parking brake on.

'No. I'll be okay.' Laura shook her head and tore at the tissues between her fingers, small fragments puffing into the air. 'Thanks, though,' she said, managing a smile.

'Okay. But you let me know if you need anything, all right? I'm still out on the farm. Well, for now ...'

'For now?' Laura looked at Tom, his face awash with a faraway look.

'Yeah, long story,' he said, shrugging his shoulders, relighting his bright, familiar smile.

She wanted to ask more, show she still cared. But the right words escaped her. Her heart shrank a little with the thought that she never really did say goodbye to Tom when she left.

'All right,' Tom said, tapping his hands on the steering wheel. 'Better get inside before those clouds open up.' He pointed to the thickening gray clouds that had engulfed the sky from horizon to horizon.

Laura swallowed the wave of emotion rising to her throat and opened the door. 'Thanks,' she said, stepping onto the grass, the dandelions tickling at her ankles.

Tom tipped his hat and slowly drove away down the road.

Laura waved goodbye before turning and staring at the house, a deep ache inside of her reminding her that it was now empty.

6

CRADLING HER CUP of hot tea, Laura stepped out onto the back patio. It was early, not quite seven a.m., and the cool morning air nipped at Laura's ears. Small puddles of water had gathered in the low spots of the yard after last night's rain. And although the morning had brought patches of blue sky, dark clouds loomed ominously on the horizon. Laura pulled up an old outdoor chair, wiped off the beads of water with her sleeve, and sat down, her eyes wandering over the backyard.

The yard, once tended lovingly by Judy, was now sad and over-grown. The deserted chicken coop and broken woodshed were far from what they once were, both no doubt now home to many a huntsman and redback spider. Laura hated spiders. She'd inher-ited her fear from Judy. Boy, were they a sorry pair when a huntsman decided to pop into the house uninvited. It was a wonder their screams didn't send the entire spider population of Banyula away for good.

Laura closed her eyes, imagining the yard as it used to be and conjuring the memories it brought. Digging in the vegetable patch with her own special garden fork and pink gardening gloves her mum had given her, bouncing on the trampoline, collecting the eggs from the chickens, which was always such an exciting experience. 'An egg! An egg!' she'd sing out excitedly to her mum.

Laura's earliest memory was not long after her father had passed away. He was a truck driver. Faulty brakes, wet road, tree. She didn't remember much of that time—she was only five—but she did remember her mum. The tears always close to the surface, spilling over each time she held Laura or kissed her goodnight. Her mum hardly got out of her dressing gown that winter. It was always pulled tight around her fading frame. Then one morning, as spring kissed the sky outside, her mother pulled on her jeans, cooked up a stack of pancakes, and announced they had to fix up the garden in preparation for a special delivery. Chickens!

Laura remembered her five-year-old legs running as fast as they could outside, tearing around the yard and giggling with Judy close behind, the smile Laura had missed so much taking over her mother's face once again. They laughed and tickled, giggled and danced. That was the best sound in the world, her mother's laugh.

Mum's laughter, she thought. Something she'd never hear again.

Laura's eyes filled with tears. She'd wasted so much time on anger and hurt. So much time refusing to let the past take any place in her present. Selfish. That was what she'd been. Too wrapped up in her own world, trying to make something of herself. Laura harrumphed. *Look how that turned out.*

Laura's sadness turned to anger. This time at her own mother, for not telling her about the cancer sooner. And at herself for not picking up on the signs. *Why hadn't I seen the signs?*

A school bell rang in the distance and forced Laura to focus once again. It was time to say goodbye. To the house. And to Banyula. To the past. But the more she stared at the backyard, the more it tugged at her. Pulling her. Grounding her. Memories of her and Rachel spread out on colorful beach towels under the hot summer sun. The sweet smell of coconut oil lingering in the air suddenly appeared out of nowhere. Laura mentally pushed them aside. A run. That's what she needed.

Laura pulled on her Nikes and headed out the front door. She avoided the Smythe Street rail crossing and headed west along the sleepy streets. It felt like it had been forever since she'd done any form of exercise, but she fought the initial burning in her throat and heaviness in her legs and fell into a slow jog. She'd usually have music or a podcast blaring in her ears to distract her from the city, but here she wanted to hear the morning.

Laura didn't realize just how much she'd missed the early mornings in a country town. The tweeting of myriad birds somehow blending into a glorious symphonic chorus, and the rustle of the mint-colored eucalyptus leaves overhead were the only sounds. No tooting horns, no roads jammed with cars bumper to bumper, no dirty smog to inhale. Just clean, crisp, country air.

In a trancelike state, Laura concentrated on putting one foot in front of another, inhaling the sweetness of the familiar lemon-scented gums. She found herself on the outskirts of town in ten minutes. As she paused to catch her breath and massage her calf, which was hinting at cramping, Laura realized where she was. Stretching out before her was the vast, open plain of the cemetery. Gravestones dotted the expanse of green lawn in lonely remembrance. She bent over and leaned on her knees, inhaling deep, oxygen-filled breaths. Her lungs felt as if they were on fire.

Spur of the moment, Laura walked to the entrance of the cemetery. She'd just go and see her mum's grave. See if any flowers that had been left needed attention. She made her way to the grave, where the freshly patted-down rusty clay was packed solid thanks to the overnight rain. As the sun crept over the east, Laura thought of the inscription her mother wanted on her headstone. *The most wasted of all days is one without laughter.* It was a quote from e e cummings, her mum's favorite. She hoped it wouldn't be too long before the headstone was mounted. Laura leaned down and rearranged the bunches of flowers, whispering, 'I miss you, Mum.'

She paused at the grave for a few moments, letting her eyes dry in the breeze. Inside, she felt lost. A little girl with no direction, yet she was almost twenty-eight years old. She'd spent so much time running without a finish line in sight. And now that she'd stopped, she'd lost sight of the finish altogether. Her thoughts began to unravel, each one ending with one single name: *Ryan.*

A wave of guilt washed over her as her mum's words knocked at the back of her mind. *Promise me you'll say goodbye properly.*

She didn't even know where his grave was, but still she wandered up and down the manicured rows of the lawn cemetery, each one laid out with immaculate precision. It took her a good five minutes to locate Ryan's headstone. It was located on the boundary fence under a lone Japanese maple, its fire-red leaves littering the small concrete plaque. Laura bent down and brushed off the leaves to read the simple font.

Ryan Adam Taylor
21 August 1992 – 7 November 2009
Loved son of William (dec) and Jane (dec)

RYAN. What happened that year had changed Laura forever.

Laura's mind drifted back to the first time she skipped school with him and went down to the nearby river. She was so nervous she thought her heart was going to gallop right out of her chest in a mixture of excitement and the thrill of being caught. And the adrenaline. Ryan had asked her—nerdy, never-had-a-boyfriend Laura—to go to the river with him.

Laura sat down, crossing her legs, the image of them sneaking out the rear gate of the school visualizing before her. She remembered how she had held her breath the whole way, until they reached the worn track leading to the river, only a few hundred meters away. Almost hyperventilating, she had finally sucked in some oxygen to fill her burning lungs and slow her racing heart.

'You don't do this often, hey?' Ryan said, grabbing a handful of leaves off one of the river gums and scrunching them in his hand as they walked. Laura had to duck to escape the whip of the branch as it flicked back toward her.

A few minutes later they were down on the coarse sand at the river's edge. The river was low thanks to an unusually dry spring season that had continued into summer, the current barely more than a trickle in some parts. Laura copied Ryan, taking off her shoes and socks and resting her feet in the shallows.

'So, what do you do down here?' Laura asked, looking around.

'Nothin' much. Depends who I'm with.' He grinned at Laura, his green eyes squinting in the sun. Laura was thankful her cheeks were already colored from the rush of skipping school to hide her embarrassment.

They sat there for a few minutes, the silence between them filled by the chattering of birds above and the gentle ripple of the river as it trickled over stone riverbed in front of them. Laura's mind started to wander. Her thoughts chided her for skipping school. What was she thinking coming down to the river with Ryan Taylor?

'Seen any good movies lately?' Ryan broke into her thoughts.

'Um, well, Rachel and I watched *The Proposal* on the weekend.'

'Oh yeah, cool.'

'It was pretty good,' Laura said, throwing a rock into the river and watching the ripple on top of the water.

'You seen *The Fast and the Furious*?'

Laura twisted her lips as she thought, then shook her head. 'Don't think so.'

'It's probably more of a guys' movie. Lots of car chases and shit.'

'Hey, don't judge me! My favorite movie is *The Terminator,* you know.'

Ryan's eyebrows shot up. 'Really? Well I'm impressed. And I'm not judging. I get a lot o' that myself.'

There was a pain to Ryan's comment. 'Yeah, I guess you do.'

'People think that just 'cause I act up a bit, I'm a loser.'

'Well, I guess it doesn't help you playing it up all the time.' Laura was surprised at how casual she was with him, but something about him made her feel oddly comfortable.

'I'm just playing a role. Someone's gotta make life interesting 'round here.' He sighed.

'What do you mean?' asked Laura. He looked a million miles away, as if shuffling through years of memories to find what he was looking for. Lost. He seemed to ignore the question, so Laura didn't push it further.

'It's just you and your gran, isn't it?' Laura asked.

Ryan's eyes shot across to Laura, and she suddenly felt she'd hit a nerve. She wished she could rewind three seconds.

'Yeah.'

'It's only me and my mum. My dad died when I was five. Truck accident,' Laura said, wishing she had more memories of her dad, but she was way too young. All she had were photographs and stories her mum told her. She didn't really miss him as such, just missed the opportunity of having a dad. But really, her mum was all she knew.

'That sucks.' Ryan dug his heels into the sand in front of him. 'My folks died when I was a baby. I don't remember them.'

'What happened?'

'House fire.'

'Shit. Sorry.'

'Don't be sorry. Not your fault.' Ryan smiled at her. 'No one's ever asked me what happened to them before.'

Laura's heart skipped. She'd done the wrong thing. Her thoughts must have shown on her face, as Ryan was quick to respond.

'Nah, it's okay,' he said lightly. 'It's kinda nice.'

Laura's eyes caught Ryan as he looked at her, and for a split second she thought he was going to kiss her. Her heart thrashed with nerves that made her jump up to her feet. She kicked her feet in the water and turned away from Ryan. She'd never felt this nervous before. She'd had little experience with boys. A random kiss—more of a peck—at the school disco last year, but that was about it. Unless you counted Tom. But that was just child's play when they were ten years old, mucking about at Tom's farm as they often did. They'd never spoken of the two-second peck since.

'Guess we'd better head back,' Ryan said, sliding his socks on and tying the laces on his sneakers. Laura noticed he used the bunny ear method like she did.

'But we still have ten minutes?' Laura said, looking at her watch.

'You gotta do this properly.' He laughed. 'You gotta get back before the bell so it looks like you were never gone!'

Laura blushed. There was something so purely innocent about Ryan's smile. It made Laura's insides turn to water.

LAURA REMEMBERED how for the rest of the day she couldn't wipe the smile off her face, so excited to tell Tom and Rachel after school. But now, Laura's hands began to shake as the memory became blurred by those from later that year. When Ryan's smile faded and a darkness clouded his eyes.

She picked up a leaf from Ryan's headstone as tears fell down her face, all the pent-up emotions too much to hold inside any longer. *Why Ryan? Why?* It was a question she had asked so many times. Not to anyone. Just to herself. Usually during the long, dark, sleepless nights following his death. Still in shock and unsure of anything, Laura would lie in bed staring into the nothingness, feeling much the same inside. Her cloudy memories crashed into themselves as she lay there, unsure of what was real and what wasn't, so she did the only thing that made her stop feeling. She locked them away in a box at the back of her mind and concentrated on forgetting.

Now, sitting here in the quiet of the autumn morning next to Ryan's grave, her memories began to move from black-and-white to color. She remembered the few months they were together had been fraught with a melting pot of emotions. Moments of perfection sat alongside instants of hurt. Days where she thought happiness would burst from her insides, and other days where the dark clouds of angst and confusion hovered over them both. Ryan could move from affectionate to distant in the blink of an eye. The memories were so visceral. Every emotion crawled over Laura's skin. She shivered and looked toward the sky, as if it held the answers to the questions she'd tried to push aside for years. But all it held now was a foreboding darkness that had swallowed the morning sun whole.

Checking the weather app on her phone, Laura saw patches of yellow and orange on the radar; heavy rain was coming. At that moment, as if a sign, the wind whipped up the maple leaves into a whirlwind of crimson red. Laura jumped to her feet and began to run, hoping she'd make it home before the downpour.

7

LAURA THREW THE heavy garbage bag into the bin. The past few days she'd spent emptying cupboards, packing boxes, and shifting between sadness and fond memories. Stella had called around a few times to give her a hand, bringing with her casseroles and slices, which was good, because the last thing Laura had felt like doing was cooking.

Laura had spent the rest of the morning cleaning out the laundry and bathroom cupboards. But now the rain had eased off, Laura decided to make a start on the backyard. She needed some fresh air. She gathered a few tools from the shed and began tackling what once was the vegetable patch, now overgrown with marshmallow weed and curly dock. The rain had at least made it easier to pull them out.

'HEY,' a voice broke through the sound of weeds being ripped from the soil, and Laura sprang up from her position on all fours to see Tom leaning over the side gate, his wide toothy grin taking up most of his face.

'Oh my god, you scared the life out of me!' she said, trying to brush off the wet dirt that covered her hands and had soiled the knees of her jeans.

Tom laughed. 'Sorry, Lauz. Been working hard?' He nodded toward the pile of limp weeds gathered near Laura's feet.

'Yeah, it's a big job,' she replied, surveying the vegetable patch that now looked slightly better than when she'd started. 'But someone's gotta do it!'

'Want some help?'

'Oh, no. It's fine. I'm sure you've got your hands full with the farm and everything.'

'Nah. It's cool. Got the farmhands out today checking the fences. I can spare an hour or two. I've even got a few tools in the back o' the Ute. I'll go grab 'em.' Tom disappeared out of sight down the driveway.

A few moments later he reappeared carrying a shovel and pitchfork. 'I came prepared,' he said, unlatching the gate.

A smile crept across Laura's face. Of all the people she'd left behind after Ryan's death besides her mum, Tom was the one she had missed the most. He had always been there for her. Ever since they were kids running around his farm chasing Bessie, his beloved golden retriever, Tom had been there for everything. He picked up the pieces every time Laura fought with Ryan that fateful year.

Ryan. Laura had tried so hard not to think of him, but everywhere she looked, she saw him. Sitting on the back steps, walking up the front path, outside her bedroom window ...

'Tom, you really don't have to,' she said, regaining her composure.

'Shut up and get to work.' He smiled and handed Laura the pitchfork.

An hour later, they stood back and observed their progress. The vegetable patch was weed free, the black soil turned over loosely and the organics bin overflowing with weeds and pruning. The garden bed along the back fence actually looked like a garden bed again rather than a mass of tangled plants. It was almost starting to resemble the backyard Laura remembered.

'Do you want a drink?' Laura asked, wiping the trickle of sweat from under her nose. Her fingernails were thick with black dirt, and slight calluses were beginning to appear on her palms. It felt good to be grubby for a change. So very different from her clean, respectable life in the city. Luke would almost fall into fits of laughter if he could see her now.

'I reckon!'

She kicked off her muddy boots and headed inside, returning with two plastic cups filled with orange juice. They sat down on the back step, Laura relieved to have her legs stretched out in front of her rather than squatted down in the garden.

Tom slurped on his juice and wiped his chin with the back of his hand as it trickled downward. 'So, you regret not going to uni?'

Laura sighed gently. She'd wanted to study law, but as her final year of school progressed, her grades dropped, and even before Ryan, she doubted she'd get the marks. Then, after she fled to the city and wound up at the beautician's, life just carried on.

'Laura?' Tom pulled her back to the present.

'Sorry? No, I guess not.' She shook her head and swallowed a mouthful of juice. 'I don't think it would've been for me, anyway.'

Tom nodded.

'How's Bessie?' Laura asked, hoping to break the silence.

'Bessie? She died a few years back.'

Laura's mouth gaped when she realized how stupid she was.

Bessie, Tom's beloved golden retriever who followed him every-where, would have been a very old dog by now. Of course she would have passed. 'Oh, Tom, I'm so sorry. Of course.'

Tom shrugged. 'She was a good dog.'

Laura could see his eyes glistening. 'She sure was. Did you get another dog?'

'I thought about it. Just never got around to it. Anyway, the farm Kelpies keep me company enough.'

'How is farm life? Still loving it?'

Tom shrugged. 'It has its days, but yeah.'

'I couldn't imagine you anywhere else.'

'That's all I'm good for, I guess.' Tom's tone hardened ever so slightly.

'Hey, I didn't mean that. I know how much you love that place. And you're doing something you love. I mean, how many people can actually say that?' Laura said, trying to make amends. She didn't mean it the way it sounded.

'It's all you ever saw me as though.'

Laura paused, processing her response. It was true. That's what she saw Tom as. But it wasn't a bad thing to her. He was just Tom—loveable, wouldn't-hurt-a-fly Tom. But she felt awful looking at him now, not only for making him feel small, but for the way they'd parted. No words. No explanation. He deserved so much more, yet it was a guilt Laura was still not ready to face. 'I'm sorry,' she said, placing her half-empty cup on the ground. 'Sorry for turning my back on you like I did.'

'I know you are, Lauz.'

The breeze had picked up again, sending the grass clippings scattering from the top of the organics bin. The sun was now a shadowy circle behind the gray clouds, which looked like they were threatening to break open again at any moment. The gloom matched the queasiness in Laura's stomach. She never thought she'd feel awkward around Tom, but time had built a wall between them that she wasn't sure how to knock down.

'I've missed you round here, Laura,' Tom said, tapping his foot up and down. 'When you left ...'

'Don't.' Laura held up her hand to stop more words escaping his mouth. She wasn't ready to go back there. She wasn't sure if she ever would be ready.

'I know you don't want to talk about it, but maybe you need to. I need to,' Tom said, his eyes burning into her.

Laura stared down at the cracked concrete beneath her feet. The cracks were worn and tired, like a road map weary from being folded too many times. Just like her thoughts.

Tom was right. She'd spent so much energy mentally searching for answers and then suppressing every emotion, pretending that part of her life never happened. That *that* Laura never existed. She was lost and running for all these years. Maybe it was time to stop. If only facing the truth wasn't so hard.

'You're right. I do. Mum made me promise I'd, you know, get closure or something,' she said, wrapping invisible quotation marks around the words. 'But, I'm not ready yet. I will be. I just need to sort everything out with Mum.'

'I get it. One thing at a time.'

At that moment, the clouds decided to release fat raindrops, and the wind whipped up and sent the side gate crashing closed. Laura and Tom bolted for the back door, covering their heads.

The rain sounded like golf balls on the tin roof as they tumbled inside to the back TV room.

'Bloody rain,' Tom sighed.

'I thought you'd be glad for it?' Laura said.

'Not as much as they're predicting. The ground is as hard as a rock, and it's got nowhere to go. Too much rain in a small window will set us on flood watch.'

Thankful for the change of subject, Laura glanced around the room. It was next on her list. 'Want to help me pack up some boxes?' she said, raising her voice over the rain. 'If you have time, that is.'

Tom shrugged. 'Sure. Why not.'

'I CAN'T BELIEVE how much stuff Mum has in here,' Laura said, pulling old notebooks, dried-up pens, and hand-scribbled scraps of paper out of the desk drawer. Old electricity bills, rates notices, and even some of Laura's old school reports had already been purged into a box to be thrown into the recycling bin.

Tom was tending to the timber bookcase, loading old Mills & Boon paperbacks into another box and sorting through the myriad VHS tapes and DVDs now covered in thick dust, untouched for years.

'Hey,' Tom said. 'Remember this one? Man, I loved this movie.'

Tom was holding up a DVD of *The Dark Knight*. Christian Bale's eyes peered from behind the dark façade of his Batman costume out through the cracked plastic cover.

'Oh god, yes! How could I forget!' Laura threw her head back. 'You used to make me watch it over and over again!' She rolled her eyes.

'I thought you loved it?'

'I only watched it for Heath Ledger, you know?'

Tom instantaneously broke into his best Joker impression. Hands stretched out, eyes and mouth wide, doing his best imitation of Heath Ledger's husky cackle.

'That is THE worst impression ever!' She laughed. The knot in her stomach began to slacken, and for a moment it almost felt like old times.

'Okay, so I'm no Heath Ledger,' Tom replied, 'but I'm keeping this DVD!'

'Be my guest,' Laura said as she dug her hand into the back of the desk drawer, grappling with a tin and pulling it out. It was an old shortbread tin, the kind you found on the supermarket shelves at Christmas. She gently pried off the lid, the buttery smell of Danish shortbread still faintly lingering. Laura's brow furrowed as she peered inside at the yellowed newspaper clippings. She flicked through them, picking up one announcing her birth and then another—her father's death notice. There was a picture from the *Banyula Times* of Laura grinning from ear to ear, holding up a picture of a pink cow that she'd entered in the local agricultural show coloring competition. She smiled as she remembered winning the seven-and-under age category: two tickets to see the local theater company's stage production of *Annie.*

Laura rifled toward the bottom of the tin when another clipping caught her eye. This one wasn't as discolored. November 8, 2009 was the date printed on the mast. Laura leaned back on the roller chair and unfolded it, the paper soft under her fingers.

'Community in Shock as Teen Found Dead on Train Tracks' was the heading in bold black ink. And as much as she wanted to shove it back in the tin and throw it all in the rubbish pile, Laura couldn't take her eyes off it. She began to read.

POLICE BELIEVE *the body hit by a train on the Smythe Street railway tracks in the early hours of Sunday morning is that of a local teenage boy. Although the teen's name has not yet been released, police have stated that the 18-year-old male was one of the revelers at an end-of-year-twelve party that got out of hand the previous evening.*

.   .   .

'WHAT YOU GOT THERE?' Tom said as he moved toward Laura. 'Oh god.' He reached down to grab it from her, but Laura pulled it away.

'No, Tom. I need to ...' Her voice trembled.

'Why, Lauz? You don't need to read it.'

She pulled out more clippings, all about Ryan's death. Another caught her interest. 'Teen's Death Not Straightforward.'

'Not straightforward?' she said, continuing to read aloud with Tom crouched down beside her.

ALTHOUGH FIRST THOUGHT A SHOCKING ACCIDENT, *the death of local teenager Ryan Taylor is still a mystery as police remain tight-lipped on the theories behind the tragedy.*

'We need to rule out every possibility before making a statement,' said Senior Detective Roy Makin yesterday afternoon.

'I DON'T UNDERSTAND,' Laura said, brow furrowed. Tom rose to his feet, avoiding her eyes. 'Tom? What does it mean?'

'I don't know. It was all such a blur. You know that.'

'What were they alluding to? That he was,' she had to force the word out, '*murdered*?'

She stared at Tom, whose eyes met hers for the briefest moment and then quickly diverted. He opened his mouth to speak but paused as if considering something of great importance. Then he threw his hands in the air and sighed. 'I don't know, Laura. It was nine years ago. I guess they were just doing their job. Maybe if you had stayed around—' He stopped abruptly.

Laura bit the inside of her cheek, feeling the harshness off his words combine with the heat that flushed across her face. She stuffed the clippings back into the tin and sat it onto the desk.

'You're right. It doesn't matter. It's in the past,' she said, busying herself in the drawer once more. Tom didn't move from his standing position next to her. Laura kept tidying.

'I guess I should be going,' Tom finally said. He picked up his Akubra off the side table and moved toward the back door, adjusting the hat onto his head.

Laura, still unable to meet his eyes, stuffed some papers into the recycling box. 'Yeah, sure.' She shrugged.

Tom paused at the screen door. 'I guess I'll see you around,' he said as he lifted his hat briefly before disappearing into the rain.

Laura picked at her nails and stared at the tin sitting innocently on the desk, holding both her favorite memories and her worst. With her heart thumping, she picked up the tin, sat down cross-legged on the floor and spilled the contents in front of her.

Ryan's olive-skinned face stared back at her from one of the clippings. His sandy fringe half covered his left eye, and the collar on his gray school shirt was twisted. The dimple on his cheek was pronounced as he smiled. The tears welled in Laura's eyes and then spilled out onto her knees.

What if it wasn't an accident? What if there was more to it like the police alluded to? Something prickled at Laura's insides. She'd always accepted that his death was nothing more than a tragic accident. After all, that's what her mum had told her, wasn't it? But what if there was more to it? The more she thought about it, the more unanswered questions appeared in her mind. Memories she couldn't piece together.

She began sorting the articles, putting anything relevant about Ryan aside. After a few minutes, she realized there was nothing left in the tin. She shuffled all the clippings and photos into a pile and scooped them back into the tin, feeling empty and exhausted, but she still couldn't shake the doubt that had entered her mind. *Why on earth would the police suspect foul play in the first place?*

8

TOM SLOGGED TOWARD the riverbank, his gum boots sinking into the waterlogged ground. Thunder cracked overhead, another downpour threatening as the clouds swirled above him like black smoke. Tom sighed at the thought of more rain. As much as they needed rain after the dry summer, the entire autumn average in the space of a fortnight wasn't what he had in mind. The river was nearing its peak, and if the rain kept up, he would have to move the cattle. The last thing he needed was losing them to floodwaters. It had already been a tough year, losing one of his prized bulls to a freak accident over the summer. He still felt sick at the thought of the bull he'd found after a particularly wild summer storm. He couldn't' tell what had happened at first, but on closer inspection and sighting the patch of singed hide, there could only be one conclusion. A lightning strike. The poor bull was in the wrong place at the wrong time.

Tom pulled back the heavy branches of a gum tree, revealing the water marker. Eight meters. The high level—the record flood of 1993—was marked at 8.4 meters. He furrowed his brow, wondering how much longer he could put off moving the cattle. It was a pain. He would have to bring most of them up to the paddock closest to the house, away from the river. But the heavily pregnant cows were already there, and he needed to keep them separate, which would mean moving them into the loading paddocks. He scratched his head. The last thing he wanted was to move stock at the last minute though. He made a mental note to get online that night to check the river levels upstream and the forecast. That should give him an idea how fast it was rising, then he could decide what to do.

He jumped back into the farm Ute and made his way toward the house, Laura's face springing to his mind as he bumped over the track. He'd been keeping himself busy all day to keep from thinking of her. But whenever his mind wandered, it wandered to Laura. He wished it was easy just to close that chapter of his life, like closing the gate on a paddock. As if nothing had happened. And then maybe he and Laura … He shook his head at his stupid whimsical thoughts.

He pulled up to the paddock closest to the house to check on the pregnant cows. There were still three that hadn't calved. It would be any day now. He jumped out of the Ute and opened the gate. Two of the cows, bellies round and bulging, were gnawing on the green pasture. The other cow was sitting, facing away from Tom, under the shelter of the peppercorn tree in the corner of the paddock. He jogged over, careful not to disturb her. It was his best cow—super fertile, great strength, and calved easily. This year he'd had her inseminated with semen from one of the top sires in the state. Cost him a small fortune, but it would be worth it to continue the strong heritability and improve his herd quality. And that's what he needed in order to join the certified breeding program.

The cow jerked her head at his arrival but didn't get up. He checked her udder. It had enlarged again since earlier that morning, the teats now firm and smooth. He swore it looked ready to burst. 'Mustn't be long now, girl,' he whispered. The cow looked at him with wary eyes. He gently lifted the cow's tail to inspect the vulva, again enlarged, but it hadn't changed much over the past twenty-four hours. Her tail was still limp—a sign labor hadn't started. He'd check on her first thing in the morning.

Back in the Ute, Tom pulled up at the house and sat down on the grayed wooden porch to take off his mud-soaked boots. Instinctively his arm reached down to pat Bessie, and he shook his head. She'd been gone three years now. He'd wanted to get another dog but couldn't bring himself to, feeling as if he were being disloyal. Good ol' Bessie; she was a good dog, always there at his heels as he worked around the farm, following him from paddock to paddock or even hitching a ride on the quad bike. Always there each night curled up at his feet. She was his shadow and constant companion for the longest time. It sure was lonely without her.

Life on the farm was a lonely pursuit, full stop. Out in the paddocks all day or stuck in the drenching yards. Gone at dawn, not back till dusk and smelling of a lovely combination of sweat, manure, and cows. It was hard work, but Tom loved it, although he could understand why others didn't. Hit and miss too. Good years relied on good weather for successful calving, not to mention premium prices at the sale yards. Yet years of drought or too much rain were becoming all too common. Farm life wasn't as stable as it was in his grandfather's or even his dad's day.

But as much as Tom loved it, he was lonely. He'd return home at the end of a long day and wonder what all the hard work was for in the end when he had no one to share it with.

Tom drew in a deep breath. He missed Bessie almost as much as he'd missed Laura.

Spending time with her earlier that week made his heart pang with the familiar feelings he'd had all those years ago. Feelings he'd thought were long gone. But seeing her in the flesh—her long wavy hair and porcelain skin—had unlatched the box he'd stuffed those feelings into. And slowly, they leeched out, surfacing once more.

It was difficult to move on after Laura left. Especially under the circumstances. There was so much she didn't know. Especially his feelings for her. After all, it was unrequited love, and he had to accept that. His mates had tried to help, dragging him along to every gathering under the sun to find a 'Missus,' but no one came close to Laura. And who was he kidding? No one wanted to marry a farmer these days. All the girls hightailed it to the city as soon as they could for a life of high heels and cocktails, not cow pats and mud.

He rose to his feet and kicked his boots into the wall of the house, sending the farm cat, who'd been waiting for nightfall on the window edge, scurrying around the corner.

Once inside, Tom switched on the nightly news on the TV in the kitchen. His normal ritual while he cooked dinner, it made him feel less alone with the background noise. And it reminded him of his parents. Their TV was always on at night. The news, *Four Corners*, then whatever soapie was favored at the time. He glanced at the photo of his mum and dad sitting next to the TV. Their wedding portrait. His mum in a simple white dress and veil, his dad looking like his tie was choking him. They were perfect for each other, and even though they'd been through times of drought, flood, and poor calving seasons, every year they'd stood by each other. That's what he wanted. That sort of honest, loyal love.

He grabbed a couple of potatoes out of the pantry and began peeling them. It wasn't easy finding someone who shared his love of the land, and as time went on, finding someone was becoming less and less of a possibility. There were so many single farmers around the district, guys who had taken over their parents' farms. Bachelors. It was hard to find love when you were tied to a property. Sure, there were the odd exceptions, but they were usually childhood sweethearts. You only had to watch reality TV shows like that one a few years back called *Farmer Wants a Wife* to see how many single farmers there were. All lonely and longing for love. Maybe he'd end up on some TV show looking for love himself.

He imagined himself showing three lovely lasses around the farm, watching them in awe of the beautiful sunsets and sunrises, getting spooked by the cows as they turned unexpectedly, and getting their hands dirty stringing fence lines. The problem with his vision was that every girl he imagined looked like Laura.

The rain began to din on the verandah, gathering momentum until it had drowned out the sound of the pork sausages splattering in the pan. He shook his head. As much as he tried to deny it, Laura was his perfect girl. She always had been. Ever since she would come out to the farm with her mum when they were kids. Those days were clearly etched in Tom's mind as if they were yesterday. The days when the two of them would run down to the dam at the east side of the property and try and catch the tadpoles, or they would wander down to the river with the fishing rods, never catching anything but having a great time laughing and talking about nothing in particular. Other times they would just sit side by side on the tire swing that his dad had made for them. A large worn-out tractor tire secured by six ropes to a branch off one of the huge, strong peppercorn trees at the back of the house. They would sit and swing for hours.

Being with Laura felt easy. They would laugh until their eyes leaked. Deep belly laughs, the sort that made you feel like there was nowhere else in the world you'd rather be. And for Tom, there wasn't. Even now. Even after what happened.

Tom plated up his meal and sat down at the wooden table. Ryan. The emotions stirred in Tom's gut. Memories of Laura always had to bring Ryan along for the ride, didn't they? Years of great memories all quashed by one tumultuous year that threw all of them around like washing on a spin cycle. Except they didn't come out clean and shiny. They all came out battered, bruised, and brokenhearted. Tom stabbed at his sausage, the anger bubbling once again as he thought of *that night.* What if things had turned out differently? A sliding doors moment. A split second. A different decision. Maybe everything could have been different.

Tom sighed and pulled himself to his feet, his appetite quashed by the memories.

He'd almost slipped. Almost caved into Laura's desperate eyes earlier that week when she'd found the newspaper clippings. He'd had the chance to tell her the truth. Oh, how free it would have felt being honest. To get the weight of it off his back like a ton of hay off the Ute. He imagined Laura's face as he told her. Imagined it twisting with hurt, her molasses eyes breaking before him.

There was no way.

He couldn't risk her ever knowing the truth.

9

LAURA TAPPED HER fingers on the arm of the lounge chair as she read another message from Luke. Again apologizing, saying he'd change, do whatever she wanted. Laura felt her resolve waver. Maybe she should give him another chance. After all, they did have some great times together. Maybe she'd be ready to move forward after her visit home, after getting the closure she needed. She tapped out a short message.

You just need to give me some time.

Her mind wandered for the umpteenth time to Ryan. Since finding that article, she couldn't shake the feeling that there was more to what had happened. If she only had ignored the short-bread tin and not let her curiosity get the better of her.

She glanced out the window and noticed Mrs. Hatfield on her front porch, staring into the rain. She'd always been the town gossip. If you ever wanted to know anything, all you had to do was ask her. Maybe she knew something. In fact, you didn't even have to ask most of the time. She'd simply tell. There was a running joke around town when Laura was younger that if you wanted something to get out, tell Mrs. Hatfield.

Buoyed by the thought, Laura jumped up and grabbed the umbrella leaning by the front door and crossed the road, giving Mrs. Hatfield a wave as she let herself into the front gate.

Mrs. Hatfield was dressed in a blue floral dress with a pink cardigan buttoned up halfway. Her white hair was pulled up into a messy bun with wisps falling around her deeply lined face. Her eyes were rimmed by deep pockets, as if she hadn't slept in years. She was pulling the dead rosebuds off her much-loved rosebushes that lined her front porch, their thick stems twisted and black.

'Hi, Mrs. Hatfield,' Laura said as she made her way up to the porch, lowering her umbrella and lifting the hood of her jacket from her head.

The old lady looked up at her, brow furrowing for a moment before raising her eyebrows in recognition.

'Oh, Laura! How lovely it is to see you, dear.' Mrs. Hatfield's voice was almost as creaky and worn as her front gate.

'I'm so sorry about your mum.' She shook her head. 'Too young. Too young.'

'Thank you.'

'Are you back for long?'

'I'm not really sure yet,' Laura answered, tucking her hair behind her ears.

'It must be hard for you after all this time. With everything that happened.' She paused, looking toward the railway line. 'Anyway, that's all in the past.'

'I actually wanted to ask you something about that.'

'About what, dear?'

'About Ryan.'

Mrs. Hatfield frowned. 'Ryan?' She paused as if shuffling through old memories. 'Oh, it was so long ago. I think things like that are better put to rest, don't you? No use dredging it all up again now,' she said, wiping her wet, wrinkled hands on her dress. 'How's this rain? Never ending. Just like in '74. They're saying if it doesn't stop soon, the rivers'll break. Don't reckon that stupid levy bank they built will hold them back,' she tutted. 'Stupid councilors in their cushy offices thinking they know everything.'

Laura nodded politely. 'No, but Mrs. Hatfield, about Ryan. I found something. A newspaper article that mentioned they thought perhaps Ryan had been ...,' she chose her words carefully, '...well, maybe his death wasn't an accident? I was wondering if you remembered hearing anything like that at the time.'

Mrs. Hatfield pursed her lips and exhaled. 'I try not to think about it. That poor boy. I don't know anything more than anyone else,' she said, shrugging and shifting her stance. 'And even if I did, it's not my place to tell ...'

Laura hesitated. 'What do you mean, not your place to tell?'

'Not to worry, love. It's all in the past. Best be off. Go on and get in out of the rain, or you'll catch yourself a cold.' And with that, Mrs. Hatfield hobbled toward her front door, her dress flapping in the breeze and slippers scraping along the ground.

'Mrs. Hatfield?' Laura urged. But it was too late. She disappeared inside and clicked the front door closed behind her.

Laura popped up her umbrella. What did she mean it wasn't her place to tell? She began down the porch steps when the motorcycle postman pulled up. 'Would you mind, love? These'll get soaked in here.' He held up a couple of letters.

'Sure.' Laura walked out and grabbed Mrs. Hatfield's mail.

'Cheers,' he said, motoring on in his yellow raincoat.

Laura traipsed back up the porch, about to slip the letters under Mrs. Hatfield's door before changing her mind. She knocked on the door and waited. Nothing. This time Laura rapped on the window. She cupped her hands over her face and peered through the lace curtain and saw a shadowy figure moving down the hallway.

'Ah, Laura!' Mrs. Hatfield said as she opened the door. It was as if she hadn't seen Laura for days, not minutes. Maybe she *was* losing her marbles.

'Sorry, Mrs. Hatfield. I didn't want your mail to get ruined,' Laura said, holding up the envelopes.

'Oh, you're a dear, aren't you? Come in! Come in!' she motioned, shuffling inside.

Laura smiled to herself and stepped into the house and onto the threadbare carpet, the Turkish rug pattern faded to a dull red. She followed Mrs. Hatfield into the front living room, where she was greeted by a smell of old mothballs and dampness. She tried hard not to screw up her nose.

'Sit,' said Mrs. Hatfield, pointing to the wood-framed vintage green lounge suite. The dark varnished wooden arms and legs were chipped and discolored. It would have been an expensive piece back in its day.

'Would you like a cuppa? Or a biscuit? I don't have much,' Mrs. Hatfield continued as she shuffled into the adjacent kitchen. 'Don't have many visitors nowadays.'

'No, no. It's fine, really. I'm okay,' Laura said as she heard cupboard doors being opened and tins clattering. Laura waited, gazing around the living room, every spare space taken up with dust-covered china ornaments of cats and miniature teacups. She noticed an old ginger cat on the adjacent lounge chair curled up in an orange ball of fur, oblivious to Laura's presence.

'Here we go!' Mrs. Hatfield returned with a plate of Iced VoVo biscuits and sat them on the coffee table in front of Laura. 'My favorite. Can't go past the old Iced VoVo!' Mrs. Hatfield smiled, picking one off the plate. She slowly lowered herself into the corner chair across from Laura. Laura swore she heard the old lady's bones creak as she sat down.

Laura picked up a biscuit out of politeness and took a bite, trying to catch the coconut flakes in her cupped hand as she did.

'Mrs. Hatfield,' Laura began. 'I know it was so long ago, but it's just what you said before, about Ryan's death. Do you know something? Something that maybe you thought wasn't important back then but maybe, in hindsight, is now?'

Mrs. Hatfield cocked her head to the side as if Laura had been speaking another language. Laura sighed and decided to start fresh.

'Okay, so I was sorting through Mum's things the other day and I found this newspaper article.' Laura pulled the soft piece of news clipping out of her pocket carefully, so as not to rip it. She unfolded it and passed it across to Mrs. Hatfield.

Mrs. Hatfield squinted her eyes and held the paper out at arm's length, then scrambled for her glasses on the side table. 'Eyesight's not what it used to be,' she said, pushing the thick-rimmed glasses upon her nose. She squinted, furrowed her brow, and read.

'What I don't understand,' continued Laura, 'is why they questioned it being an accident. It was like they thought someone might have ...'

Mrs. Hatfield tutted and pulled her glasses off, discarding them onto the arm of the chair. 'Well, I s'pose that's my fault.'

Laura's breath caught in her throat.

'It was me who pointed out the army material,' she continued, shaking her head. 'I just thought it strange, y'know? I'd seen that odd fellow a few times hanging around the track there, probably on his way back from the pub, I guess.'

Laura leaned forward, hanging on every word but totally confused. 'What odd fellow?'

'He was new to town. Everybody knew he was a loner. Homeless, y'know?'

'You think he had something to do with Ryan's death?'

'Well, I don't know.' She shook her head again. 'The whole tragedy of the thing. Poor kid. His whole life ahead of him.'

'But what about the homeless man? What was it that made you think of him?'

Mrs. Hatfield leaned back in her chair, crossing her legs at the ankles and smoothing down her dress. 'Well, I'd been sitting on the front porch that night. Y'know I could hear that damn party from here?' She raised her eyebrows. Laura smiled sheepishly.

'And anyway, I stayed out there longer than usual. It was the first warm night of the year. And the mosquitos didn't seem to be out yet, so I was enjoying it, just sitting there. Apart from the noise, of course.'

Laura shifted in her seat, scratching the side of her neck, wishing Mrs. Hatfield would get to the point.

'Anyway, it was late, and I thought it time to call it a night, but then I heard some sort of kerfuffle up at the railway line. An argument of sorts. The noise carried well—must have been the way the breeze was blowing. I didn't know the voice, but it was drunk, slurred words and all that. I wandered up toward Janet's house there on the corner before the line and poked my head out from behind her front tree. The homeless fellow was there. Dressed as usual in his army greens, boots, and torn T-shirt. He was on the track yelling at some kids farther down the line. "Get off my track! This is my track!"' Mrs. Hatfield flailed her arms around. 'And some other choice words, mind you! And anyway, he picked up something, I think it was a bottle. Beer probably. Whiskey. Doesn't matter. And stumbled along the tracks and down under the cutting toward the river. I couldn't see him after that. But, anyway, I didn't think that much of it. Thought he was just heading back to his bridge.'

Laura slumped her shoulders. Mrs. Hatfield didn't really have much to tell her. At least not the knowledge Laura thought she had.

'Well, it wasn't till the next morning when...' The old woman hung her head. 'Never forget it, I will. How the train driver didn't know he'd ...' She inhaled quickly. 'Anyway, when I was up at the track with the whole bloody neighborhood, I saw a piece of green and black material just like that fellow's pants not far from ... So, I thought I should tell the coppers. Turns out it wasn't anything. Well, I don't reckon so, as they never found him. Seemed he'd moved on.'

Laura bit the inside of her cheek, trying not to let the tears that had backed up behind her eyes escape. She swallowed. 'I guess we'll never really know.'

'Well ...' Mrs. Hatfield paused and stared at Laura as if she were about to tell her something important. But the intent in her eyes vanished, and she shook her head.

'Mrs. Hatfield?'

Mrs. Hatfield dismissed Laura's question with a wave of the hand and nibbled on another biscuit.

This was all beginning to seem like a waste of time. She was just a wannabe Mrs. Marple.

Laura thanked Mrs. Hatfield and returned home. An uneasiness still hung over her. Would it make it any better if there was someone else involved? Surely, that would be worse. But still, she couldn't slow her racing thoughts. She noticed her mum's library card on the kitchen bench and an idea sprang to mind. Yes, the library. Maybe she could find some more articles from around that time that would help piece things together. There had to be more to it than what was initially reported. She glanced at her watch. The library would be closed now, but she planned to go there first thing in the morning.

10

LAURA SHOOK OUT her umbrella and swung open the heavy wooden doors to the library. The rain had set in again, endless clouds covering the sky in a gray blanket. She placed her umbrella against the wall and inhaled the familiar scent of old books and carpet freshener; nothing had changed.

She hadn't set foot in the library since high school, and it was like stepping back in time. As before, the nonfiction shelves were to the left, fiction to the right, and there was a small children's room complete with a long beanbag caterpillar that Laura remembered sitting on when she was little, its faded fabric now covered in colored patches where it had been mended. The only change was the small café that had sprung up where the meeting room used to be. Instead of bland board tables, the café held small round tables and cute mismatched chairs. The walls were decorated in posters of classic book covers. But as inviting as the café looked, Laura was here for a purpose.

She veered toward the back of the library, where she knew the periodicals and archives used to be housed. It was eerily quiet.

The only noise was the gentle hum of the heating unit. There were a couple of people browsing the fiction shelves, and a young girl with her back to Laura sitting at one of the private cubicles tapping away on a keyboard. On second glance, Laura was sure it was Gemma and glanced to her left as she walked past, recognizing Gemma's profile.

'Gemma, hey,' Laura said, turning to speak with her. Gemma looked up from the computer, and her eyes widened and face flushed. She quickly shut the lid to her laptop.

'Ah, Laura. Um ... hi,' she said, fidgeting with her hands.

'Day off school?' Laura said, pulling up the chair across from her.

Gemma's eyes glanced from side to side. 'Um, kind of. I wasn't feeling well so, um ... slept in, and then I thought I'd, ah, come to the library to study instead.'

Laura nodded, trying not to furrow her brow. Something was up. Gemma was acting strange, and her story didn't seem to make sense. But Laura shrugged it off.

'So, you must be in what, year twelve now?'

'Um, yeah.'

'Wow! Time flies. Any thoughts on what you want to do when you finish?'

Gemma rolled her eyes and shrugged.

Laura couldn't put a finger on what it was, but she knew something wasn't right. The Gemma she once knew seemed like a stranger now. Gone were the joyful dancing eyes, wide smile and enthusiasm for life. It was replaced by dark clothes, kohl-rimmed eyes, and a permanent glower.

'Is everything okay, Gem?'

Again, Gemma shrugged, her eyes darting around the room before gathering her laptop and sliding it into her backpack. 'I'd better go. I'm feeling a bit light-headed again,' she said.

Laura rose to her feet. 'Sure. Hey, did you want a lift home? It's raining cats and dogs out there.'

'Nah, it's fine,' Gemma said, pushing her arms through her hooded parka.

'Okay, well. I'll see you again?' It was more of a question than a statement. Gemma's eyes narrowed, and Laura noticed her posture stiffen. It looked like Gemma was about to say something, but then she simply nodded and walked toward the door.

Laura didn't want to pry, but an uneasy feeling was lining her gut about Gemma. She made a mental note to talk to Stella. Not that she wanted to be nosy, just out of concern. After all, Stella had mentioned she was worried about her. And Gemma's dark mood reminded Laura so much of Ryan in those last few months.

Laura's thoughts pushed back through her memories to the first time she'd experienced Ryan's sudden mood change.

They were lazing about down at the river one blue-skied Saturday afternoon. Lawn mowers hummed in the background, and a group of kids on bikes and scooters passed by the walking track, disturbing a flock of galahs in the branches hanging over the river, their piercing screeches echoing as they flew off in a flurry.

Ryan had been in a good mood, at least until then. Laura would say it was his usual mood. Carefree, light, and laughing about the latest episode of *How I Met Your Mother*.

And then his mood began to change.

'What are you doing at uni next year, Ry? You are going, aren't you? Don't you want to do graphic design or something?' Laura had asked, staring up at the gum trees overhead, her head resting on Ryan's stomach.

Ryan remained silent.

'Ry?'

'Yeah. I s'pose, something like that,' he said with a sigh.

'What does that mean?'

'It just means what it means. I s'pose it's what I'll do. That's all.' He shifted up onto his elbows, and Laura sat up to face him.

'You should. Do it, I mean. You're good at it. Amazing, actually.'

Ryan stared past her again, staying silent, a sullen expression on his face.

'I've got it!' Laura said, speaking at a hundred miles an hour as an idea formed in her head. 'We'll move to the city, go to uni. I'll do law, if I get in of course, you'll do a design course, and we'll rent a little flat somewhere nearby and get some part-time jobs. It will be perfect, Ry. Maybe Rach could live with us to help with the rent? And we can all come back every few weeks to visit Tom on the farm. It'll be awesome! What do you think?' She hardly paused to take a breath, pleased with herself and her ingenious plan.

Ryan's face, however, clouded further, and his eyes changed from soft green pools to angry oceans. His lips were pursed and his body tense. Then, all of a sudden, as if he couldn't hold it back any longer, he exploded.

'What does it matter what I think?' he barked. 'Sounds like you've got it all planned out.' He jumped to his feet, flicked his towel over his shoulder, and turned to walk up the bank.

'Ryan! Wait!' Laura called to him, her voice hard to control thanks to the lump in her throat.

He turned back to Laura with narrow eyes and stormed toward her. 'What about what I want, Laura? Did you ever even ask what I want?'

Laura stood there, her bottom lip trembling as Ryan seethed before her. She'd never seen him like this. And then, almost as quickly as he exploded, Laura saw Ryan's face drop, the anger sliding away his head fell forward.

Laura was frozen, not wanting to move, unable to muster any words.

'I'm sorry. I didn't mean to snap at you,' Ryan said, his voice barely a whisper. He reached his arm out toward Laura, who flinched momentarily before letting him pull her into his arms.

'It was only an idea. I didn't mean that ...' She sobbed into his shoulder.

'I know. I know,' he said, stroking her hair. 'It's just, everyone keeps talking about next year, and I just want to enjoy this.' He moved back slightly and looked down at Laura. 'This. Us. You know? Our last year of high school.'

Laura nodded as Ryan bent down to kiss her head. 'I just lose myself sometimes,' he said.

Laura didn't know what he meant, but she didn't want to ask either.

'I'd better go,' Ryan said. 'I promised Gran I'd help her in the garden this afternoon. I'll call you later, okay?' He pecked her forehead again and turned and made his way up the riverbank.

Laura sat down on her towel, hugged her legs into her chest and cried into her arms.

Looking back on it now, Laura wished she had done more than feel sorry for herself. Maybe Ryan was trying to tell her something. Maybe things could have been different if she'd noticed. She sighed. That thundery look Ryan had was so similar to the one drawn on Gemma's face just moments before. Laura had to talk to Stella.

'Can I help you?'

Laura let out a sharp breath as she unwrapped herself from her thoughts, startled by the young woman who had stepped out from behind one of the rows of shelves.

'Oh, I'm sorry. Didn't mean to frighten you.' She smiled. She wasn't Mrs. Roberts, the librarian whom Laura remembered, old and stern and with a lisp that she found hard to contain if she was grumpy, which was most of the time. No, this woman—girl— looked barely out of school. With a peroxide pixie cut and square, black-rimmed glasses, she looked like she'd be more at home at a hipster café in Fitzroy.

'No. That's fine. I just didn't see you there,' Laura said, clutching her phone.

'So, are you looking for something in particular?'

'Um, yeah. I'm after the newspaper archives.'

'Oh, okay,' the young woman replied, as if it were an odd request. 'A particular date?' she asked as she motioned for Laura to follow her into a darkened room behind the periodicals.

'Um, November 2010.'

'That's easy then. All on digital now,' she said as she clapped her hands together. 'We've been working on getting all the news- papers computerized for the past few years. Big job,' she said, her eyes widening with excitement. 'But we started with the present, which was easy as the first seven years back were digital already, and then it was manual scanning. You know. Takes time. But we're already back to 1987, can you believe?'

Laura smiled politely.

'Right over here.' The librarian showed Laura the computer and how to search the program, and then left her to it.

Fifteen minutes later, Laura found another article discussing Ryan's death. It was the only other one apart from Ryan's eulogy, which she couldn't bring herself to read. She squinted as she read the pixelated print.

POLICE HAVE RULED *the death of local teenager Ryan Taylor a 'tragic accident.' The teen was discovered on the tracks near the Smythe Street* crossing three weeks ago, with the police and coroner only now ruling on the cause of death.

'Our investigation has concluded, and we've determined that the death is not suspicious and was simply a tragedy that could well have been avoided,' local detective Roy Makin said in a statement released late yesterday. He went on to say that the potent mix of alcohol and marijuana, presumed to be consumed at an end of exam after-party, had resulted in the youth straying onto the tracks. Due to the extent of injuries, the coroner was unable to conclude if Ryan was already passed out before he was hit, or if he stumbled onto the tracks in his intoxicated state. Although it could not be officially confirmed, the police ruled out any evidence of foul play, further dismissing the green army material found on the tracks.

'We hope, if anything, that the local youth realize that excess alcohol and illicit drug use can have very permanent consequences,' said Detective Makin. He went on to say that steps will be taken to install guardrails on this section of the track, which is so easily accessible to the general public.

LAURA SAT IN SILENCE, her stomach now a collection of knots, her brain feeling like it was being cut open, raw memories burning behind her eyes. Ryan's death was an accident. An unfortunate, tragic accident. A case of too much alcohol and god knows what else. That was all.

'Did you find what you were after?' the librarian asked Laura as she was about to leave.

'Well, yes, but no,' Laura said, glancing at the girl's name tag.

She smiled and raised an eyebrow. 'Ah, very cryptic. And hi,' she said, stretching out her hand. 'I'm Shea.' Laura reached across and shook her hand.

'Don't get a lot of girls my age in here too often. I'm guessing you're my age. Mid-twenties?'

Laura nodded. 'Yeah. I'm Laura.'

'I'm twenty-four. So, kind of out of touch with the oldies that come in, as lovely as they are, of course. And then there's the little ones with their mums. They're all nice.'

A thought jumped to attention in Laura's mind. 'What about Gemma, the girl I was talking to at the tables when I came in?' Laura motioned toward the now empty group of study tables.

'Ah, Gemma, is that her name? Mmmm. She's a bit of a quiet one. She's been coming in quite a bit lately, I've noticed. Mainly to log into the free Wi-Fi on her laptop. Don't think she's ever borrowed anything. Kind of keeps to herself. You know her?'

'Yeah, well, I used to. I grew up here but left after year twelve. She was one of my mum's friend's daughters.'

'Oh, right! A local. I can't call myself a local yet, only been here for a couple of years, but I love it compared to the city. So much quieter and simpler. Is that why you've moved back?'

Laura swallowed. 'Oh, I haven't moved back. Just, um, visiting.' She paused to take a breath. 'My mum passed away, and I have to pack up her house to sell it, then I'll be back to the city.'

'Oh. You must be Judy Murphy's daughter?'

Laura nodded.

'I'm sorry for your loss. I didn't know her to speak to, but I know she was well liked. I'm so sorry.'

Laura smiled politely as a customer approached the loans desk where Shea was standing. 'Well, better let you get back to work. Nice to meet you,' Laura said.

'Yeah, you too. Let me know if there's anything else I can help you with.'

'Thanks. I will.'

Laura stepped out of the library and popped up her umbrella.

The water was welling in the gutters, creating a mini river rushing by. She ran to her car, trying to avoid the puddles that were now almost lakes across the parking lot. Once in the car, she started the engine and pumped up the heater, switching the vent to the floor. The air warmed her cold feet while her mind again asked questions she didn't have answers for. As she drove across the bridge over the railway line, Laura tried to keep away the images that had plagued her imagination so intently, night after night, day after day. At times, the snippets flashing before her felt so real, but she knew it was just her mind playing tricks on her. Tormenting her. She'd learned to switch it off, but now with the memories of Ryan at the forefront of her mind, and seeing the tracks, the collage of images had flickered to life again.

Light-headed and heart racing, Laura pulled to the side of the road to catch her breath once across the tracks. *It's time to move on, Laura. Time to move on.* Replaying memories wasn't going to do any good. What's done was done. But still, she couldn't shift the unsettled feeling that had lodged in the pit of her stomach, keeping her thoughts flapping from one page to another like a book in the wind. She needed to hear it from someone who knew. She wanted to hear it from the source: Detective Makin. Laura bit her fingernails as a flash of Makin's face entered her memory. It was the morning she found out about Ryan.

Laura had sat in the living room of her home, eyes fixed straight ahead as she fingered the holes on her mother's crochet blanket that lay across her legs. It was doing little to warm her. She was so cold. Her skinned knees stung, and her bones ached. Muffled voices and road noise echoed irregularly through the open window, and the morning breeze stung her red and swollen eyes. A cup of tea sat untouched on the side table next to her. The milk had separated, fat floating in ribbons on top of the cold liquid.

Her eyes flickered as she heard voices approaching. Heavy, unfamiliar footsteps creaked on the hallway floorboards.

'Are you sure this is necessary, Detective? Now?' Her mother's voice.

'It's only a couple of questions, Judy. I promise it won't take long.' The male voice was deep and raspy. Laura didn't look up as their shadows appeared at the doorway.

Her mum walked over, knelt, and placed her hand over Laura's. The warmth of her mother's hand made her realize how bone cold she was. Cold and empty.

'Laura, honey? Detective Makin just needs to ask you a couple of questions. Is that okay?'

Laura shrugged, the slight movement threatening to break her.

Detective Makin sat on the worn couch opposite Laura, his large frame sinking into the cushions. He cleared his throat before speaking.

'Laura, I know this is hard, and I'm very sorry for your loss, but I need to ask you a couple of questions. Is that okay?' He paused for a response, which Laura didn't offer, and then continued. 'When was the last time you saw Ryan?'

Laura felt the tears well in her eyes at the mention of his name. She swallowed. 'Last night.'

The detective began scribbling in his black, vinyl-bound notebook, the concentration forming in thick lines between the bridge of his nose. 'Do you know what time?'

'I don't know. Late.'

'Was this after the party down the road?'

Laura nodded.

'Do you remember where you saw him?'

Laura's hands began to shake.

'It's okay, honey. It's okay.' Her mother folded her hands over Laura's.

'On the train tracks.'

Detective Makin looked up over his square-rimmed bifocals. 'The tracks? Here? Just down the road?'

Laura nodded.

'Can you tell me what state Ryan was in? Was he intoxicated? Had he taken any drugs? What was his frame of mind?'

Laura stared past Detective Makin into the distance, trying to urge her memories to clear. Everything was still a blur. She remembered seeing Ryan and arguing, then storming off, leaving him sitting on the tracks. She remembered being in her bedroom and sobbing into her pillow. And then she remembered nothing but smudged and hazy images. Images of Ryan. At her bedroom window? At the front door? His head bleeding? The train? But that wasn't right. She didn't trust these memories. There was nothing to ground them. The line between real and imagined had twisted in knots in her mind, strangling every thought and memory into tight balls of confusion. Every time she closed her eyes, the memories would skip and change like a broken movie reel playing different images simultaneously. She couldn't trust the tricks her mind was playing on her.

'Laura?' Detective Makin prompted.

'I ... um ... yes, he was drunk. He was slurring his words.' The tears began again, and she feverishly brushed them away.

'Had he taken any illegal drugs?'

Laura shook her head. 'I don't know. Maybe. I'm not sure.' Laura remembered the sweet smell of marijuana and gagged. Her shoulders began to shake with the deep sobs that rose from her chest, unable to be held back anymore. Her mum shuffled to her feet and put her arms protectively around Laura's shoulders.

'I'm sorry, Detective, I think we should continue this another time. It's too soon.'

'With all due respect, Mrs. Murphy, it's imperative we get as much information as early as possible for the investigation. Just one more question, please?'

Her mum pursed her lips.

'Laura, did Ryan have any reason to want to end his life?'

With that, Laura caught her breath and looked sharply toward the detective. 'What? You think Ryan …'She cupped her mouth with her trembling hands.

Detective Makin sighed with heavy shoulders. 'I'm sorry, Laura. We have to look at all possibilities.'

Judy moved between Laura and Detective Makin. 'Obviously she doesn't have an answer for that,' she said. 'That will be all for now. I'll show you out.' She gestured forward and walked to the door with her head held high.

Detective Makin sighed as he heaved his body off the couch, leaving a sunken impression in the cushions. Pausing at the door of the living room and the hall, he turned to Laura. 'I'm so very sorry, Laura.'

Laura startled as a group of teenagers crossed the road noisily in front of her, their raucous laughter vibrant against the backdrop of the gray sky. Laura noticed her white knuckles and slowly uncurled her hands from gripping the steering wheel. Behind her, a passenger train rattled rhythmically along the tracks as it slowed toward the station. It felt to her like it was tearing along at a speed of one hundred miles per hour, right through her heart. She turned the key in the ignition, her heart pounding, and drove home.

Once inside, Laura's breathing calmed. She switched on the kettle, grabbed a cup off the sink drying rack, and dropped in a tea bag. Part of her wished she hadn't come back. As much as she felt centered here, safe within the confines of her home, she realized the memories that her hometown held simply couldn't be put aside like she had done over the past years. Was finding out what really happened to Ryan going to make any difference? Why couldn't she just say goodbye and be done with it, just like she'd promised her mum? She didn't know why it didn't seem like enough. It was as if everything inside, from her core right through to the marrow in her bones, ached to know. It was a compulsion now, a drive like nothing else she'd experienced. She just had to know.

The kettle switch flicked off, and she poured the boiling water into the cup, the tea bag shrinking and then relaxing. As she let the tea steep, Laura pulled the telephone book from a kitchen drawer. 2013. It was a few years old, but it was a start. She flicked through the soft paper to find the right page and then scanned her finger down the list of names. Maddison, Maguire, Makin. There were two listed:

Makin A.R., 17 Allison Crescent

Makin D.M. & P.D., 2850 Clear Springs Road

Neither began with R for Roy, but it was worth a try. Forgetting about her tea, she pulled on her raincoat, slipped on her boots, and decided to check out the listing on Allison Crescent. It was only a few streets over.

Laura drove carefully down the cul-de-sac, a wave of nostalgia washing over her. Familiar houses with neat nature strips and concrete driveways. She remembered cutting through the adjacent alley as a shortcut to Rachel's house when she was younger.

Laura came to a stop in front of a cream, triple-fronted brick veneer, a brass number 17 adorning the matching brick mailbox. The gardens were immaculate, albeit a little waterlogged. Pruned hedges and manicured conifers stood symmetrically on either side of the house. A row of apricot roses in full autumn bloom lined the front fence. Laura inhaled their fresh scent as she walked toward the porch. Knocking on the security door, Laura froze. What was she going to say? She didn't have long to think about it, as a large man wearing thick bifocals and sporting a neatly clipped gray beard opened the door with a cautious look on his face. His frame took up the whole of the doorway.

'Yes? Can I help you?' The man towered over Laura by a full head and looked down at her over his glasses, his brow creased.

She recognized his raspy voice immediately. 'Detective Roy Makin?' she questioned timidly, feeling as if she were seventeen again.

The man jutted his head back, still frowning. 'Who wants to know?'

'Sorry,' Laura said, shuffling from one foot to another. 'I'm Laura Murphy. My mother was Judy Murphy.'

The man's face softened in recognition. 'Laura, right. So sorry to hear about your mum. She was a good woman,' he said, tutting. 'Much too young to be taken.'

Laura looked down at her feet. 'Yes, thank you. But that's not why I'm here.'

The man opened the door further and folded the newspaper he'd been holding, placing it under his arm as he ushered her in. 'I know why you're here,' he said as Laura followed him into his kitchen, taking a seat at the kitchen table covered in crossword puzzles and red pens. 'Sorry, wasn't expecting company,' he said, shuffling the papers and pens into a messy pile before sitting down with a sigh. 'You're here about Ryan, no?'

Laura's face shifted into a frown. 'How did you know?'

'Saw Mrs. Hatfield at the supermarket earlier. She said you were back. Asking questions. Well, Laura. There's nothing to tell. Nothing more than you probably already know.'

'I just can't believe it was an accident. Ryan wasn't stupid.'

'Don't need to be stupid with a mix of alcohol and marijuana in your system, love. That takes care of stupidity for you,' he said, shaking his head.

Laura's face fell.

'Look, I know how hard it was for you and his friends, and I wish I could tell you more, but there's nothing to tell. All the evidence led to a stupid bloody lack of judgment.'

'What about the green material you found on the tracks nearby?' Laura asked.

'Bloody wild goose chase, that's what,' Mr. Makin said, crossing his arms.

'But wasn't there a ... well, a homeless man hanging around at that time?'

'As I said, bloody goose chase. Yes, we followed him up, but it was a dead end. He admitted to being on the tracks that night, but he had an alibi for the ETD.'

'ETD?'

'Estimated time of death. He was,' he cleared his throat, a flush creeping up over his cheeks, 'otherwise entertained.' He raised his eyebrows.

Laura's brow furrowed.

'He was shacked up with, well, let's just say a lady friend.'

Laura twisted her mouth. 'But how does that prove anything? Maybe she was covering for him. How can you be sure?'

'The green army material didn't match any of his clothing either. He had no priors. He was harmless. Moved on to Clear Springs a couple of days later.'

Laura's shoulders dropped.

'Look, I know you want a better answer than that, but really, I don't know why him being murdered would be a better outcome.'

He was right. It would be horrible if Ryan was murdered, no

matter the circumstances, but it would at least be a clear answer. Something she could draw a line at accepting, maybe.

Mr. Makin reached his hand over to Laura's and patted it affectionately. 'I know you took off back then. But you need to move on. Put it behind you. You're still so young, Laura. You've got your whole life ahead of you. Okay?'

Laura squeezed her mouth into a thin smile, forcing herself not to cry. She nodded.

'It's such a shame, you know. Youth of today are no better. Worse, in fact,' Makin said, leaning back in his chair.

'What do you mean?'

Detective Makin shook his head. 'Boredom. Depression. Underage drinking. Drugs. It's a bloody shame, and there's only so much law enforcement can do. This bloody town needs some help. Counsellors. Youth programs. I don't know, but something. They're just not getting the support they need.'

Laura felt awful that the town she loved was falling apart from the bottom up. If the youth weren't supported, what was the future for Banyula?

'Anyway, that's a whole other story. I'm sorry I couldn't help you more, love.'

Laura thanked Detective Makin for his time and walked toward the front door.

'Laura?' Detective Makin said as he removed his glasses and opened the door for her. 'I hope you can move on from here. There's nothing to be gained from living in the past. Believe me. I know.'

11

TOM LEANED BACK against the cattle race, rubbing his five-o'clock shadow. 'I'm sorry, Mum. I meant to tell you. I just got sidetracked, that's all.'

'I had no idea until I read it on Facebook. On Facebook, Tom!' she said through the phone.

'I know, Mum. It's just things have been busy here. And I was going to email you the night before the funeral. I'm sorry.'

Tom heard her sigh. 'Well, how was the funeral? Was Laura there?'

'Of course she was there, Mum!'

'Well, it's just she hasn't been back to Banyula since. I'm surprised she didn't bury Judy in the city.'

'Mum!'

'Have you seen her?'

'Who? Laura?'

'Yes, of course Laura.'

'Yeah, a couple of times. I drove her home after the funeral. Helped her clean up at Judy's a bit.'

'How's she holding up?'

'She's upset. Sad. But she's strong too. She just wants to clean up the house and get back to the city.'

'Well, have you spoken to her?'

'Mum, you're not making any sense. Did I talk to her about what?' Tom was getting frustrated. It wasn't like his mum to talk in riddles. Maybe the holiday had affected her thinking.

'Bloody hell, Tom, do I have to come out and say it?'

Tom didn't reply.

'Have you told her how much you miss her?'

'Mum!'

'Don't think I don't know. You've missed that girl ever since she left. You need to tell her. You mightn't get another chance. She'll up and go, and you'll likely never see her again if she goes this time. I just want to see you happy. You deserve someone. And Laura's a good one.'

Tom felt his face burning. Was he really having this conversation with his mother? He didn't even know what to say.

'Anyway, think about it. I'd better go for now. Your dad's trying his hand at beach fishing. I think he might have caught something the way he's carrying on down there. Give our best to Laura.'

'Okay. I will.'

'And tell her how you feel. If this trip's taught me anything, it's that life is too short to waste.'

Tom slipped the phone into his shirt pocket and sighed.

As much as it embarrassed him to admit to it to his mum, he knew she was right. This might be the only chance he would get to tell Laura how he felt. Maybe he could take a chance and tell her. There was nothing to say he had to be honest with her about everything. Just his feelings. Things had been forgotten and had been kept secret for so long, it was probably best to let it all be buried in the past anyway. No use dredging things up.

He headed over to see off Nigel, one of his farmhands.

'Sorry, I gotta leave early today, mate,' Nigel said.

'Nah, don't worry about it. You be here tomorrow?'

'Yeah, no worries, mate. Gotta finish that fence down in the east paddock. Didn't ya say you had Matty coming to help with the worming tomorrow?'

Tom shook his head. 'He pulled out on me. So hard to get good bloody help these days.'

Nigel nodded. 'Yeah, I hear ya. I'll give ya a hand with the worming before I do the fence, how's that sound?'

'That'd be great. Cheers, mate. See you tomorrow.'

Tom watched Nigel head off. It was true. It was hard to get farmhands these days. None of the young blokes wanted to work. Tom rolled his eyes. He was starting to sound just like his father. Not that it was a bad thing. His dad was a bloody good farmer. Well respected and a hard worker. That's where Tom learned everything he knew. And that's why Tom had to make things work.

He crooked his neck to the side, thinking about the other issue he had with the bank. He just needed more time. Needed the cows to finish calving and get the two-year-olds to market. He might even drive them over to Yangaville. They were getting good prices over there. He decided to finish off in the yards, then head inside and check out what was lining up at the markets.

As he clicked the gate behind him, he also made a conscious decision to ask Laura around for dinner. Or he could take her to that new Thai place in town. Maybe not tonight. Maybe tomorrow. He needed to work up the courage first. And then if she said yes and the right moment came, he might even take a chance and tell her how he felt. Like his mum said, this could be his only opportunity. Better to die of embarrassment than to die wondering. That's what his mum'd say. What was the worst thing that could happen?

12

LAURA ARRIVED HOME with Detective Makin's words still echoing in her ear. He was right. There was nothing more to know. Laura had to accept the fact that Ryan's death was an accident. Something that should never have happened but had. It would always be with her, but she had to come to terms with the fact that she'd done everything she could. It was time to face the rest of her life and move forward once and for all. Face Luke and say goodbye to Ryan and Banyula. Start a new life. Maybe she would go and finish that counseling course. It was time to be an adult.

Laura grabbed her phone, Googled the local real-estate agent, and made the call.

'Today? That would be great. Three o'clock? Sure. Thanks, Mick, see you then.' Laura ended the call and placed her mobile on the kitchen bench. This was it. Time to sell. Laura felt her gut begin to form a knot. *No. Keep a level head. You're going back to the city for a fresh start. That's the plan. Stick to it.* The knot in her gut twisted a little more.

. . .

THE BROWN PACKAGING tape screeched as Laura stretched it across to seal up another box. She'd been through everything: clothes, knickknacks, Tupperware. She was surprised how so many memories were associated with everyday items. Dresses she remembered her mum wearing on special occasions or Christmas, tea towels that she'd bought for fifty cents from the Mothers' Day stall at school, unopened photo frames still in their packaging with the faces of nameless models smiling beneath. So many things, so many boxes. Life. That was what was in these boxes. Laura's heart quickened as the finality of it all hit. Once she said goodbye, that was it. This chapter of her life was finished. The book would be closed forever. But she couldn't help but feel that this place was beginning to seem like home again with every minute she spent here.

She shook off the feeling like the dust that had gathered on the doilies she'd packed earlier. It was only her grief talking. There was nothing for her in Banyula. She'd pack up the beautiful memories of her mum and move on. That was the way it had to be.

MICK KNOCKED on the front door right at three. He'd been a year below Laura at school, and Laura noticed he'd hardly changed, apart from his attire. He'd swapped the football jersey for a navy suit and striped tie. But that self-assured smile-cum-smirk was still the same. *Yep, real estate is the perfect career choice for Mick*, Laura thought.

'Hey, Laura,' he said, shaking her hand firmly, if not a little awkwardly.

'Hi, Mick. Good to see you,' she said. 'You've done all right for yourself, I see.' She nodded toward the shiny black BMW sitting in front of the house.

'Yeah, I guess. Gotta look the part, right? You're looking great,' he said, followed by a sudden flush of color to his cheeks. 'I'm sorry to hear about your mum,' he said, tightening his mouth. 'She was well respected around here.'

'Thanks,' Laura replied, forcing a lightness into her voice. 'Time to move on though. Let someone else enjoy this little cottage, I guess.' If only she felt as convinced as she sounded. 'Come in out of that rain. Looks like it's set in for the day.'

'Yeah, we're all a bit sick of it. Rivers will peak soon if it doesn't stop,' Mick said as he stepped inside and wiped the droplets of water off his iPad.

'Well, the house is old and unrenovated,'Laura said as she walked Mick into the living room. 'But it's in good condition. Mum looked after it as best she could.'

'Neat and tidy, that's all we need. It's the location that will sell it.'

After ten minutes showing Mick around the house and yard, they got down to the nitty gritty.

'So how much?' Laura asked as they wandered back to the kitchen. The rain formed a diagonal drizzle that slid slowly down the windowpane.

'Well, considering the location and its original state, it's certainly a renovator's delight. But, what I can really see is a developer snapping it. It's a ripper parcel of land.'

Mick's words began to take shape in her mind. Was she really ready to sell this place and let some rich, fat cat developer knock down her childhood home and build a block of soulless units?

'Laura?'

'Sorry.' She snapped back to attention. 'What were you saying?'

'I'll have to do a few comparatives, but I reckon around the $380,000 mark.'

Laura's mouth dropped. 'Three hundred eighty? Thousand?'

'Yep. Market's good at the moment, and there's not a lot around coming into winter. Could be even more if we went to auction, you know.'

Mick pulled the chair from the kitchen table and motioned for Laura to sit down.

'Look, if you're not ready, it's fine. I know it's a big decision for you. I've had a look now, so you can just call me when you're right to go. Or feel free to get another appraisal. Jenkins is a good guy.'

In city terms, $380,000 wasn't a lot, but here in the country, Laura knew it was decent money. She could move back to the city and even find a small one-bedroom apartment in Carlton or Fitzroy.

'So, you planning on staying here in Banyula?' Mick asked as he continued tapping away on his iPad.

'I'm not really sure.' The words were out before she thought them through.

Mick laughed. 'Well, I know a great real-estate agent who has a few bargains if you're looking.'

Laura chewed her bottom lip. No. This was it. As much as her heart pulled at her, she knew this had to happen, especially for the money Mick was talking.

'No. Put it on the market. Let's see what happens,' she said before she could reconsider.

Mick raised his eyebrows. 'You sure?'

Laura nodded.

'Okey dokey. Just give me a minute and I'll fill in the details.'

A few minutes later, Laura signed on the dotted line, but not before almost falling off the chair when Mick told her the commission fees. No wonder he could afford a BMW!

'Okay, I'll send someone around to grab some photos, and then we'll get it on the books. I have a few people in mind already. I reckon they'll be hot for it.'

LAURA WAVED Mick and his Beemer off as her phone began to ring in her hand. It was Luke. She sucked in a deep breath. She had to talk to him sooner or later.

'Luke, hey,' Laura said, pacing on the porch as the wind caught the door behind her and slammed it shut.

'Laura. Thank god I got you this time.'

'Sorry. It's just—'

'It's fine. You don't need to explain. How are you?'

'I'm doing okay, I suppose. I got the house appraised.'

'Oh, right? How much?'

'Three hundred and eighty thousand, they reckon. I've put it on the market.'

'Wow. That sounds like good money.'

'Yeah.'

'Laura, I—'

'Luke, don't. I ...' She paused and slumped down against the weatherboards and peered out into the drizzling rain, searching for the right words. 'I meant what I said.'

'Laura, c'mon. Let's not do this now. This isn't the time to be making rash decisions. You've been through a lot. You'll be home soon. We can talk then.'

Laura closed her eyes. She never was good at confrontation, even over the phone. She picked at a thread on her jeans, contemplating whether or not to feign a bad connection, but Luke kept talking.

'If you don't want me to, I won't go for the promotion.'

Laura's throat constricted as the tears trickled down her face.

'It's more than that, Luke,' she said, searching for how to tell him she wasn't in love with him. An icy shiver crawled up her spine as images of Ryan and Rachel flashed through her mind. She had to be honest. She'd promised her mum.

She cleared her throat. 'I'm not sure if I'm in love with you.'

'What?' Luke's voice was almost a whisper of disbelief.

'We fell into the relationship so quickly and I ... I don't know if ... I just feel so lost. I need to sort myself out. What I want out of life. For the future.' Laura cringed at the way the words sounded. Cliched. It was no better than the age-old excuse, *It's not you, it's me.* But it was so much more than that. She was caught up in decisions and hurt from the past that had cut deep, the scars still not healed.

'I don't get it. I don't know what to say.' Luke sighed. She could imagine him pushing his hand through his hair in frustration, like he would when they'd argue about issues much less important than this.

'There's nothing to say.'

Laura slid down onto the porch deck and blinked away the tears.

THAT EVENING LAURA switched on the TV and flicked between the local channels, nothing capturing her interest. She couldn't focus on anything anyway. Since speaking to Luke, she had become even more determined to be honest with herself and others from now on. She'd finally realized what closure meant. That closure allows you to move forward. It may never help you get over something, but it helps you to pack the bags and store them away rather than carry the baggage with you every day and let it weigh you down. Laura ached for her mum. She'd always supported everything she'd done. Every decision she'd made, even the one to never return to Banyula. Always happy to travel up on the train to visit Laura in the city. She was selfless. And Laura had been selfish. But she was going to change. She wasn't going to hurt anyone anymore. She was going to pack up those bags, zip them up, store them away for good, and finally move forward.

13

CLEANING. LAURA HATED it, but it needed to be done, and it kept her mind off the fact that she was dismantling her life piece by piece. She wiped the pantry shelf down, the smell of eucalyptus and lemon making her sneeze each time she squirted the cleaner onto the Laminex. She hated this cleaning spray, but it also reminded her of walking into the bathroom just after her mum had cleaned it. She smiled at the memory and was then interrupted by a sharp knock on the front door.

'Yoo-hoo! Laura, you home?' Stella's voice echoed down the hallway.

'In the kitchen, Stella,' Laura called, climbing down from the stepladder.

'Oh darling, look at you. Come here.' Stella pulled Laura in for one of her warm hugs. 'How are you?' She stroked Laura's hair, which was half falling out of its loose ponytail.

'I'm okay.' Laura sighed, gently prying herself from Stella's well-meaning embrace. 'What about you, Stel? You're so busy running around after everyone all the time. How are you?'

Stella batted her arm at Laura. 'Me? I'm fine.' Stella dropped into one of the kitchen chairs. Laura noticed the worry lines gather between Stella's eyes as she sat down across from her.

'Are you sure? You look a little tired.'

Stella began fidgeting with her wedding band, twisting it round and round as she stared at it. The corners of her mouth flinched before she spoke. 'Well, actually …' She shook her head. 'No, it's nothing.'

Laura reached her hand across to Stella's. 'Stella, you don't have to always be the one that looks after everyone, you know? It's okay for you to be sad. Mum was your best friend. You don't have to put on a brave face, especially in front of me.'

Stella gave a thin smile, her eyes filling with tears. 'Oh, Laura. I miss your mum. She was such a beautiful soul. Life's not fair sometimes, is it?'

'Are you sure that's all it is?'

Stella sucked in a deep breath. 'Well, it's Gemma actually.'

'Gemma? Why? Is she okay?' Laura thought back to the uneasy feeling she had at seeing Gemma at the library.

'I don't know. I just don't know what to do anymore.'

'What do you mean?'

'She's not herself. Late last year she dropped out of school. Said she wanted to get a job, be a hairdresser. I was able to talk Debra at the salon into giving her a trainee position, but she lasted a week. She enrolled in a TAFE course this year—hospitality—just to try and get a job, but I don't think she's been going. When I confront her, she ignores me and locks herself in her room. That's when she's actually home. Most of the time I have no idea where she's gone. I know she's smoking. I just hope that's all it is, but I don't know, Laura. I'm so worried about her. And I feel so helpless. It's like she's a different person these days.' Stella pulled a tissue from her bra strap and wiped her eyes.

'Oh, Stella,' Laura said.

'I just don't know what to do. She's so ... oh, stuck in her own world. I've tried to reach her, but she pushes me away. And Art's never home. He works away a lot these days, not his fault. Just the way it is. I even tried to convince her to see a counselor, but the closest one is in Clear Springs and they have a three-week wait. Not that Gemma would go even if I got her in. That's the thing. There are so many kids like Gem. It's not just her. Depression, anxiety. I see it at school, the kids withdraw from life, and then ... I know the day will come when I'll have to stand up at the school assembly because one of our students ...' She shook her head, unable to continue.

Laura's heart felt heavy for Stella. And for Gemma. And for Banyula. 'I saw her at the library the other day,' Laura said.

'The library?'

Laura nodded. 'She had her laptop with her, but I'm not sure what she was doing. She wouldn't talk to me much either, looked a bit embarrassed that I'd run into her.'

Stella's shoulder's slumped. 'I suppose there are worse places she could be,' she said, shaking her head. 'I just wish there was someone she could talk to about whatever it is that's making her feel this way.' Stella shot an intense look at Laura. 'Maybe you could talk to her. She looked up to you so much when she was little. She was always talking about you. You really were like a big sister to her.'

Laura smiled, remembering how Gemma used to beg Laura to play Monopoly with her or watch her perform her latest acrobatic trick. 'Well, like I said, she didn't really want to talk to me the other day.'

'Of course, no, I'm sorry. That's too much to ask. I'm just being silly.'

'No, it's okay,' Laura said, seeing the distress in Stella's eyes. 'I'd be happy to try again.' Laura thought back to the few months of the counseling study she'd done. She vaguely remembered covering the child and adolescent unit. Maybe she could help Gemma. 'I can try at least,' Laura said, patting Stella's hand.

'Oh, Laura, would you?' Stella smiled beneath her sadness.

AFTER STELLA LEFT, Laura continued cleaning the pantry, but her thoughts were racing. For a moment, she felt positive. Maybe there was something she could do to help Gemma. She vowed to go and see the girl. After all, it couldn't hurt.

LAURA WAS HALFWAY through cleaning the oven when Tom called. She pulled off the thick rubber gloves, now covered in a greasy brown residue, and answered.

'Lauz, hey,' Tom said. 'I'm coming into town shortly, wondering if you wanted to catch up for dinner or something. There's a new Thai restaurant where the bookshop used to be. I haven't tried it yet, but well, I thought maybe we could, you know, see what it's like?'

Laura looked at her watch. It was almost six thirty, but the last thing she felt like doing was heading out. She was covered in grease and grime and knew she must have smelled like a chemical warehouse. Her stomach did stir at the thought of food though. 'I'd love to Tom, but I'm halfway through cleaning the kitchen. How about pizza? Takeaway?' Laura suggested, secretly hoping Tom's offer would extend to maybe helping her clean the top of the cupboards after pizza.

'Yeah, of course. That sounds great. Want me to call in and grab it?'

'Nah, it's fine. I'll get it delivered.'

'No pineapple!'

Laura laughed. 'Ha! Of course I remember!'

'No worries. I'll see you soon.'

Laura shook her head. Tom could always bring a smile to her face. She was glad the awkwardness from the other day had seemed to disappear. She wondered how she'd managed without Tom all these years. His quick wit and dry comments always made her smile. He'd always been there, especially when things got rough with Ryan, even though she knew Tom wasn't keen on her seeing Ryan for some reason. She never did figure out why. Her mind drifted back to the first time she realized Tom had mixed feelings about Ryan.

LAURA AND RACHEL were hanging out at the shops one afternoon after school.

'You wanna go down to the basketball game on Saturday?' Rachel asked Laura as they wandered past the bakery. The sweet smell of cinnamon and sugar made Laura's mouth water.

'Um, yeah. I guess so.'

'C'mon, it'll be fun. Stacey and the others aren't too bad, you know.'

'Yeah, I just feel so weird around them all. I want to go to watch Ryan, but ...'

Rachel shrugged. 'It's not like you don't see enough of him anyway,' she said sarcastically.

'Hey!' Laura said, pretending to slap her away. It was true though. She had been spending all her spare time with Ryan, and it had been great. Although the last few days, he'd been a little weird.

Laura paused to check out what was on the sale rack outside

Popsicle, the only place for decent fashion in Banyula. 'Anyway, you jealous, are you?' Laura said playfully.

'I'm not jealous,' Rachel snapped a little too sharply before softening her voice. 'Just missing my best friend.' She put her arm around Laura, planting a big kiss on her cheek.

Laura laughed. 'Hey, these would look good on you,' Laura said, holding up a pair of crisp white jeans.

Rachel rolled her eyes. 'They're so last year. Ugh. I'm just so over this,' Rachel said, flicking through the dresses. 'I want to get out of here so bad.'

By here, Laura knew Rachel meant Banyula. All the kids in their school year had grand plans to get out of Banyula. Laura wanted to as well. At least to go to university. But she also felt a pang of sadness thinking about leaving it all behind. Her mum, their little house, long days out on Tom's farm, fun times down at the river with Rachel, Ryan, and Tom. So many good times. Sure, Banyula wasn't vibrant like the city. People here moved at a slower, laid-back pace. Laura didn't think there was anything wrong with that.

'Laura? Are you even listening to me?' Rachel said.

Laura spied Ryan across the street outside the local fish and chip shop with some friends. 'Of course I am! Oh, hey, there's Ryan! Come on!' she dragged Rachel by the arm across the street.

'Maybe you can hook up with Mick or Dean?' Laura whispered as they approached the boys, who were digging into a pile of hot chips wrapped in newspaper. The salty smell increased as they got closer.

Mick and Dean were the school football heroes—tall, handsome, and barrel chested. The only problem was that they knew it. Laura didn't really understand why Ryan hung around with them, but hey, who was she to try and understand the workings of the opposite sex's minds? Boys were so different. An alien species.

As they neared, Laura heard Dean clear his throat and nod to Ryan. 'Ball and chain at two o'clock.'

Laura ignored him. 'Hey, Ry,' she said, slipping her arm around his waist.

Ryan stepped back as the other boys nudged each other and smirked, and Laura felt the hot embarrassment race up her neck and burn her face.

'Come on, Lauz, let's go,' Rachel said as she grabbed Laura's hand. 'We've got better things to do than hang out with these losers anyway.' She whipped her long blonde ponytail around. As they walked away, Laura could hear the laughter behind them, including Ryan's.

'Why did he do that?' Laura asked Rachel, the tears welling behind her eyes.

'Stupid boys, Lauz,' she said. 'Who needs them when we have ice cream?' She pointed to the bright yellow façade of Scoops - the local ice creamery. 'Come on! My treat! Vanilla or chocolate?'

Half an hour and a double chocolate waffle cone later, the sun had fallen toward the horizon. Shopkeepers were rolling down blinds and closing doors. Laura waved goodbye to Rachel, who went off to the pizza shop to see if they had any part-time jobs, and Laura began toward home.

'Lauz!'

Laura swung her head behind her to see Tom running across the street, his long, lanky legs hanging out of his school shorts.

'What are you still doing in town?' Laura asked as Tom caught up with her.

'Mum had some errands to do before we go home, so I've just been hanging out. Whatcha doing? Where's Ryan?'

Laura twisted her mouth.

'What's wrong?'

She shook her head. 'Nothing. Ryan's just being a jerk, that's all.'

'What d'you mean?'

'Just hanging out with the boys and acting all tough and everything. Sometimes I wonder what I see in him.'

Tom smirked. 'Yeah, me too,' he said under his breath.

'Hey! That's not nice! You like Ryan, don't you?'

'It's not that I don't like him. Anyway, you're the one who just said he was a jerk!'

'Yeah, he can be. In front of others. But on his own, he's, well, he's different.'

Tom rolled his eyes.

'Wanna walk me home?' Laura asked.

Tom paused, a serious look on his face as if he had more to say. He sighed and checked his watch. 'Yeah, sure. Mum's still going to be another ten minutes.'

They crossed the road at the roundabout, shielding their eyes from the late afternoon sun, and entered St. James's Park, the shortest way to Laura's house.

The park was one of Laura's favorite places in Banyula, but even it was showing signs of the heatwave overstaying its welcome. The trees hung with a tiredness, and the grass, normally thick like a green blanket, was tinged brown and patchy in places.

'Sick of this heat,' Laura said as she kicked stones on the path.

'Yeah. Our dam's gone dry. We're having to move the cows closer to the river. But even that's bloody low,' Tom said, shaking his head.

As they neared the far side of the park, only a block from her house, Laura noticed Ryan perched on the boundary fence near the rosebushes. She paused, causing Tom to look up too.

'I better go, Lauz. Mum'll be pissed off if I'm late.'

Laura looked between Tom and Ryan. 'Tom ...'

'It's fine, Lauz. I'll see ya tomorrow.' Tom gave a halfhearted wave of acknowledgment to Ryan and turned back.

Laura walked toward Ryan, who jumped off the fence to greet her.

'Look, I'm sorry about what happened back there. You know, with the guys,' he said, his hands shoved deep in his pockets.

Laura shrugged and squinted into the setting sun.

'Are we okay?' he asked.

'I s'pose.'

Ryan put his arms around Laura and gently kissed her nose.

'I don't get it, Ry. If you want to be with me, you have to acknowledge I'm your girlfriend.'

'I know. I do.' He paused. 'I'm sorry.' Ryan shifted on his feet, dropping his arms from around Laura. 'What were you doing with Tom, anyway?'

'I wasn't doing anything with Tom. He was just walking me home. Geez, are we really doing this, Ryan?' Laura began to walk out the gate.

'Hang on. I'm sorry,' Ryan said, grabbing her and sighing. 'It's ... everything just gets to me sometimes.'

'What do you mean?'

'It doesn't matter.'

Laura sucked at the side of her cheek as she leaned against the fence, and then Ryan tilted her head up to look at him. He had turned on his cheeky grin, the one that indented his left cheek in a cute little dimple and widened his doe eyes, and she couldn't help but smile, even though she still wanted to be annoyed at him.

'Come on. I'll walk you home,' Ryan said, planting another kiss on her nose. He took her hand. Laura glanced behind her as they left the park, noticing Tom in the distance staring at them.

. . .

LAURA'S GRIP on the oven door loosened, and it slammed shut, jolting her back to the present.

'Hello?' Tom's voice called down the hallway as he opened the door.

'In here!' Laura replied, grateful for the distraction from her crazy thoughts. It was the house that did it. All these crazy memories swirling around crashing into each other, confusing her. It was time to forget them.

Tom walked into the kitchen. 'I even cleaned up a bit for you,' he said, holding his hands out and smiling.

He did look all spiffy in a clean pair of jeans and button-down check shirt. He smelled of soap and musk, his curls still tight with dampness.

'You shouldn't have. Really.' Laura smiled.

'Ah, it was nothing.' Tom blushed.

'No, I mean really you shouldn't have,' Laura said, handing Tom a screwdriver. 'Those hinges up there need tightening. Would you mind?' Laura pointed to the overhead kitchen cupboards.

Tom shook his head. 'That'd be right. I should've known you had ulterior motives.' He grinned, pulling over the stepladder and tackling the cupboards.

'Looks like you've packed up most things,' he said as he wrangled the cupboard door into alignment.

'Yeah. I can't believe how much stuff Mum had hoarded away,' Laura said. 'I mean, look at this.' Laura reached into one of the boxes and pulled out a green plastic alligator-shaped grater and held it up.

Tom laughed. 'That's fantastic! Who wouldn't want one of those?'

'And then there's this.' She held up what looked like a cross between a stapler and a hole punch.

'What the heck is that?'

'I believe this is a cherry pitter.'

'A what?'

'You know, gets the seeds out of cherries.'

'Right.'

'Yep,' said Laura, throwing the item back into the box. 'This was mum's claim to fame—hoarder of useless kitchen gadgets.'

Tom laughed as he knocked another cupboard door into alignment. 'So, you decided what you're doing with the house?'

'Yeah,' Laura said, wrapping a glass in newspaper. 'It's going on the market. Tomorrow.'

Tom looked at Laura, raising his eyebrows. 'Wow. That was quick.'

'Well, no use faffing around with a decision,' she replied, leaning back against the kitchen bench and itching her cheek.

'I guess not. I mean you've got a life in the city to go back to,' he said.

'Yeah.'

Just then, the cupboard door Tom was holding slipped from his grip. He stumbled off the stepladder and grabbed above Laura's head just in time.

Laura found herself positioned between Tom and the kitchen bench. Her heart quickened as she felt his strong arms balance the cupboard door above her and then place it down on the bench. Neither of them moved. As her eyes caught in his, she felt a palpable tension between them. An involuntary, rush of heat coursed through her body. A visceral reaction to his masculine scent and the heat radiating from his body so close to hers. As if in slow motion, she watched his lips part and form a smile. And then he reached his thumb to her cheek.

'You have newsprint all over your face,' he said quietly as he wiped her cheek with his thumb. He leaned closer, his face so close it made Laura's palms sweat and voided her mind of all thought. She closed her eyes, leaning in to meet his lips, losing all her senses in the warmth of their touch. At that moment, the ring of the doorbell caused her to jump and break the moment.

'I'll get it!' she said, quickly ducking under his arms and almost running to the front door, her heart in her throat. She took some deep breaths to calm herself and steady her shaking hands. What just happened? She was filled with a mix of emotions— adrenaline, excitement, confusion. She didn't know how to feel. She pulled herself together, tucked her hair behind her ear, and opened the door. As she did, the color and excitement quickly ran from her face.

'Rachel?' Laura said, staring at the face she hadn't laid eyes on in so long. Gone was the long blonde tussle of hair, replaced by a sharp bob. Her eyes were still a vibrant blue, yet were now flanked by dark circles and fine lines. The denim shorts and cropped tee were replaced by black trousers and a black Banyula Pizza Parlor polo shirt with a colorful cartoon pizza slice on her right pocket.

'Hi Laura,' Rachel said in a soft voice. 'I've been sitting in the car for ten minutes trying to get the courage up to knock on your door. Sorry. I hope your pizza's still hot.' Rachel's smile flickered, a flush falling across her cheeks.

Laura tried to think of something to say, but her mind was a mess of thoughts crashing violently into each other. That night. Ryan. The unanswered questions. So much hurt. Laura's hands began to shake.

'Oh-kay,' Rachel said awkwardly when Laura failed to respond. She tapped on the pizza box. 'Um, that's eighteen twenty-five,' she said.

Laura took the box silently and handed her the twenty-dollar note she'd put in her pocket earlier. 'Keep the change,' she said, and stepped back to close the door.

'Laura, wait.' Rachel put her hand out to stop the door.

Laura shook her head. 'I can't do this, Rachel. I'm sorry.' Laura closed the door and felt emotions catch between her chest and shoulder blades, the smell of salami and cheese making her stomach churn. Rachel. The person she thought was her best friend. The person she'd trusted with every secret. The person who'd betrayed her. She took a deep breath and swallowed it all back inside.

'You okay? You look like you've seen a ghost,' Tom said as Laura plonked the pizza on the kitchen table.

'Here, have some pizza. I'm not hungry anymore,' Laura said, sliding a plate across the table. Her initial shock had quickly turned to irritation.

'Ah, what just happened' Tom said, taking a slice of pizza and biting into it, the cheese stretching from the pizza to his mouth in a long, melted thread.

'You know who delivered the pizza?' Laura said, her eyebrows raised.

Tom licked the cheese off his lips. 'Ummm ... is this a trick question?'

'Rachel. That's who. Why didn't you tell me she was back in Banyula?'

Rachel had left Banyula around the same time as Laura. Or so Judy had told her. Laura had assumed it was because she couldn't take the shame of what she'd done with Ryan behind Laura's back. Served her right. After Judy telling Laura to try and smooth things over with her a few hundred times, which Laura had ignored, of course, time passed and it—she—was forgotten. Or at least pushed into the farthest corner of Laura's mind.

Tom stopped chewing and put down his slice of pizza, eyes wide.

'Wow! Well, I mean, I'd heard she was back in town, but I didn't know she was working at Mac's.'

'So, you knew?'

'Well, yeah, I guess, but I didn't think you'd want to know.'

Laura sighed. She shouldn't be angry at Tom; it wasn't his fault. 'Yeah, you're right. I wouldn't have wanted to know. It was just a shock, opening the door and seeing her face. I haven't seen her since ...' Laura pulled her sleeves over her hands and tucked her legs into her chest on the chair.

Tom took another bite of pizza. 'What did she say? What did *you* say?'

'I didn't say anything. I couldn't.' Laura's eyes welled.

'Maybe you should give her a chance. I dunno, let her apologize properly?' Tom shrugged as if it were as simple as that. 'You know, closure.'

'Closure? Are you kidding? She's had ten years to get *closure*.' But so had Laura. She knew the vast distance between them was as much her fault as it was Rachel's.

'Yeah, well how do you know she didn't try and contact you after you took off? You wouldn't speak to anyone, remember? Not even me.'

Laura hung her head, knowing it was true. She'd cut everyone from her life after Ryan's death. Everyone except her mum. But that was the only way her seventeen-year-old self knew how to deal with all the emotions.

'I guess I don't know if she tried to contact me. I wouldn't have talked to her anyway. What did you expect me to do? It was a whole hell of a lot to handle, you know.' Laura's voice had risen. She grabbed a piece of pizza and took an angry bite to quell her emotions. 'The sooner I'm out of here the better.'

Tom paused eating. 'What do you mean?'

'Out of Banyula and back to the city.'

Tom's shoulders dropped.

'There's nothing here for me, Tom. Nothing but hurtful memories.'

Tom shook his head. 'That's all you would see.'

'What's that supposed to mean?'

'Nothing,' Tom said as he rose to his feet and put his plate in the sink. 'I'm really sorry about everything, Laura.' He walked toward the hall to leave.

'What do you mean you're sorry?'

Tom stopped in the doorway and turned around, the dull yellow light from the kitchen highlighting his misty eyes. He scratched his head and sighed as if he needed to choose his words properly.

'What?' Laura asked.

'I knew,' he said softly.

'You knew what?'

'I knew about Ryan and Rachel.'

Laura felt like the wind had been knocked out of her. Like the time she fell off Tom's horse on the farm when she was fourteen. Only this time, her breath didn't return as easily. 'You knew?' Her face contorted as the realization hit her. The only person she thought had been honest through everything had betrayed her.

Tom looked to the ceiling as he slumped his shoulders. 'I didn't know how to tell you. I knew I should have. I knew it was wrong. But Ryan promised he was going to sort it out.' He paused. 'None of it matters now. I just ... I just didn't want to be the one to hurt you.'

'You didn't want to be the one to hurt me? You knew and you didn't tell me! How long had you known?' Laura's throat constricted as she pushed the words out. She knew she was being irrational, but in a split second she'd been transported right back to that night. Her emotions were seventeen again.

He hung his head. 'Too long.'

Laura covered her face with her hands.

'I loved you, Laura,' he said, almost whispering. 'I—'

'No. No. That's not true. If it was, you would have told me!' Laura didn't want to hear another word out of his mouth. She'd heard enough words to last a lifetime. She pushed past Tom, ran down the hallway, and flew out the front door, tears streaming down her face.

'Laura!' Tom called from behind.

She stopped at the edge of the porch and stared into the rain, which under the arc of the streetlight looked like a sheet in the black night. The cool air did little to relieve the heat surging inside her, the urge to run.

'Laura, don't. I'll leave. I'm sorry.' Tom reached out to her, but Laura shrugged him away, thankful the rain blowing on her face hid her streams of tears. She heard Tom's footsteps as he ran down the path, him opening the door of his Ute, followed by the rumble of the engine as he drove away. Laura went inside, closed the door, dropped to her knees, and felt more helpless than she ever had.

14

AFTER A RESTLESS night, Laura pulled on her running gear and headed out into the morning air. A fine mist of rain fell feather-like from the gloom overhead, but it wasn't enough to deter her.

After Tom's admission last night, Laura was bombarded by emotion. She felt seventeen again—naïve, stupid, emotional, and irrational. She kept trying to summon memories from that year. Memories that could, in hindsight, make her see what was happening. Maybe Tom did try to tell her and she just didn't listen. The only night she remembered Tom acting a little strange was the night of Rachel's eighteenth birthday.

THE LAWN TENNIS clubhouse had been lit up like a Christmas tree, straining with the weight of bodies and loud music that it was seldom used to. Black, purple, and white helium balloons clung to the ceiling, their gold ribbons tickling the heads of the partygoers. And silver fairy lights twinkled around a foil sign with the words "Happy 18th Rachel."

After a few too many vodka cruisers, and another argument with Ryan about why he was late to the party, Laura stepped outside to clear her head. Ryan had turned up an hour late, drunk. The smell of beer seeped through his pores. She wasn't going to say anything at first, but he had stumbled and almost knocked over the table of presents, so she'd pulled him aside and told him to go outside to sober up. He'd ignored her and told her she was being lame.

As she stepped outside, Laura's eyes stung in the cold air. Another fight. That was all they seemed to do lately. It was like they were on different pages. In fact, Ryan's book was closed. She'd found it almost impossible to get him to talk about anything lately.

Laura walked toward the nearby playground and noticed Tom's shadowy figure swinging on one of the swings.

'Hey,' she said as she wandered toward him.

He looked up. 'Hey.'

Laura joined him on the adjacent swing, and they both rocked back and forth in unison. The moonlight threw a blue hue over their shadows on the mulch, and the breeze tickled the oak trees overhead. The dull boom of the party still thumped through Laura's chest. Her stomach had begun to churn from the alcohol, so she slowed herself down to a more subtle movement on the swing.

'Good party?' Tom said, his words slightly slurred. Laura wasn't sure if it was a question or a statement.

'Yeah,' she replied. 'Rachel's having a blast.'

'Yeah, Ryan too from what I saw.'

Laura didn't answer.

'He just slammed down a whole bottle of Jack before,' Tom said, shaking his head. 'I dunno what's with him.'

Laura twisted her mouth. 'I know. I think he's struggling with school, that's all. All the pressure. His gran's always reminding him he'll be the first in the family to go to uni and all that. He's just really stressed, I guess.'

Tom grunted.

'What's that supposed to mean?'

'You're always making excuses for him, Lauz. He's been a real jerk lately. To everyone. Especially to you.'

'I'm not making excuses for him. I just understand what he's feeling. You need to give him a little bit of a break. It's not like he's got something like a family farm to fall back on like you have.'

'I'm not falling back on anything. It's what I want.'

Laura's shoulders slumped. 'I know. I didn't mean that. Ryan hasn't got much though. And sometimes he still doesn't even know what he wants. I know he's been acting weird. I think he needs space. That's all.' Laura saw Tom's eyebrows rise. 'As soon as exams are done and all the stress is over, he'll be back to the Ryan we know, right? And anyway, it's not like you're Mr. Innocent. How many beers have you had?'

Tom ignored her comment, and they sat in an uncomfortable silence, Laura wondering why this year was so much of a letdown. Instead of being the fantastic senior year she'd thought it would be, things just hadn't turned out that way. Everyone was acting weird and stressed. Even normal, laid-back Tom she could usually crack a smile from hadn't been himself. This was their final year of school. It was supposed to be fun and carefree before they became adults and headed off into the real world. But it was nothing like that.

After a few more moments, Tom broke the silence. 'Lauz, I need to tell you something.'

Tom's tone caught Laura off guard. He was too serious. Her mind raced, trying to figure out what it could be. She hoped it wasn't his parents. His dad had been unwell lately.

'What is it?' she said, trying to be upbeat, hoping it wasn't bad news.

Tom stopped swinging and stared at the ground, digging his heel into the bark chip below him, but he didn't say anything.

'Tom?' Laura prompted, the worry pricking at the hairs on her arms.

'I really care for you a lot, you know,' he blurted out. 'I don't want to see you get hurt.'

Laura furrowed her brow, puzzled by his ambiguous meaning.

'Okay.' She paused. 'What do you mean?'

'I don't think Ryan's the one for you.'

The words floated around Laura's ears. She wondered if she'd heard wrong.

'Sorry?'

'Ryan. I just don't think you and him are, y'know, a good match.' He shrugged.

She hadn't heard wrong, and all of a sudden it felt like the world had stopped turning. She couldn't hear the music in the distance or the cars passing on the nearby road. All she could hear were Tom's words. Why would he say that?

Tom remained silent and kept digging at the ground. The thud was beginning to annoy Laura.

'What are you talking about?' she said, snapping at him. 'I mean, why would you say that?'

'I have my reasons.'

'You have your reasons? What the hell?' Laura's voice was increasing in volume and agitation, her knuckles white as she gripped the swing chain tightly.

'Forget it. I shouldn't have said anything.' Tom stood up and threw the swing behind him. It clattered into the steel frame, echoing in Laura's ears.

'Hang on. You can't just say something like that and not justify it.'

Tom stopped and turned around. Even in the pale moonlight, Laura could see the anger flash in his normally happy eyes.

'There's things you don't know, all right?' He paused. 'You know what? I thought I should tell you, but I'm not the one you should be asking. And what would it matter? You wouldn't believe me anyway.'

'Tom!'

Tom turned away, ignoring Laura's calls for him to stop. He walked straight past the clubhouse and to his Ute. The engine roared, and the wheels screeched as he took off into the distance.

THAT NIGHT, Laura had swallowed back the emotion and ignored Tom. She put it down to too much alcohol and Tom just being weird. Now, as she pounded rhythmically on the footpath, the rain catching on her eyelashes, she wondered if he'd been trying to tell her about Ryan and Rachel. She wondered if maybe, deep down, she knew and she just didn't want to hear it.

She paused at an intersection as a car signaled. Sucking in oxygen, Laura looked at the street sign and realized where she was. Ryan's street. Nostalgia tingled through her. She pictured her and Ryan walking hand-in-hand toward his grandmother's house, laughing, joking, talking about school and the latest crazy gossip. She had a sudden urge to turn around and run home, but she had a stronger desire to see Ryan's grandmother. It was something she should have done well before now. Well, there was no time like the present.

She turned down into the street and followed the worn foot-path in large strides to avoid stepping on the joints as she and Ryan used to do, and then she saw the house. A simple cement sheet-clad, flat-roofed building. Pale pink walls and potted plants full of pink and white geraniums lining the verandah. The same lace curtains hung from the front windows, and Mrs. Lincoln's old brown Toyota Corolla took its usual place in the driveway. Laura walked to the front door and was just about to knock when a voice came from somewhere.

'Can I help you there?'

Laura spun around to see Ryan's gran emerging from the side of the house, her frown quickly turning into the wide eyes of recognition.

'Laura?'

Laura looked at Ryan's gran. Her face harbored more wrinkles than she remembered, and her hair was much grayer, but the warm smile and friendly eyes were the same. Laura swore she was still wearing one of the hand-knitted jumpers she always used to favor. 'Mrs. Lincoln,' Laura stammered as her face heated.

'Laura!' Mrs. Lincoln repeated as she shuffled up onto the porch, her aging now even more evident in her hunched-over posture. She stopped and regarded Laura, a soft look gathering on her face as she grasped her hands.

'Let me look at you. Well,' she said, smacking her lips, 'if you don't look more like your mother every day! Rest her soul. I was so sad to hear of her passing. I was visiting my friend on the coast for a week or so and only heard about it when I came back the other day. I'm so sorry, Laura. Oh, come here.' She pulled Laura into a hug.

As Laura broke the hug a few moments later, she noticed the wetness around Mrs. Lincoln's eyes.

'Bah, look at me! An old sook!' she said, wiping at her eyes with the back of her hand. 'It's just ... when I see you, I can't help but think of Ryan.' She squeezed her face tight, prompting Laura to put her arms around her.

'I'm sorry, I didn't mean to—'

'It's okay. It's so good to see you,' she said, swatting the emotion away. 'Come inside.'

A few minutes later, Laura was sitting at Mrs. Lincoln's kitchen table. The decor hadn't changed. The orange benchtops and brown Laminex cupboards were still spotless, and the royal-blue carpet only faded where the scraping of the kitchen chairs had worn it down. Laura remembered Ryan bringing her here for the first time. They'd stolen two chocolate Tim Tam's from his gran's not-so-secret stash.

Mrs. Lincoln put a cup of tea in front of Laura and sat down next to her.

Laura took a sip of her tea, the steam dampening her nose. Placing the cup back on the table, Laura searched for what to say. 'Mrs. Lincoln, I ...'

'It's okay,' Mrs. Lincoln said, placing a veined hand on top of Laura's. 'You don't need to say anything. I wish things had turned out differently for you. For you all. Especially for Ryan. And I know you do too. I don't know how many sleepless nights I had blaming myself for everything.'

Laura's brow furrowed. 'You have nothing to blame yourself for! Ryan thought the world of you.'

'I know. He was a good kid. Wasn't he?' Mrs. Lincoln asked Laura, as if wanting reassurance.

'Yeah, he was.'

'I mean he had his moments. I know that. And well,' she sighed, 'he just, ah, lost his way.'

'I can't help thinking I should have done more. Been there more for him or something. Stayed with him after the party. Maybe then he'd still be here,' Laura said, staring into her tea.

'Laura, honey, you can't think that way. None of us can. I mean, I should have been more attentive, you know? Seen the signs.' She wiped away some crumbs off the table with the back of her hand. 'Tarred with the same brush. Well, that's what he thought. But it could have been different. If he'd just had some help. If I'd stepped in and found the help for him ...'

Laura's shoulders tensed. 'What do you mean?'

Mrs. Lincoln tilted her head to the side. 'How much did he tell you?'

'About what?'

'His parents.'

Laura shifted in her seat, cupping her mug. 'Not a lot, just that they died in an accident when he was younger.'

Mrs. Lincoln's shoulders fell, and she shook her head. 'I should have known as much,' she said. 'Tried to deal with it all himself, as usual.'

'I don't quite understand,' said Laura.

Mrs. Lincoln stood up from the table and left the room, leaving Laura feeling uneasy. Moments later she returned with a tattered notebook. Laura remembered the standard-issue notebooks from school. The ones with the colored world map on the front and times tables on the back. This one was scribbled over in abstract patterns of black ink—Ryan's patterns. She'd recognize them anywhere. Laura felt shivers rush over her arms, and she tensed in her seat.

Mrs. Lincoln sat down and held the book close to her chest. 'I always knew Ryan wasn't one to share his emotions. I thought he might have to you though. I'm guessing not.' She smacked her lips again. 'Well, that was our Ryan. Here,' she said, sliding the book across the table. 'This was Ryan's journal. I found it under his bed when I was...,' Mrs. Lincoln continued clearing her throat, 'cleaning up his room. I couldn't bring myself to go in there for months after it happened. And then, when I found it. It was all too late. It was no use to anyone. Except maybe you. Your mum told me how hard you'd taken it, and after reading this, I knew why.' She shook her head again. 'Ryan made some bad decisions, but at least if you read this, maybe you can understand why. It's not an excuse for what he did, but well ... just read it for yourself.' She pushed the book toward Laura.

Laura stared at the worn corners and ran her fingers over the softened cover and deep indentations made by the pen. She wanted to grab it and pull it up to her nose. Embrace it. Inhale Ryan once more. 'I ... I don't know if I can,' she mumbled, her voice catching in her throat.

'Laura, it had been brewing for such a long time. Longer than I ever imagined. I thought after we moved here, I could just move on. Start fresh. I was naïve. I never gave it a thought that Ryan would want to know the truth. I didn't think it would serve him, only hurt him. I was right in the end. But I was wrong for not being upfront with him sooner.'

Laura's tears welled, a look of confusion on her face, unsure of what Mrs. Lincoln was trying to tell her.

'Ryan's father was sick. Mentally ill. He cracked one day and took my Jane with him. I am only so grateful Ryan wasn't there too.'

Laura's hand shot to her mouth. 'Oh my god,' she whispered.

Mrs. Lincoln nodded. 'Ryan was such a beautiful boy. I do blame myself, but I can't fixate on it either. I've come to terms with it. I know I did what I thought was best. I mean, in my day, it was all different. You kept all that stuff private. I didn't know what else to do. I only wish ...'

Laura reached over and embraced Mrs. Lincoln, the two of them sharing in the heartbreak of loss, grief, and a mutual longing to change the past.

A few moments later, Mrs. Lincoln regained her composure. 'Here, take it with you. Read it when you're ready. He cared for you, Laura. If anything, I want you to know that, and maybe, to remember him. In the good times.' Mrs. Lincoln pulled a hanky from her sleeve and blew her nose, then stretched out her fingers with a grimace. 'Damn arthritis. Can't even blow my own nose,' she said, letting out a deep, husky laugh before allowing her tears to fall freely. Laura reached across the table to hold her hands, her own tears spilling from her eyes.

'Come on.' Mrs. Lincoln smiled. 'Drink your tea. Nothing worse than cold tea.'

15

WHEN LAURA ARRIVED home, she sat down cross-legged on the living room floor and placed the journal in front of her on the carpet. Her heart thumped beneath her chest, echoing loudly in her head. She swallowed to calm her nerves; the sound of her uneven breathing permeated the air around her. Laura picked up the journal, pulled it toward her face and fanned through the pages, closing her eyes and feeling the cool air and the ever-so-subtle smell of Ryan—his shampoo, his aftershave, his warmth.

A photograph, its edges slightly worn, dropped into her lap. She picked it up. On the back, in Ryan's black handwriting, it simply read: *Us*. She turned over the photo, and saw the faces of herself, Ryan, Tom, and Rachel staring back at her. The foursome were sitting on the back of the farm Ute at Tom's. Laura stared at the photo as the memory of that day appeared, hazy at first, before materializing into vivid color. It was not long after Ryan had asked Laura out. The three of them had been helping Tom clean out the old chicken coop and move the chickens to their new home that Tom had spent the last two weekends building. The afternoon had been spent in raucous fashion. Tumbling over each other, throwing handfuls of straw and feathers, and laughing until they gasped for air. By the end of the chore, they were covered in a sour mix of sweat, feathers, and dirt, the autumn sunshine warm on their faces. Laura remembered Tom's mum barreled over laughing at the sight of them all, and his dad shaking his head with a broad smile. Mrs. Gordon had gone inside and returned with her camera, insisting on getting a photo of the four of them. They piled into the back of the Ute, shaking with laughter, so much so that they couldn't sit still. The edges of their faces smiling out from the photo were slightly blurred, but the happiness of that moment was in sharp focus, evident by the carefree smiles, squinting eyes, and arms entangled over each other's shoulders.

Laura traced over the photo with her forefinger. The memory seemed so distant, almost surreal, as if those days had been blown away with the storm that passed through later that night. Laura caught her breath as hot tears trickled from her eyes. Not long after that photo, life changed. Relationships became murky with emotions, hormones, and the confusions of youth. They were just kids. Kids turning into adults trying to find their way, memories of childhood fading with the dust and feathers. Laura felt the loss deep within the crevices of her body. It tightened her chest, making her limbs heavy and lifeless. She placed the photo carefully beside her and picked up the journal and opened to the first page, wiping her eyes as the first words came into focus:

Last night I asked Laura out. She said yes.

16

～

Ryan's Journal

<u>22 February 2009</u>

    Last night I asked Laura out. She said yes. I was so nervous when I asked her. I can't believe she said yes. There's something about her that's different from the other girls. Like she doesn't judge me or something. I've liked her for a while but never thought she'd notice someone like me. The someone who isn't Ryan Taylor the class clown. Then, a few days ago, I convinced her to skip class with me. I was surprised she did. She's a bit of a good girl, follows the rules and stuff. But I think that's what I like about her. Testing her out. Seeing how far she'll go. We went down the river, and we sat there and just talked. It was good. I guess I felt like she was really listening to me. Like the real me. She saw past the clowning around and the rebellious stuff. It was like she really wanted to know me. A few days later, she asked if I wanted to go out to Tom's farm with her and Rachel.

It was different being with them at Tom's farm. They all sort of made me feel like one of their gang. Well, Laura and Rachel did, anyway. I'm not sure what Tom thinks of me. I think maybe he thinks I'm moving in to take over or something. It's not that he wasn't cool about it. I dunno. It's just a feeling I got. Mostly he was cool though. Rachel seems pretty cool too. I don't really know much about her, but she seems nice. I reckon she was flirting with me at the river though. She saw me when I was watching her take off her top to go swimming. I didn't mean to be looking. And then she wanted me to come in for a swim. But I didn't. I was into Laura. I waited for the right moment to get her alone, and then I kissed her. She had soft lips. Warm. Her skin was so soft. It took all my strength not to do anything else. I had to be a gentleman. Gran taught me that.

Even though it was nice, the kiss, I mean, it wasn't like in the movies. It wasn't like all tingles and fireworks and stuff. It felt right, though, if that makes sense. Like it was meant to happen. I know that sounds all woo-woo and shit, but I really like her. And I think she likes me. She must, because she said yes when I asked her out. I blurted it out really stupid like. Got all tongue twisted or something. I really thought I'd blown it, but after a minute, she said yes.

LAURA CLOSED the book and squeezed her eyes tight. Ryan's words seemed so simple. She remembered that night like it was yesterday. She remembered the river, the sounds of the crickets, the warmth of the summer night air, the electric feeling that jolted through her when Ryan asked her out. She shuffled through the memories in her head and pressed play on the events of that day.

LAURA'S BIKE skidded along Tom's gravel driveway, whipping up the dust. She felt it settle on her skin, sticking to the sweat seeping out of every pore.

'How long till you get your license, Ryan?' Rachel yelled as they neared Tom's farmhouse, her voice wobbly from the rough terrain.

'Still five months away!' Ryan laughed.

The afternoon sun was sinking in the west, its last long rays still burning the already parched fields. It was mid-March, and this was likely to be the last heat wave for the summer. Laura, Rachel, Ryan, and Tom had planned on making the most of it by the river on Tom's farm. As they reached the farmhouse, they leaned their bikes against the tired date palm that towered over the ramshackle weatherboard house. The threesome wandered up the concrete path to the front door, Laura avoiding the cracks. *Step on a crack, break your mother's back.*

Tom's family farm was like Laura's second home. Her mum and Mrs. Gordon were friends through the Country Women's Association, and Laura had spent many weekends and school holidays hanging out with Tom. The days felt longer out on the farm, and she loved how Mrs. Gordon always welcomed her with a smile.

'Hiya!' Tom's mum yelled as they clattered down the hallway. The timber boards creaked under their feet as they made their way to the kitchen.

'Hi, Mrs. G,' Rachel and Laura chorused in unison.

'Hi girls. And who's this?' Mrs. Gordon said, gesturing to Ryan, who was lagging behind Laura and peering out from behind his fringe.

'This is Ryan,' Rachel said.

'Hi, Mrs. Gordon, thanks for having me,' Ryan said. Laura blushed.

'Hi, Ryan. Good to meet you. Tom's out the back; he's just finished feeding the dogs,' Mrs. Gordon said as she continued preparing a salad. 'And, yes, grab a muffin,' she said, shaking her head. 'I can see you eyeing them.'

The three of them leaped at the blueberry muffins sitting on the bench still in the tray, the warm smell making Laura's mouth water.

'And grab a drink from the fridge out back. It's hot as Hades today.'

Once outside, they grabbed a can of Coke each and went out to find Tom hosing down the back of the farm Ute.

Tom's grin broadened as he saw them approach. He looked good with his short hair curling over his ears and his white teeth contrasting against his nut-brown summer skin.

Turning off the hose and wiping his wet hands down the front of his grubby jeans, Tom beamed. 'Party time!' he cheered. 'Mum's made us some salad and cold meat stuff. And I've got some coldies in the esky.'

'All right!' Rachel high-fived Tom as he jumped off the back of the Ute. 'Let's do this.'

Ten minutes later, Tom pulled the farm Ute up to the bank of the river that snaked through the property. It was a touch cooler under the shadows of the tall gums.

They threw a couple of towels on the sand, and Rachel switched her iPod onto shuffle as the sun melted into the ranges on the horizon.

Laura pulled her long brown hair messily into a ponytail to cool the back of her neck and sprayed herself with mosquito repellent before grabbing a beer out of the cooler. She sat down next to Ryan on the blanket. It had been Rachel's idea to ask him to come along. Laura was hesitant, still feeling nervous after their time at the river. It was almost like she didn't want to share the time they'd had, worried it wouldn't be the same, but Ryan was keen to come.

'So, how'd you do on the English test?' Laura asked Ryan.

'Yeah, I dunno. All right, I reckon. That Mr. Cooper's an arsehole though,' Ryan said, rolling his eyes.

'Oh, you got Coops! Man that sucks,' Tom said, perched on the cooler, shaking his head.

'Tell me about it.'

'I had him last year. Broke my balls.'

The foursome chatted and laughed about school and the latest gossip, and before Laura knew it, the sun had almost disappeared. The twilight made everything appear like an overexposed Polaroid in hues of burnt orange. Laura glanced at Ryan out of the corner of her eye, noticing how the orange glow highlighted his tan face. He was old-school handsome in a James Dean kind of way. Smallish nose, crooked grin, moody eyes. His blond hair flicked across his forehead, gently resting on his right brow. Laura was overcome by the overwhelming instinct to brush it away. Embarrassment crept up her neck at the thought.

Rachel wandered down to the riverbank. 'Who's coming in?' she asked, pulling off her T-shirt and tossing it on the bank as she waded out knee-deep into the water. Rachel was wearing her black bikini top and denim cutoffs, her body curving in all the right places. Laura tugged at her own top and pulled it down over her stomach. Laura didn't have curves like Rachel. Her nickname had been surfboard up until about year nine.

'Come on, Ry! It's beautiful in!' Rachel said, stretching her arms above her and smiling.

'Nah, maybe later,' Ryan said, dropping his head.

'I will!' Tom yelled, jumping up and pulling off his T-shirt over his well-defined abdominal muscles. He'd filled out over the summer from all the farmwork. Tom was now almost a man. He bounded into the water, entering with a shallow dive before surfacing next to Rachel with a wide grin.

'Don't you dare!' Rachel screamed just before Tom dunked her underneath his weight. She resurfaced, squeezing her eyes and pulling at her wet hair that was plastered across her face. 'I'm going to kill you, Tom.' And it was on. A full-on water fight. Laura and Ryan watched from the dry safety of the riverbank.

'Go on, your turn,' Laura said to Ryan, who looked as if he'd love to jump in.

He smiled and shook his head, taking another swig from his almost finished beer. 'Nah, I'm good,' he said, watching them splash around. 'They'd make a cute couple.' He nodded toward them, where Rachel was monkey-like on Tom's back, trying to dunk him under with little success.

Laura looked at Ryan with a puzzled look, and they both burst out laughing.

'No, they wouldn't!' She laughed.

No way. Rachel and Tom were as opposite as north and south. Rachel hated getting her hands dirty, and Tom was rarely clean, all calloused hands and grimy fingernails thanks to the farm.

Laura and Ryan sat in silence for a few minutes watching Rachel and Tom, who had now settled down and were having a floating competition, both on their backs staring up into the sky, the water gently rippling around them. Although the sun had disappeared behind the gum trees, the late summer heat hung in the air so thick you could almost touch it. Beside her, Laura felt

Ryan glance toward her, and her heart increased in speed. She lifted the back of her ponytail off her neck to cool herself down, not knowing if it was the stifling evening air or being so close to Ryan that was giving her hot flashes.

'Hey, see that?' Ryan said, pointing past Laura into the trees in the distance.

'See what?' she asked, looking toward the nearby scrub. 'Oh god it's not a snake, is it?'

'Nah, a possum, I think. Come on!'

Ryan grabbed her hand and pulled her to her feet. The grasp of his hand was firm and strong. Darkness had now descended, and the moon, full and round, glimmered through the scraggly eucalyptus branches. Laura strained her neck backwards, peering up into the tree following Ryan's gaze.

'I can't see anything,' she said. The trees rustled, and the hot breeze fluttered at her shirt. Apart from that, the night was silent. Laura turned to Ryan, who was staring directly at her, the full moon making his sea-green eyes shine. The corner of his mouth twisted, accentuating the dimple on his cheek.

'What?' Laura smiled back, tucking her hair behind her ear and secretly hoping her face wasn't as flushed as it felt.

'Nothing! You just ... I dunno. You look nice tonight.' He stumbled over his words.

Laura glanced down at her tattered denim shorts and cropped black T-shirt and folded her arms across her stomach. Then Ryan moved closer, resting his hand gently on her waist, his eyes boring into hers. Laura's heart leaped up into her throat as he edged toward her. He was now close enough for Laura to feel his warm breath, and she instinctively crooked her neck and mirrored his actions until their lips touched ever so gently. Laura closed her eyes. His lips were soft and full, his mouth hot. Her stomach fluttered and a warmth swirled from her neck down to her toes. The kiss was like a perfect summer storm, hot and lingering.

Laura broke away, trying to hide her search for air, then Ryan whispered, 'Do you want to go out with me?'

A nervous giggle escaped unexpectedly from Laura's mouth, and she covered her face with her hands, mentally beating herself up for ruining the moment.

'Well?' he said.

Under the moonlight, Laura noticed the slight fleck of freckles along Ryan's nose for the first time. They danced up toward the corners of his eyes as he stood there almost holding his breath.

'Okay,' Laura whispered back.

Ryan leaned in and kissed her again. His lips barely grazed hers before he took her hand and they walked back to the blanket on the bank. This time, they edged closer to each other as they sat down. *A couple now*, Laura thought, her heart doing a happy dance. Goose bumps pricked at her skin. The tingling feeling inside was like nothing she'd ever experienced. Her entire body from head to toe buzzed with electricity.

Laura's stomach continued to flutter as she looked around and breathed in the summer evening. She wanted to soak in everything. How it felt, how it looked, the smells, sounds, everything. She etched the first sprinkling of stars in the evening sky into her memory and drew the warm summer breeze, teasing the gum trees, and then added the soundtrack of cicadas trilling and Jason Mraz in the background. She never wanted to forget this moment. And then she noticed Rachel in the water, staring at her and Ryan. Laura couldn't stifle her excitement and grinned from ear to ear, but Rachel mustn't have noticed, as she turned away.

· · ·

LAURA'S EYES SPRANG OPEN, pulling her back from the memory. It was like reliving the moment again, yet this time it was filled with angst and confusion. Why did Rachel turn away? Why did Ryan write in his diary that he didn't feel sparks? Laura surely did.

All the energy drained from Laura's body. Her bones suddenly felt tired right down to the marrow, as if she couldn't possibly move a muscle. But Ryan's diary called to her. She had to read on.

17

Ryan's Journal

16 March 2009

I used to think I was bulletproof. Like I could do anything. No sense of fear and all that. Just fun at all costs. That's what I used to feel like. I've felt different the last couple of weeks. I guess it's been longer than that, like a niggling feeling of something I can't quite explain. But these last few weeks it's been more than usual. It's like I think I should be happier. I have a girlfriend now. And Laura's great. Always so happy, so excited to see me. She's changed me. For the better. When I'm with her, she makes me feel worth something. But the more I try to lose myself in her, it's like the more awake my head becomes. Questioning me. Planting doubts in my head. Like I'm not good enough for her.

The last few weeks have felt like they've dragged on, each day heavier than the last. My mind gets really confused and overthinks everything. It's like I'm trying to solve a complex algebraic equation that keeps going to infinity, and I just can't get my head around it.

I can't work out why I feel like this. I should be happy, right? Then today, my anger just built up inside me. I couldn't control it. It was as if a freight train was pounding in my chest, thundering up toward my head, demanding to be released. That's the only way I can explain it.

It wasn't the first time it's happened. I felt bad about the last time when I went off at Laura for no real reason. This time, us boys were on the basketball court at lunchtime. Laura and Rachel and a couple of others looked on. Everything was cool until one of the boys started ribbing me about Laura watching, saying I was trying to show off as I'd just shot two three-pointers in a row. I knew he was only teasing, but I lost it. I threw the ball into his groin and stormed off. If I were a cartoon, steam would have been coming out my ears. That's how hot and burning with anger I felt. All I saw was black. Rage. Frustration. I pissed off down the river for the last two periods 'cause I couldn't face anyone. Then I walked home and locked myself in my room. I didn't know what to do. The feeling didn't go away. It kept building inside me. I don't know why I did it. Like I had to get it out, I guess, but I took a pen and began digging it into my thigh. The pain actually felt good. When I broke the skin, it was like relief trickled out with the blood. Like I was letting out all the poisonous feelings that had built up. Then I felt calm. The throbbing of my leg felt good. I deserved it. But the calm feeling didn't last long. After that, I felt shit again. Heavy. I don't know what's happening to me. I don't know who I am anymore. And I hate it.

. . .

3 April 2009

IT WAS EASTER THIS WEEKEND. Gran gave me a chocolate rabbit. I gave her a box of Cadbury chocolates, those roses ones. They're her favorite. Then last night there was a party out at Tom's farm. Most of the year twelves were there. I was looking forward to it, but at the same time I felt weird. Things with Laura were weird. I don't know how to explain it. I miss her when I'm not with her, but when I'm with her, I wish I was elsewhere. Sometimes I just feel smothered by her, or by my own feelings. I don't know. It frustrates me. I kind of think that maybe I expect too much. Like everything has to be perfect. Like those stupid romance movies. All electricity and fireworks. Sometimes I want her so bad, yet other times I just want to be alone. I know it's hard on her. She'd spend every minute with me if she could. I know it's wrong not wanting to be with her. It makes me feel crap. Like I'm a bad boyfriend. I am really. I like being with her, but. See? I can't work myself out. There's like this feeling in the pit of my stomach. A queasiness. I got so frustrated with myself Friday night that I slammed my fist through my cupboard door. Fuck, it hurt. Way more than I let on. Gran was pissed too. I tried to pretend it was an accident, but she isn't that stupid. She's worried about me too, which I guess is only natural. But she's a bit overly worried, like trying to hug me and tell me I can talk to her anytime. Which I can't. This stuff isn't for her.

Then at the party last night I did something really stupid. I kissed Rachel. We ended up alone in the shed after Tom showed us his HQ Ute his dad's restoring for him. Man, it's cool. He's so lucky. Anyway, Tom and Laura ran back to the party to miss the downpour of rain, but me and Rachel got caught out behind, so we sheltered in the shed to wait for the storm to pass. It was really pissing down. We were both a little drunk. I know that. And her white shirt was wet and sticking to her. She looked really sexy. And she came on to me too. It wasn't just me. Not that that's an excuse. But I kissed her, and it felt so good. She kissed me like she wanted me. Actually wanted me. Then I got really shitty at myself for cheating on Laura. I know it was wrong. But Rachel didn't seem to care much. She told me she's liked me longer than Laura has. And she kissed me again. After the rain stopped, I ran to find Laura. I was going to come clean, but she was in such a good mood, how could I tell her something like that? Instead, I told her I wasn't feeling well and rang Gran to come and pick me up.

And now I feel like shit. I can't stop thinking about what I did. But I can't stop thinking about Rachel either. I'm a fucking asshole.

30 MAY 2009

TODAY IN ART class I kind of lost it. We were supposed to draw an abstract charcoal sketch of what was inside our minds. Mine turned out to be a huge smudge of gray twisted lines and dark shadows. As I drew, I pressed harder and harder until the charcoal smashed into a powdery mess in my hands. I screwed up the paper. More proof that I fuck everything up. Just like I'm fucking things up with Laura. I know she's so good for me.

But I'm scared of hurting her. I know I've hurt her already, especially if she found out what happened with Rachel. I don't understand how Laura sees any light inside me at all. I feel so ugly. If she only knew what I was really like.

I've been texting with Rachel a bit, which I know is bad. But she gets me. She's got her own shit with her parents pressuring her to be as smart as her older sister who's studying medicine. They want her to study medicine next year too. But she doesn't want to. She feels trapped. Like I do. We like, have common ground. Which I know sounds lame. And it's no excuse.

I knew it was wrong to kiss her in the shed that night. But I can't stop thinking about how it felt. It was a fast and furious relief. Feeling her body on mine, with as much, if not more desire. Rachel tastes different than Laura.

Laura is different, being with her is different. It's calm. Like only one emotion. Just the opposite of what's going on in my head. Life isn't calm and perfect at all. Life is fucked.

I don't know why, but I feel like Rachel gets that, which makes me want her even more. She's like a drug or something, and I can feel my addiction building. I want that feeling of kissing her again. I need to tell Laura. It's not fair to her. She's done nothing wrong. I'm the asshole. But I also don't want to hurt her. I have to break it off with her though. She deserves someone much better than me. I'm just making a mess of not only my life, but hers too. But I can't find the right moment to tell her. It's as if I'm two different people half the time. Two different people constantly fighting with each other to go opposite ways. But one of them always seems to win. The bad one gags and silences the other one—the good one— unable to stop the darkness of the other.

All I want to do is make Gran proud of me. But if she knew this, she'd be so disappointed in me. I know it. She's done so much for me. Being my mum, dad, and gran. I've been thinking about that a lot lately too. The accident. I've never been told much about it. All Gran has said is that it was a car crash. They were driving back from Melbourne on the back roads, not far from home, when Dad lost control and the car ended up wrapped around a telegraph pole. I want to know more. What happened. It's like I don't know who I am, and I feel that finding out about them more would ground me or something. It sounds stupid, but I feel like I'm lost. I was only like two or something when Gran moved us here. I can't remember the place I was born in, where I lived with Mum and Dad. It was out in central NSW, somewhere remote. Maybe I should go there one day. See where I used to live. Go see their graves or something. I don't even know why Gran chose to move here to Banyula. Just said she picked somewhere on the map and chose it. Weird. Maybe I should Google what happened. I know Gran doesn't like talking about it. And I don't want to upset her. It's all I seem to do lately. Upset people.

18

LAURA WIPED HER eyes and closed the diary. Outside the living room window, the gray clouds of day had turned to a black moonless night. Laura hadn't even noticed the rain begin again, the gentle monotonous tone on the roof. She looked at her watch. It was almost nine, and she hadn't eaten, but she wasn't hungry. She couldn't stop thinking about Ryan. It began to make sense now. His mood swings, his pushing her away. Why couldn't she have seen it more clearly then and tried to help him?

Acid had crawled through her skin when she read about Ryan kissing Rachel. It hurt all over again. Anger built as she thought of Rachel. How could she? There was more to their relationship than a kiss. They had deep conversations, something Laura never had with Ryan. The betrayal cut deeper now than it did before. It's one thing to have your boyfriend kiss your best friend, but another for them to share intimate details and their thoughts and feelings. Why couldn't Ryan do that with her? She tried to analyze where she'd gone wrong. Where they'd gone wrong. Were they ever right? Laura's feelings for Ryan were so much stronger than it appeared his ever were. If she'd realized then, if she'd paid more attention, she could have stopped the heartache. She could have tried to help him.

Laura tried to think of the first time she felt their relationship sour. There wasn't an incident as such, more a series of weird moments that caught her off guard and unsettled her. Of course she'd shaken them off, but now in hindsight ...

She thought back to one time in particular. At the time it had bothered her, but she'd pushed it aside. Even thinking back now, it wasn't a huge watershed moment, but it was a point where the dynamics between the four of them, especially her and Rachel, changed.

It wasn't that long after Laura had started seeing Ryan. Laura and Rachel were sitting underneath the line of gum trees along the school boundary fence eating their lunch.

'WHAT'S GOING ON, RACH?' Laura had asked after they'd sat there in silence for a few minutes against the backdrop of the noisy schoolyard.

'Huh? What d'you mean?'

'Well, I haven't seen much of you.'

'I see you every day at school! What are you talking about?' Rachel took another bite of her ham sandwich.

'Yeah, I know. But we haven't caught up after school for ages. And whenever I text, it always takes you forever to reply.'

Rachel seemed to chew on that one mouthful for a long time. 'I dunno. Guess we're both just doing different stuff.' She paused. 'I mean, you're hanging with Ryan or doing homework, and now I'm working. And mum's still on my back about my grades.'

Laura shrugged, not convinced. Rachel had been weird since Laura had started seeing Ryan. She was sure of it. Just subtle changes like whenever Laura would start talking about Ryan, Rachel would change the subject.

'I guess,' Laura said, unable to question her more as Ryan and Tom sauntered over to them.

Ryan sat down next to Laura with his sausage roll and leaned over to kiss her on the forehead before jamming the roll into his mouth, the pastry crumbling and sticking to the corners of his lips.

Laura noticed Rachel roll her eyes.

They sat there for a while, eating their lunches and surveying the school ground. The cool kids were hanging out in a pack by the common room, the boys jack-arsing around and the girls pretending to laugh at their antics, secretly thinking they were tools. There was a group of boys on the basketball court dribbling and joking around.

Laura noticed the group of popular girls sitting in the middle of the oval, their legs stretched out in front of them. She immediately felt self-conscious. They were all so much prettier than Laura with their long legs, clear skin, and pouty lips. But here she was with Ryan. The most popular boy at St. Joseph's liked *her*. Plain Jane Laura. She mentally pinched herself, still not believing it was real. *A boy likes me. Me, plain old Laura.*

'So are you guys coming over this Saturday? Mum said we can camp out in the sleepout,' Tom asked after finishing his pie.

'Yep. I'm good,' said Rachel.

'Sure,' Ryan replied.

'Lauz? You coming?' Tom asked again.

'Yeah. Course,' she said.

'Cool. If it's still hot enough, we can go down the river for a swim.'

'Hey, did you see Sam's tattoo?' Ryan asked no one in particular.

'Tattoo? Ya kidding?' said Tom.

'Yup. Some weird shit. A Chinese symbol or something. Come on, he's over there.' The two boys jumped up and headed over to the basketball courts to check out the tattoo.

Laura watched Ryan as he sauntered off across the grass, tilting her head and smiling.

'You really like him, don't you?' Rachel said.

Laura's cheeks flushed, and she averted her eyes.

Rachel shook her head.

'What?' Laura asked.

'Nothing.'

'It's not nothing, Rach. Something's up with you. Is it me going out with Ryan?'

Rachel brushed the crumbs off her skirt and casually frowned. 'Nah. Don't be stupid. Why would that worry me?'

'I don't know. Well, if it's not that, what is it then?'

Rachel exhaled. 'It's just ... I dunno, you haven't even been going with him for a month, and well, it's like he's everything!'

Laura sensed a change in her tone. 'He's not everything. It's just the first real relationship I've had. You know that. You'd be the same.'

'I just think you should slow down a bit. You know.'

'What do you mean?'

'I just mean don't rush into it.'

Laura wasn't really sure what Rachel meant, but an uneasy feeling twisted silently in her tummy, tightening and making her queasy.

'I'd just hate to see you get hurt. That's all.' Rachel cut the silence, shrugging it off as if it were nothing.

'I'm a big girl, Rach. And anyway, I've got you.'

Rachel smiled. It was a faraway smile, and Laura could see the lines between Rachel's eyes deepen.

'Rach?' Laura reached across and touched her hand. 'What's wrong?'

She shook her head. 'It's just ... you are so happy, and ... well, it's not that I don't want you to be happy, but ...'

'But what?'

'I don't know. It's just like everything is changing, that's all. I don't want things to change, especially us. You guys are the only ones who get me, who don't expect me to be like Amy.'

Amy was Laura's older sister. She was smart, beautiful, and could never put a foot wrong in the eyes of their parents. She'd moved to Canberra to study medicine and had just graduated. Their parents expected the same from Rachel.

'It's okay, Rach. It's not going to change anything,' Laura said. 'I promise, okay?'

Rachel nodded before jumping up. 'I've got to go and see Mr. Tait, get the math homework,' she said before heading toward the main building.

Laura watched her walk away. She paused next to the group of popular girls, and one of them looked like she was asking her something. Rachel looked back at her, and then turned back to the group of girls, said something, and continued walking. Laura saw the stares from the group as they giggled behind their hands. Laura's face reddened, and she quickly looked away.

LAURA'S PHONE RANG, causing her to jump back from the memory. The queasiness she'd felt on that day seemed to have manifested into the present. She quickly grabbed her phone to see who it was. Stella? That was odd. Stella wouldn't normally call this late at night.

Laura cleared her throat and answered. 'Hi Stella, is everything okay?'

'Oh, Laura. I'm so sorry to ring you this late,' Stella replied. Her voice was tense, and she spoke a million miles an minute.

'It's fine. What's wrong?'

'It's Gemma.'

'Is she okay?'

'Well, yes. And no. Um, I'm actually out in front of your house. I'd really like to talk to you.'

'Of course! Come in right now.'

Laura went to the front door as Stella ran up the porch.

'Oh, Laura!' Stella said. 'You've been crying. Are you okay? I'm sorry. I shouldn't lump you with my problems.'

Laura put her arms around Stella, happy to feel her warmth. 'I'm fine, Stella, really.'

Once in the kitchen, Laura filled up the kettle and put it on the stove. 'Right, now tell me what's happened?' Laura said, pulling up a chair next to her.

Stella looked down and fiddled with her wedding band as she spoke. 'Well, we had a little tiff earlier today. Gemma and I. It wasn't much. I was just trying to get through to her. Talk to her. She shuts me out all the time, and I have no idea what is going through her head.'

Laura nodded.

'Anyway, she stormed out of the house, and that was that. I didn't think much of it. She's always storming out or leaving without telling me these days. I guess that was about six o'clock. Then about half an hour ago, the phone rang and it was the police.'

'Oh my gosh. Is Gemma all right?'

'Yes, she's fine. Mostly. They were ringing to tell me they had her there at the station. She was in St. James's Park with some others. They were all drunk. So the police brought them in. Not to charge them. Just to give them a scare and keep them till they sobered up a bit.'

Laura sighed. Poor Stella. She handed her the box of tissues from the bench.

'I wanted to come and get her right then and there, but they told me I had to wait an hour for her to settle down. Let the alcohol wear off. I was heading there now and just going to wait outside, but ... Oh, Laura. I just don't know what to do.' Stella dabbed her eyes.

'I'm sorry I haven't been around to see her,' Laura said, dropping her eyes.

'Oh, darling. It's not your fault. You've got so much on your plate. This is our mess and,' she wiped her nose, 'we've got to deal with it.'

'Where's Art?'

'He's in Sydney again. He's so busy with work, I don't want to burden him with all of this. He tries to talk to her when he's home, but it's the same thing. She listens, doesn't say anything, and goes to her room.'

'How about I come with you? To the station and wait with you. Then we can take her home and I can have a little chat with her?'

Stella looked across to Laura, considering her offer. Then she shook her head. 'No, I think it's best if I bring her home. Let her sleep it off. But, do you think you could come around and have a chat with her tomorrow? First thing? I know it's a lot to ask of you, but ...'

'Not at all. I want to help.' Laura smiled gently. She got up to pour the hot water into the cups. 'You know, Stella, I think Ryan was suffering from depression. I've been thinking about it a lot lately. He didn't have anywhere to turn either. I think maybe Gem's depressed too.'

Stella began to sob, and Laura felt awful. 'Oh god, Stella. I'm sorry. I didn't mean to upset you. I just don't want Gemma to feel alone. Like Ryan did. We can try and get her some help, someone she can talk to.'

Stella sighed. 'The problem's bigger than her. It's half the kids her age. There's nothing for them here. That's what they think. The council say they don't have the funding to put things on for them. Won't even fix up the skate park. There's no money. People are losing jobs. There's no hope for these kids, especially the ones who aren't academic. They just get left behind. Just last week I had to ring up a parent and explain her daughter hadn't been to class in two weeks. She had no idea! This poor girl is failing. And her mother had no clue! As a teacher, this is my responsibility, but everyone is fighting their own battles ... I just don't know what the answer is.'

Laura felt a wave of emotion build up inside. A wave that she couldn't hold back. Her shoulders began to shake and she cried.

Stella pulled Laura in for an embrace. Laura felt Stella's chest rise and fall with her sobbing. Crying for Gemma. For Ryan. For loss. For grief.

Half an hour later, Laura said goodbye to Stella. Her mind instantly drew back to Ryan's diary, but she couldn't face it tonight again. Instead, overcome by a weight of sudden exhaustion, she pulled back the covers on her bed and climbed in, fully clothed, and closed her eyes.

19

LAURA WOKE EARLY the next morning to the sound of the garbage truck collection. The shrieking of the brakes every few meters, the clunking of the bin being lifted and emptied and then released back to the nature strip with a thud. She pulled herself up to a sitting position and reached to her bedside table. She opened up Ryan's diary, noticing there was no date for the next entry, and Ryan's writing was messy, almost illegible in parts. She began reading again.

~

RYAN'S JOURNAL

SOMETIMES WHEN I'M ALONE, a blackness grips hold of me, pulling me down into a vast space of nothingness.

That's the only way I can describe it. It sounds dramatic, but that's the way it feels. One minute, I feel fine. I guess like an average teenager, and then the next I feel like there's a thousand drums beating in my head and someone is standing on my chest crushing my lungs. That feeling is happening more often and lasting longer each time. When it happens, I want to both run and hide. It's like I'm spiraling down a black hole, looking up at the top and screaming inside for someone to help me, but the light gradually disappears and no one listens.

LAURA SLOWLY CLOSED the book and stared at her ceiling. *Is that what Gemma feels like? As if there's no hope? As if she's screaming and no one is listening?*

'I would have listened, Ryan,' Laura whispered. 'If you'd let me.'

A couple of hours later, after a strong coffee, a creamy bowl of porridge, and a hot shower, Laura walked into the library with a box of books.

'Hi, Shea,' she said, plonking the box on the counter.

'Laura, hey! What've you got there?' Shea peered in the box.

'Just some books from my mum's house. Some of them are pretty old, but most are in good condition. I wanted to donate them to the book sale you're having in a few weeks. I saw the posters the other day when I was here.'

'Fantastic!' Shea said, rummaging through the books. 'These Nora Roberts are always popular. And even these old Mills & Boons are still in demand. For a couple of our oldies.' She winked.

Shea placed the box under the counter. 'So how are things going with your search?'

Laura tilted her head.

'You were looking in the archives the other day.'

'Oh yeah. It's kind of complicated.'

Laura went on to tell Shea about her efforts to find out what really happened to Ryan. It felt good to share the story. Shea didn't judge her.

Laura held her breath as she spoke. 'I don't know, but I think he may have meant for the train to hit him.' It was so hard to get the words out. But everything in his journal pointed to it.

If Shea was shocked by Laura's summation, she didn't show it. She simply nodded. 'I'm so sorry, Laura. I can't imagine how awful all this must be for you. I wish I knew what to say.'

Laura smiled. She felt a small weight had been lifted off her shoulders. Shea was so easy to talk to.

'My cousin hung himself when he was only fifteen,' Shea continued. 'We weren't really close. They lived in Brisbane, but it was weird because his parents, even his sister, had no idea he was feeling that way. He wasn't being bullied or anything. They couldn't explain it.'

'Oh, that's horrible.'

'Yeah. I don't know if it's more common now—depression—or just that we hear about it more these days. I see a lot of kids come in here, and a few of them, you can tell they're pulling a mask on to hide what they're feeling inside. I didn't notice at first, but I do now. They seem fine with their friends around, but you can tell there's something going on behind the façade. I think a lot of it is that they don't see much hope here in Banyula. And for the ones who don't want to or can't get into uni, there aren't many options work wise. They end up bumming around or moving to the city, only to return broke or addicted to ice or whatever. It's hard to make them see what a beautiful place they have here, if they only gave it a chance. If the town only gave them something back. It just makes me sad to see the younger ones so, well, despondent, I guess.'

Laura sighed. 'I wish I had the answers, but I can't even figure out my own mess of a life.'

'Laura, no. You're doing something positive. You're facing your past. Trying to move forward. I think you're really strong for doing that.'

Laura felt her eyes well up. She hadn't thought of herself like that.

A lady cleared her throat at the borrowing counter, and Shea smiled. 'Won't be a moment, Mrs. Jackson.'

'Anyway, if I can help you with anything, just let me know. I'd better go.' She jokingly rolled her eyes toward Mrs. Jackson.

'Of course. Thanks for listening to me babble on.'

'Ha, no dramas at all. And thanks for the books.'

Laura stepped out of the library and paused. Was she strong like Shea saw? She wasn't convinced. But she knew she had to at least try to be. She wanted to help Gemma. She didn't know how, but she at least knew she had to try.

A few minutes later, Laura arrived at Stella's. As she went to knock on the door, Stella swung it open. Her eyes were swollen with exhaustion. Laura wondered if she'd managed to get any sleep last night.

'Laura,' she said. 'Thank you so much for coming.' She held the door open, and Laura followed her to the kitchen and placed her bag on the table.

'How is she?' Laura asked.

'She's still in bed. Well, she's in her room. I don't think she's sleeping.'

Laura nodded. 'I can come back later if that's better. You know, after you've had a chance to talk to her first, maybe?'

Stella shook her head. 'No. It's fine. I haven't told her you were coming. I was hoping, if you don't mind, that we can pretend it's a surprise visit?' Stella said, leaning toward Laura and speaking in a hushed tone.

'Sure. Whatever works.'

'Okay.' And with that, Stella's demeanor changed, and with a loud voice she said, 'Laura! Oh, it's so good to see you. I didn't know you were coming over! You're here to see Gemma? Oh, that's wonderful. I know she'd love to say hi! Just wait here a tick and I'll see if she's up. You know teenagers and sleep-ins!'

Laura smiled at Stella's noteworthy acting skills as she disappeared into the hallway.

'Gemma?' Laura heard Stella call out as she knocked on Gemma's bedroom door. 'Are you awake? Laura's here to see you.'

A muffled tone responded, and then Stella returned. 'Yes, she's awake. Give her a moment and you can go and see her.'

'Thanks, Stella,' Laura said, playing along.

A few moments later, Laura knocked on Gemma's door.

'Yeah,' Gemma replied.

Laura opened the door and saw Gemma sitting on a beanbag in the corner of the room, headphones around her neck and a blanket covering her body. The curtains were drawn, and the room gave off a sweet, musty smell. Laura well knew it was a combination of stale marijuana and air freshener.

'Hi, Gem!' Laura said, smiling. She looked around for somewhere to sit among the debris of clothes littering the floor, desk, and bed. She cleared a space and sat down on the end of Gemma's bed.

Gemma regarded Laura with narrow eyes and then said quietly, 'I know Mum has sent you here to talk to me.'

Laura bit her bottom lip, trying to think of what to say, then she slumped her shoulders and exhaled. 'Yeah, she has. But I wanted to. Wanted to see how you were doing. It's been ages.'

Gemma pursed her lips and nodded with an air of distrust.

'I s'pose she told you all about last night too.'

'Well, she did mention it.'

'Hmph,' Gemma grunted. 'That'd be right.'

Laura looked around the room, trying to order her words before speaking. 'Look, Gem, she's worried about you, that's all. I know you just want her to leave you alone, but she's your mum. It's her job to worry.'

Gemma shrugged.

'So, you don't write anymore?' Laura asked.

'No. Wasn't any good at it, anyway.'

'Well, I think you were. You came up with some great stories with your imagination. I remember the one about the girl whose superpower was being able to change people's minds. And she stopped World War Three! That was so clever, Gem. I think you really have talent.'

'Yeah, well. That's not going to get me anywhere. I need a real job apparently. And *an education*,' she air quoted. 'Everyone keeps telling me what I'm supposed to be doing. No one ever asks me what I want.'

Laura shivered as she remembered Ryan once using those exact words.

'Hey, Gem,' Laura said gently. 'I know you're going through a really tough time right now. And you think no one gets it. And you know? You're probably right. No one does get it. But, it doesn't mean you're alone. It just means it's tough at the moment. It won't be that way always.'

Gemma shrugged, but Laura could see the tears welling in her eyes. She hoped she was getting somewhere.

'You remember my friend Ryan?'

Gemma frowned. 'The one—' She stopped mid-sentence before continuing. 'The one who was hit by a train?' Gemma's eyes narrowed.

Laura was slightly taken aback at Gemma's blunt tone. 'Um, yeah.'

'That's when you ran away.'

'Well, I didn't run away ...'

'Yes you did. One day you were here, and the next you weren't.'

Gemma was right. That was exactly what she did.

'Was as if you had something to hide,' Gemma snapped.

Laura stiffened. 'I was in shock.'

Gemma raised an eyebrow before her expression changed, lips tight. 'I wish I could run away like that. Like you did,' she said under her breath.

'Gem, no. You don't. I ran away, because ... well, because I didn't know any better. I didn't want to face the hurt. I didn't know where to turn. But you know what? It didn't fix anything. Here I am years later having to deal with it. I have a life that I fell into that I don't want, and I'm no better off than I was ten years ago. In fact, I'm in a worse place than I was then.' Laura exhaled, shocked at her own honesty that she'd never been able to articulate accurately until now.

Laura looked to Gemma. It was hard to gage her expressionless face. She sat there with a stormy look, staring blankly ahead—not at Laura, not really at anything. Laura swallowed back her shame and reached into her handbag and pulled out Ryan's journal. 'I have something I want to you to read.'

Gemma's eyes shot to Laura. Her curiosity was piqued. She removed the headphones from around her neck and threw them down next to her before plonking down next to Laura on the bed. 'What's that?' She lifted her chin toward the notebook.

'This,' Laura said, stroking the front cover, 'was Ryan's journal.'

Gemma's mouth gaped. 'You can't read someone else's journal.'

'I know. You shouldn't, but his gran wanted me to read it, to help me understand what he was going through back then. I haven't finished yet, but I think there are some things in here that you will maybe relate to.' Laura opened to the page she had read that morning and handed the book to Gemma.

Laura watched as Gemma's eyes scanned the page. Then out of nowhere, tears dropped onto the words, the droplets sinking into the paper, blurring the ink ever so slightly.

'It's okay, Gem. You're not the only one. And you're not alone. Everyone wants to help you. We want to listen to what you want. It's not going to be easy. But you have to begin to trust us again,' Laura said. 'We're going to help you, Gem. I promise.'

Laura let her own tears fall too. Tears of shame, regret, hurt, and tears of relief. She wasn't able to help Ryan, but she could help Gemma. She was sure of it.

Gemma passed the book back to Laura without a word and then returned to the beanbag. She picked up the headphones and fiddled with the cord before turning to Laura with expressionless eyes. 'I don't want your kind of help.'

At that moment, Gemma's door flung open as Stella, who had obviously been listening, burst through. 'Gemma! There's no need to be rude to Laura. You apologize right now!'

Gemma ignored her mother and turned the music up, the heavy beat and squealing guitar leaking out the headphones in a muffled tone. Laura stood up and raised her palm to Stella. 'It's okay, Stel. Let's just leave her for a bit.'

Stella looked between Gemma and Laura, and thinking better of it, turned and walked out with Laura, closing the door behind them.

In the kitchen, Stella took a tissue out of the box on the bench and blew her nose. 'I'm so sorry, Laura. I just don't know what's wrong with her. She's been worse than ever these past few days.'

'It's okay. She's a teenager, and she's got a lot going on. I think what she read in here,' Laura tapped on Ryan's journal, 'will help.

It just might take a bit for her to process. I remember when I did my counseling course we were told that small steps make big progress.'

Stella's brow furrowed, 'I didn't know you ended up going to counseling. Did Jude know?'

'Mum made me go for one session very early on. But a while after, I enrolled in a counseling course. I almost finished it, but ... well,' Laura paused. 'I got sidetracked with life.' Laura shrugged, remembering that she'd met Luke around the same time.

'Oh, okay. Well, I hope you're right.'

Laura said goodbye to Stella at the door. 'I'm sure she'll come around. And I'm here when she's ready to talk more.'

Stella embraced Laura. 'Thank you. I know you tried.'

20

Tom loaded the last of the broken gum branches on the back of the Ute as the rain welled on the brim of his Akubra and dripped down in front of his face. The strong winds had torn down part of an old tree along one of the eastern fence lines. He would have loved to pull out the damn tree, but it did offer shade to the cattle, and getting a permit to fell this variety of native eucalyptus wasn't worth the effort. Stupid environmental red tape.

He jumped into the Ute and drove carefully back toward the house, trying to avoid the soft spots in the track. There was no end in sight to the rain, and tomorrow he would have to move the cows to higher ground. He was hoping his last cows would have calved by then.

He pulled up to the paddock closest to the house to check on the last three pregnant cows. He jumped out of the Ute, unlatched the gate, and latched it behind him. He noticed two of the cows sheltering under the peppercorn tree, the other under the tin shelter that he'd laid with fresh hay that morning. The cow was tending to a newly born calf. He leaned down next to her and saw the little one, its legs tucked under its body. Mumma cow was still cleaning the amniotic fluid off with her sandpapery tongue. Tom crawled over to check that the calf was breathing, which it was. Nothing for him to do. He smiled. This was one of his favorite parts about the farm. New life. Watching as nature took its course.

The cow got to her feet and nudged her baby to follow suit. The calf stumbled gingerly to her feet before bumbling over. She tried again, her bony little legs shaking as they tried to balance. A few moments later, the calf had balanced and was hungrily suckling, taking in all of the important colostrum that would see she got the best start to life.

Tom pulled out his iPhone from his pocket and recorded the date, time, sex, sire, and dam details before taking a quick photo and returning to the car as the rain began to fall harder. He slammed the Ute door shut and sighed, a warm feeling buzzing inside him.

LATER THAT EVENING, Tom sat at his desk shuffling paperwork and entering data into spreadsheets. His plans were slowly coming together. Although he'd had to go into the red to source the semen and embryos, they'd stuck, and the calves that were coming through were proving to be sound. His two-year-olds would be ready to sell late winter, and as far as he could see, although market prices weren't great, he had potential to do well with them. His meticulous record keeping and sound scientific breeding practices were producing quality stock with increased fertility, good temperament, and fast growth rates. Pushing boundaries to improve the genetics would see his cattle, his bulls in particular, in demand. He dreamed of one day holding his own sales, right here on the farm, like the top producers up in New South Wales. Heady dreams maybe, but he knew he could do it.

He leaned back in his chair and sighed, his eyes drawn to the desk drawer. He opened the drawer and pulled out the letter, the formal black ink on the page bold and sharp.

DEAR MR. GORDON,

This is a courtesy letter to remind you that you are now ninety (90) days overdue on your loan repayment. As we have had no formal correspondence from you during this time, we urge you to contact us immediately.

If you fail to do so, arrangements will be put into place to freeze your accounts and begin recovery proceedings.

We urge you to contact us immediately.

Sincerely,

Royal Farmers Union Bank

TOM RUBBED HIS FOREHEAD. He knew he shouldn't have extended the loan, especially with his future plans needing financial backing, but he wanted to make sure his parents had enough money to take their trip. After the balance of the farm was signed over to him, his parents only had enough to do half of what they wanted, so Tom decided to do something about it, telling them he had been saving and that the spring sales had gone extra well. At first, his dad wouldn't accept the money, but Tom had insisted. It was the least he could do.

His parents had worked hard every day of their lives. They deserved to enjoy their twilight years before they got too old. The last time his mum had called, she'd told him they were up on the northwest coast of Australia near Carnarvon. His mum babbled on with excitement about the sunset they had just witnessed while walking along the mile-long jetty. She'd said it was the most beautiful thing she had ever seen. 'The colors, Tom. Oh, the colors. I've never seen anything like it, even on the farm. Orange, auburn, pinks, and reds melting into the sea. It was amazing. Even your dad was speechless!'

Just remembering the emotion in her voice made Tom choke up. It was worth it. He just needed to find a way to hold off the hounds. Just till the sales. Then he'd be back on track. He hoped.

Tom folded up the letter and placed it back into the drawer. Loneliness began to settle in his bones once again, as it did more and more these days. If only he had someone to talk to, to confide in. Someone to talk about other things than the farm, money, and what the weather held for the next three months.

Again, his thoughts turned to Laura and the other night. The kiss. Her lips were soft like rose petals. It had taken all of his resolve not to ravish her. And then he remembered their fight. He hung his head, the guilt of not being upfront with Laura when he should have weighing him down. He still remembered the burning anger he felt the night he saw Ryan and Rachel kiss. It still made his jaw clench.

It was the night of Ryan's eighteenth, a few weeks after the Easter party.

TOM THREW another log on the bonfire. It crackled and flared into the still black sky. The cold winter air bit at his nose and he shifted closer to the fire.

'The first of us to be legal, and you're spending the night here on the farm,' he said to Ryan as he downed a beer.

'Yeah, well, who else am I going to go to the pub with? You're all too young!'

'Not for long! I'm next!' Rachel said. 'Seventeen days, in fact. And you'd better throw a much better party than this for me.'

'Hey!' Laura smiled, slapping her on the leg.

'Only kidding. Mum's insisting on throwing me a party down at the tennis club.'

'Ooh la la, the *tennis club,*' Tom said as he rubbed his hands together over the coals.

'Shut up!' Rachel hissed through a smile. 'It'll be the best party this year. I promise you.'

'Got anything else other than beer?' Laura asked Tom, peering toward the esky beside her.

'Mum's got some wine inside, I reckon.'

'Oooh, that's a bit refined. Anything sweet?' Laura asked.

'I dunno, I s'pose. Come on, we'll raid her secret stash.'

Tom walked Laura to the house, glad for some time with her. He hadn't seen much of her, since they only had one class together this semester, and any spare time she had she spent with Ryan. He missed their chats and the smell of her fruity perfume. Most of all, he missed her infectious laughter. Ryan was a lucky guy. But he had the goods. Looks, sporting ability, charisma. Not like Tom. Laura'd never see past the farm boy he was. Tom knew that. She deserved better, anyway.

Tom and Laura crept in the back door, trying not to disturb Bessie on her bed, but it was to no avail. She lifted her head in anticipation of a pat. *Thump, thump, thump.* Her tail pounded the floorboards in the kitchen in front of the combustion stove where she was curled up.

'Is that you, Tom?' Tom's mum called out from the adjacent living room.

'Yeah, Mum, just grabbing some water.'

Laura giggled. "Water?" she whispered. 'As if she'll believe that!'

'It's for Laura, she's feeling sick.' He winked.

'Oh, is she okay? Do you want me to come out?'

'No! Mrs. G, I'm okay, just a bit queasy. I'll be fine. Thanks.' Laura squinted her eyes in annoyance at Tom while trying to stifle her giggling.

Tom opened the door of the walk-in pantry. The shelves were well stocked, as always. Tom's mum loved to cook. And Tom loved nothing better than coming home to freshly baked biscuits after school or warming winter casseroles after a day in the crush, and of course, her hot buttery scones for Sunday breakfasts.

Tom reached up to the top shelf. 'Here it is. Her finest.'

Laura grabbed the green bottle out of Tom's hand, her fingers gently brushing his, resulting in his heartbeat increasing.

'Margaret River Chardonnay.' Laura read the label, her eyes wide. '*Sweet, luscious white wine with hints of peach, citrus, and nectarine,*' she read. 'Are you kidding? We can't take this. It looks expensive! And it says, *Serve chilled.*'

'Nah, don't worry about that. It's like ten degrees outside. And look, there's a whole box of it. She's a member of some wine club and orders all this shit and never drinks it. She'll never even know.'

'No, Tom. I can't.'

Tom grabbed the bottle and smiled. 'But I can! Come on!'

'Tom, you're so bad!' Laura jeered. 'Hang on, I have to go to the loo. You go.'

'Alrighty. I'll grab some plastic cups.'

'Plastic? All class you are, Tom Gordon!'

Tom watched as Laura wandered off down the hallway, an ache beginning inside him. He'd missed their banter. He grabbed some plastic cups from the cupboard near the sink, glancing through the kitchen window toward the silhouettes of Rachel and Ryan dark against the glow of the bonfire. Then he looked closer, squinting to try and understand what he was seeing. It wasn't two silhouettes, but one. Ryan was kissing Rachel. And it was no friendly peck on the cheek. He had one hand on the back of her head and the other on her waist. This was no first kiss. This was no silly, drunk, happy birthday kiss. This was a deep, passionate, familiar kiss. The kind Tom dreamed of with Laura.

'Tom? You coming?'

Tom startled and spun around to see Laura standing in the doorway of the kitchen. His pulse began to race.

'Tom?' Laura raised one eyebrow as she always did. It made her look cute.

'Um, yep. Just grabbing the cups,' he said, fumbling the cups into the sink. He scrambled to pick them up and then rustled through the cutlery drawer to find the corkscrew, making as much noise as he could to distract Laura from looking out the window.

'Okay! Let's go!' he practically yelled.

'Shh!' Laura hushed.

'You two okay?' his mum called out.

'Yes, Mum, no worries. Just heading back out to the bonfire,' he called, raising his voice louder than needed.

'Well keep it down, okay? Your father's in bed.'

Tom grabbed Laura's hand and made sure she was behind him as he swung open the back door. It slammed against the back weatherboards of the kitchen wall. Bessie barked.

'Jesus, Tom!' his mum exclaimed at the noise.

Tom looked toward the bonfire and saw that Ryan and Rachel had moved apart, and his heart slowed. As he and Laura walked back to the bonfire, his hackles began to rise. This was shit. What the fuck was Ryan doing?

'What the hell?' Rachel said as she grabbed the bottle of wine out of Tom's hands. 'This is like really expensive!'

'I hope it tastes good then.' Laura smiled.

Tom ignored them both, sat down, and sculled the last of his beer as he glared into the fire, unable to look at Ryan or Rachel.

All of a sudden Tom was hot. Sweat trickled down the back of his neck. His fists clenched.

'Tom?' Laura said, tapping his knee.

'Huh?'

'The corkscrew?' Rachel said.

He threw the corkscrew at Rachel's lap, and it hit her square on the knee.

'Hey, what's with you?' Rachel said, maneuvering the cork from the bottle.

Ryan, Rachel and Laura continued talking, but it was all white noise to Tom's ears. He just wanted to get out of there, unable to breathe the same air as them. He jumped to his feet, threw the empty can into the fire, and started walking back to the house.

'Tom?' said Laura.

'Hey, where you going?' Rachel yelled. 'More wine?' The two girls erupted into fits of giggles as they sipped the liquid from their plastic cups.

A moment later, Ryan jogged up behind him. 'Hey, man? You okay?' he asked.

'Fuck off, Ryan,' Tom replied without stopping.

'Whoa, what crawled up your arse all of a sudden?'

Tom spun around to Ryan, his mouth tight and fists clenched. It felt like the anger was bubbling out of his every pore.

'I saw you two,' he whispered through gritted teeth, gesturing toward Rachel. 'I saw you kissing her.'

Ryan's smug face dropped and he tilted his head back. 'Fuck.'

'Yeah. That's right. Your dirty little secret's out. You two make me sick,' he said, turning back toward the house.

'Hey, I can explain.' Ryan reached for his shoulder, and it took every ounce of strength Tom had not to turn around and smash his face.

'Explain?' he snapped, trying to keep his voice low and level. 'What's to explain? It's pretty obvious, mate.'

'I know. We—we're going to tell Laura. But, we don't want to hurt her either. It's just happened. We didn't mean for it to. It just happened,' Ryan said, his eyes darting from side to side.

'You're pathetic.'

'Please man, don't say anything.'

Tom fronted up to Ryan, adrenaline surging through him. 'You fix it. Or I will tell Laura.' And then he flung open the screen door and stormed upstairs.

Once upstairs, Tom looked out the window. Ryan was now back with the girls. They were huddled close, and for a split second, he actually thought Ryan was coming clean. That was until they all threw their heads back in laughter and raised their cups.

TOM HELD his head in his hands as the memory disappeared and stupid questions began entering his mind. Why didn't he tell Laura sooner? If he had, would it have changed anything? Would Ryan still be alive? Would Laura feel differently for Tom?

Maybe it was too late. He'd had his chance. And you didn't get second chances with a girl like Laura. As his mum would often say, 'You made your bed, now you gotta lie in it.' She was right. Tom had to lie in his bed every night, alone, wondering how things would have turned out if he'd handled the situation differently. If he'd had the balls to tell Laura about Ryan and Rachel when he should have. If he'd had the balls to tell her he loved her.

But it was too late for all that now. He'd blown it with Laura for a second time. There wouldn't be another chance.

Tom was about to call it a night when a message appeared on his phone. Laura.

Hi, sorry it's late, but I was hoping to come out to see you in the morning. To apologize. For everything. I understand if you're too busy. Or don't want to see me after how I yelled at you the other night.

Tom's heart picked up speed. He fought the urge to grab his phone and reply too quickly. After a moment, he tapped out a message.

Sure. I'm around. What time? I'll make sure I'm up at the house.

How's 9:30?

Sounds good.

Okay, see you then. Good night.

Night.

He put the phone down gently on the desk and leaned back on the chair, clasping his hands behind his head. Maybe it wasn't too late to make amends. Maybe he could fix this and have a chance with Laura. It was now or never.

21

AFTER A SLEEPLESS NIGHT, Laura stirred early the next morning with a thumping headache. She needed to clear her head, so she drove out to Creek View Lookout. Following the road west out of town, she turned off toward the scrubby hills and up a winding road to the top of the Banyula Ranges. She parked in the gravel parking lot and walked the five hundred meters toward the lookout, carefully dodging the muddy puddles before reaching the clearing. On a clear day, you could see for miles into the distance —Banyula to the left, and further to the right, the town of Clear Springs. Clear Creek could be seen snaking its way in and around Banyula and then over to Clear Springs and beyond. Today, however, a sheet of gray blanketed the horizon, and low-lying clouds settled in the valley along the creek.

Laura positioned herself on the edge of a smooth rock and inhaled the eucalyptus hanging in the air, its scent heightened by the dampness. Laura remembered coming up here with her mum, usually as a way to fill in a lazy summer Sunday. They'd sit on the large boulders, shaded by gum trees, with their backs to the sun.

Sometimes they'd pack sandwiches for a picnic lunch, but Laura's favorite was when Judy would surprise her with a bag of Fantales to share. They'd spend the afternoon chewing on the hard caramel lollies, taking turns reading out the trivia questions from the wrappers. Judy, a self-confessed movie buff, would usually get the answers right before Laura had even finished reading.

Laura stretched her arms above her head, feeling the tension between her shoulder blades slowly release. A lone crow echoed in the background, and the breeze made the overhead gums look like they were slow dancing. In the distance, Laura spotted a wallaby through the scrub, disturbing a honeyeater as it bounded past. Being here, surrounded by nature, made Laura wonder how life got so complicated.

How did it go from carefree Sunday afternoons chewing on Fantales to feeling like she was continually functioning on autopilot, blinkers on, eyes ahead? She was much too young to be contemplating the meaning of life. Much too young to have to deal with the tragedy and grief of death three times already. But here she stood, her mind at a crossroads.

For too long she'd had those blinkers on, content to let life take over and blindly follow the path without giving it much thought. Happier to live in the moment than ever think about the past, or more particularly, the future. Wasn't that what all those inspirational quotes on Facebook and Instagram said? To live in the moment, forget about the past, and not worry about the future?

Laura sighed and kicked a loose stone on the ground, watching as it rolled and bounced down the hill. Was that how Ryan felt? As if he were blindly rolling down a hill out of control?

The darkness of his words hadn't left Laura's mind. They were imprinted on her eyelids every time she blinked, each word detailing his spiral downwards into depression. Her heart broke for Ryan with each and every word.

In the last few days, Laura had passed seamlessly from sadness, to anger, to despair. 'Why didn't you let me in, Ryan?' she whispered to the unhearing sky. Why didn't she see it happening? See the signs. They seemed so obvious now in hindsight.

It was true, all the signs were there, but when you're seventeen, the signs are like breadcrumbs. If followed, they'd lead you to the truth, but they're so easily missed and eaten by the birds of everyday life. She'd missed them. Everyone had missed them.

Laura longed to see Ryan's face again. To try and understand what was going on behind that dimpled smile, behind his once confident, carefree façade. To forgive him for what he'd done. She felt the emotion build up inside as her thoughts questioned her memories.

She thought of Tom. Anger bit at her insides when she remembered his confession the other night. But it quickly dissipated. Things had changed. And it was time to forgive. Forgive Tom. Forgive Ryan. Maybe even forgive Rachel.

Was that the answer to Laura's confused emotions? Forgiveness? Laura wasn't sure, but the thought of it made her feel lighter.

'I'm making good on my promises, Mum,' she said out loud before squeezing the tears from her eyes. A crackle of cockatoos flew overhead, their screeches echoing through the trees. Laura watched as they disappeared into the gray sky before she returned to the car. She sat behind the wheel as if waiting for a sign to show her what she should do next. But there were none. This was a decision she had to make by herself. A decision that would help her let go of the past and move forward. Tom didn't deserve any of her anger. He deserved her forgiveness, and that's what she was going to give him. And perhaps something a little special too. For the first time in so long, Laura felt lighter. She smiled.

22

TOM CHECKED HIS watch. It was nearing 9:30 a.m. He kicked the last of the hay bales off the back of the Ute, jumped down, and stacked them with the others. Then, he began to make his way back to the house.

He wondered if there was a particular reason Laura wanted to see him. He knew she wanted to apologize, but that seemed like an arbitrary excuse. If anything, Tom needed to apologize to her. For more than Laura knew. Or would ever know, for that matter. He'd already said too much by declaring his feelings for her, and there was so much more he should have said. But there was nothing to be gained from telling Laura the one thing that he'd carried heavy on his conscience for so many years.

Tom sighed as his boots kicked up more mud onto his jeans. It was great having Laura back, but it had also stirred up so many memories, guilt, and questions from the past. Could he have done more? Should he have? He knew there was something off with Ryan back then. It wasn't that Tom didn't like him—he was jealous, of course, that he'd scored Laura. But, it was more than that. It was like Ryan had it in for Tom, had to show off about Laura. And for what reason?

He recalled the time Tom confronted Ryan in the classroom before he knew about Ryan and Rachel.

'Excuse me, Mr. Gordon, would you like to rejoin us?' Mr. Martin's voice seeped into Tom's consciousness. Tom sat up in his seat and refocused from the window to the board.

'This is not the time for daydreaming. Now, tell me,' he said, tapping the board with his chalk. 'Is the answer A or B?'

'Um ... B?'

'Correct.'

Tom breathed a sigh of relief at his guess and looked at Ryan, who raised his eyebrows, acknowledging the lucky escape. 'Lucky guess.'

'This is crap, anyway. Seriously, who needs this advanced algebra shit, anyway?' Ryan said, leaned toward him.

'Yeah,' Tom nodded. 'Hey, I can't come down the river after school. Promised Dad I'd help him.'

Ryan shrugged. 'Whatever. I think it's just me and Laura, anyway.'

Tom swallowed, the jealousy gnawing at his nerves. He began coloring in the back of his ruler, trying to ignore it, but it kept festering. He nudged Ryan. 'You and Laura,' he whispered, 'you guys serious?'

It was a weird question. He didn't even know why he asked it, apart from the fact he wanted to make sure Ryan wasn't fucking around with her. She deserved better than that.

'I guess. Why?'

'No reason.'

Tom looked away, the heat burning his cheeks, hoping Ryan wouldn't catch on.

'She told me she loved me the other day,' Ryan added casually.

The corner of Tom's lip twitched, and his shoulders froze. *She what?* he wanted to say. *She didn't. She wouldn't have. Would she? Did she?*

The bell blasted, signaling the end of class, and everyone scraped their chairs back and grabbed their books, but Tom didn't move. He could feel the anger slowly build and rise from the pit of his stomach. He stalled, wanting Ryan to leave. He didn't know what he was capable of if he had to look at Ryan right now. The thought of Ryan with Laura made him feel sicker than it ever had.

'Hey?' Ryan said, waiting by the table with his books. 'You coming?'

Everyone had piled out of the room to make their way to the next class as Tom willed his body to calm.

'Hey?' Ryan tried again.

Tom slowly pulled himself to his feet, looking Ryan in the eye. 'Laura deserves to be treated right,' he said, gritting his teeth. Then he grabbed his books off the desk.

'What's that supposed to mean?' Ryan said, fronting up to Tom as he went to pass by. 'Hey, you gotta problem, Tom? Just say it.'

'It means she's not just any girl, all right,' Tom said and walked past him. He could feel Ryan's eyes burning into his back, and it took all his resolve to keep walking.

'You had your chance with her, Tom. You've had a million chances, but you never took them. I did.'

Tom froze in the doorway. Embarrassment burned on his cheeks.

'It's not like I don't know you like her. Problem is, Laura doesn't know that. And now she's with me.'

'I don't like her like that. She's just a friend.'

'Whatever, man,' Ryan said, pushing past Tom, shouldering him as he did.

Tom turned back into the classroom to regain his breathing, the seed of self-doubt sprouting up again. Ryan was right. He had had chances with Laura. They'd come and gone many times, and he'd never had the balls to take them. Always too self-conscious, more worried about losing a friend than seeing if there was more to their relationship. That was why Ryan was with her. He'd taken a chance, and he'd won. Tom swallowed back the acidic taste in his mouth.

Tom had lost.

Tom jumped up on the verandah with those words playing on his mind all these years later. He had lost. But, in the end, they'd all lost. Hindsight wasn't any help. Recalling stupid memories and wishing things had been different didn't help either. All he could do was take the chances that were in front of him right now. If he was man enough to.

23

IT WAS ALMOST serendipitous, certainly not something she'd planned. A notice in her letterbox on the way out this morning had caught Laura's attention. And now, with a clear head, she knew it was the right thing to do. A gift of forgiveness. She had to shake any anger she felt toward Tom and release him of his guilt. And that was what this gift would do.

She drove to the address on the notice, handed the money over, and made her choice. Returning to the car, she sat the box gently on the front passenger seat and carefully closed the door before returning to the driver's seat. 'Okay,' she said. 'Let's do this.'

She drove through the center of Banyula, cars angle parked along the sides of the road in front of the tired shop façades. Laura noticed many of the smaller boutique shops had closed down. Popsicle, once her and Rachel's go-to fashion house, the bookshop, and the music store were all gone with not much to replace them. Her heart panged for the little town she used to call home. There had been rumors of a chain store moving in, which would definitely change the Banyula she once knew. But, change was inevitable, and maybe in the long run it would be the only saving grace for the town. Still, though, the thought left a small part of her heart craving the place she grew up in and knew so well, as much as she'd tried to deny it up until now.

Flicking on the indicator and turning left past the Ford dealership, now bigger than she recalled, the butterflies rose in Laura's stomach as she felt a rush of nerves tingle up the back of her neck.

The road out to Tom's farm, once scattered with old weatherboard cottages on small acreages, had now been developed into a housing estate with rendered square buildings and colorbond roofing that all looked the same. Yucca plants grew in stone-covered garden beds, and concrete driveways met double garages. Flat, boring, and lifeless. The landscape didn't match the memories inside Laura's head. It didn't even feel like it was the right road to Tom's. Only a few grand old gum trees towering near the bridge over Clear Springs Creek indicated it was.

Laura remembered how she had loved riding her bike out to the farm, not even minding the twenty minutes it took. In fact, she looked forward to it, the smell of the dry country air, the long grass, the silvery gums towering along the roadside, offering shade in the summer heat. She'd ridden it so many times she could probably have done so with her eyes closed back then. But it felt much different today.

After another minute, the road finally became more familiar. On the bend ahead, two huge weeping peppercorn trees swayed in the breeze, and before she knew it, there was Tom's driveway. Laura noted the new sign. The black lettering contrasted against the stone-white background.

Gordon Angus. Quality, Performance, Diversity.

Laura's Mazda 3 rattled over the cattle grate, memories

washing over her like she'd been here only yesterday. The expansive fields to the left and right with the big dam they used to catch yabbies in, the green pastures spotted with the black cows that Tom loved so much, and the familiar line of red gums in the distance that curved along the riverbank. The hairs prickled on Laura's arms as the old farmhouse came into view, and she felt a small lump form in her throat. She pulled up right in front of the old date palm, still as strong and tall as ever, still imagining her bike thrown against the trunk, helmet hanging off the handlebars.

Laura opened the car door and sat for a moment, taking it all in. It was like she was ten years old again, marveling at the sprawling twelve-foot verandas surrounding the weatherboard farmhouse, the four orange brick chimneys standing proudly. Laura found herself imagining it in its heyday a hundred years earlier, wondering how much effort and money it would take to bring it back to its former glory. Her eye caught Tom rounding the verandah, interrupting her daydream. She smiled.

'Hey,' Tom said, jumping down off the verandah to meet her at the car.

'Hey!' Laura maneuvred herself out of the car, and there was a moment of awkwardness between them. Averted eyes. Hands shoved in pockets. Then they both broke the silence together.

'Look, Tom—'

'Lauz, I'm—'

They both smiled.

'Me first,' Laura said.

Tom nodded.

'I'm sorry I reacted the way I did the other night,' she started. Tom began to open his mouth, but Laura held up her hand. 'Let me finish. I know you did what you thought was best back then. And it's okay. We were so young, Tom. I don't blame you. I understand.'

'Are you sure?' Tom said, glancing up with hopeful eyes.

'Yeah. I'm sure.'

Tom smiled. 'I'd do it differently if I had the chance again. I'd do a lot of things differently,' he added, tucking his hands in his back pockets.

'I know you would. Me too.'

A noise escaped the car, and Laura's eyes shot wide open.

'Oh, I almost forgot,' she said, rushing around to the front passenger door and lifting out the box. She opened it up out of sight behind the car, and then walked back around to Tom. Following close behind her, a golden ball of fuzz trotted up to Tom and began chewing on his boots. Laura watched, bursting with excitement as Tom peered at the big chocolate eyes staring up at him and the wet, black nose glistening in the light.

'What the?' Tom looked at Laura with a confused look before bending down and picking up the puppy. 'Hey, little one.' He ruffled the top of its head. 'And this is?' he questioned Laura as the puppy began gnawing on his hand with its pointy little teeth.

'I think she likes you!' Laura laughed.

'Yeah. But...'

'This is my forgiveness gift,' Laura said, her eyes wide.

As she caught Tom's eyes, her heart felt like it was going to explode out of her chest. She watched as Tom's lip trembled and his eyes began to water. The puppy squirmed and wriggled in his arms. 'Are you kidding?' His voice wavered.

Laura slowly nodded, unable to speak.

'Lauz, she's beautiful. She looks just like Bessie.'

'I know! Doesn't she? I knew she was the one as soon as I saw her. And she was the first one that came up to greet me too.'

The puppy licked Tom's face excitedly.

'I think she's a keeper.'

Tom reached out to Laura's hand and squeezed it. 'I think so.

Thank you.' Laura's skin buzzed with his touch, as if a current of electricity had just connected them. She quickly turned away and went around to the passenger seat to grab the bag of puppy supplies. 'Let's get her settled!' she said.

Half an hour later, the new puppy had collapsed with exhaustion on Tom's kitchen floor, sprawled out on its new bed surrounded by newspaper Laura had carefully laid out in case of any accidents.

'You don't mind if I have a few chores to do while I show you around?'

'Course not! It'll be like old times,' Laura said, trying to convince herself as much.

'I think she'll be okay here till we get back,' Tom said, nodding at the puppy. He paused. 'Rosie. How's that sound for a name?'

'That's perfect!' smiled Laura. 'Rosie Gordon.'

Tom closed the hallway door, leaving the little puppy softly snoring, and Laura followed behind and out through the back door.

'I just have to head down the river. Need to check the level before it rains again,' Tom said, pulling on his boots.

'Yeah, sure.'

'Here, put these on.' Tom threw Laura a pair of well-worn, dusty Blundstone boots. 'They were Mums, so they should fit okay. Those Converse of yours won't cut it down at the river. I doubt there'll be any snakes still out, but you never know.'

Snakes. Something Laura didn't miss about the farm. She remembered the time they ran into an eight-foot tiger snake down at the dam. She'd jumped into Tom's arms screaming, sending it scurrying into the scrub. Tom had laughed until his eyes watered, and Laura ended up pushing him in the water in a burst of anger and embarrassment.

Laura smacked the boots together and then on the concrete.

'Ah, you're definitely a farm girl at heart,' Tom said, grinning.

'Well, spiders, you know!'

'Tell me about it! Had a redback spider in mine the other day.'

'What!' Laura shrieked.

'Only kidding.' Tom shook his head and laughed. 'You haven't changed, have you? You're still so gullible.'

'Oh, shut up,' she said, swinging a friendly arm at Tom as they jumped in the farm Ute and set off down toward the river.

As they neared the gums, Laura realized how little the farm had changed. The worn track to the river was still the same, albeit soggy and muddy at the moment. A few Angus cows lifted their heads in the adjoining paddock as the Ute rumbled past, chewing slowly and methodically on the green pasture. The chirping of the cicadas was an annoying yet comforting chorus in the background.

They pulled up as close as possible to the riverbank, and Tom descended toward the pump shed while Laura sat down on a fallen tree log. The water was the highest she'd ever seen it. Not far from breaking the bank. Their old swimming hole wasn't much of a hole anymore, more a torrent. Broken limbs from nearby gums littered the edges, and the old rope swing hung splintered and torn. A flash of Ryan leaping from the rope swing into the water below materialized in Laura's head, taking her by surprise. She could see his strong arms rippling as he hoisted himself into the air, the sky cobalt blue behind him, with not a wisp of clouds. She could hear Rachel and Tom's laughter and the splash of Ryan into the river. And almost feel the warmth of the summer sun on her face if she tried hard enough.

Laura struggled with the memory. Part of her wanted to push it away, the other part wanting to relive the moment and every feeling it brought back to her. A time of no responsibility, no regrets, no secrets, just the naïve bliss of untouched youth. The memory blurred as the wind caught Laura's hair and whipped it behind her. She knew the time had come to let it go. It was time to let Ryan go.

'All done,' Tom said, slapping his palms together as he made his way toward Laura. 'Lauz? Hey, what's wrong?' he said, bending down in front of her.

Laura looked up into the sky above to dry her tears. The silvery blanket overhead stretched as far as Laura could see, her heart heavy, realizing how much she missed the endless skies of the country. For the first time in so long, she wanted to feel the beauty of this place, relive the happy memories and not feel burdened by the bad ones.

'It's so hard to let it all go,' she cried, letting her tears spill down her face.

'Hey, come here.' Tom put his arm around her and pulled her close. Laura could smell a sweet mix of sweat and aftershave. Such a familiar smell. Tom. The only person she could feel like herself with. The only person who really knew her. As Laura let herself relax into Tom's embrace, her heart slowly began to release the tension it was holding.

24

Tom made Laura a hot cup of tea and opened a packet of Marie biscuits. His mum always said a cup of tea made everything easier.

'Sorry, that's all I got.' He smiled and put the packet of biscuits on the coffee table.

Laura smiled back. She looked so beautiful. Her big brown eyes were endless pools, and he longed to see them again filled with the laughter and energy they used to hold. He'd give anything for that.

Tom sat down on the sofa next to Laura.

'I went to see Mrs. Lincoln,' Laura said, staring at her tea.

'Ryan's grandmother?'

Laura nodded. 'She gave me Ryan's diary.'

'His diary? I didn't even know he had one. Huh. Wouldn't have picked him as the type.''

'Me either.'

'What was in it?'

Tom listened as she told him about Ryan's journal. About

Ryan's spiral into depression. He shook his head. 'I had no idea. I mean, I thought he was just being a jerk.'

Laura reached her hand over to Tom's, and he wrapped his fingers around hers. 'I don't think any of us knew,' she said through a trembling voice. 'Well, maybe Rachel.'

Tom nodded. He tried to think of what to say. Anything to make it better, but he came up blank. They sat in silence for a few moments until he finally managed to speak. 'I'm really sorry, Lauz.' Tom gripped her hand tight.

'Sorry for what?'

'Just all of it. I should have told you earlier. I knew something was up. Maybe it would have brought things to a head. You know, we could have found out how Ryan was feeling. Got him some help.'

'You can't blame yourself. I've done that for so long, blamed myself. Thought "if only" or "what if?" I wish it could have been different, but ...'

'You're right. We can't change anything now. Just make amends, I guess.'

Tom stared out the window as the dusk disappeared into black. Hindsight told him he'd known something was off with Ryan. He'd tried to like him, and sure, they'd had some fun times together—some of his best memories actually—but there had always been something amiss. Then, after he found out about Ryan and Rachel, well that was the end of it. But that wasn't all. An unwelcome wave of guilt crashed over him.

'I should probably get going,' Laura said, breaking into his thoughts.

He didn't want her to go. Not now. Not ever. His mind raced for something to say.

'Still like lasagna?'

She looked at him puzzled. 'Ah, yeah, why?'

'I've got some for dinner. It's only store bought. Not homemade or anything. But if you want to, like maybe, stay for tea or something.' He felt like he was fourteen years old again, awkward and uncomfortable.

'Oh, Tom, I should really get back.'

Tom stared at her blankly. What did she have to go back to? An empty house, memories of her mother. Of Ryan.

'Seems silly going back to an empty house when I've got food here.' He shrugged. The puppy rounded the couch and tilted its head toward Laura expectantly. 'And Rosie wants you to stay too.'

Laura sighed. 'How can I say no to that face? Okay, I'll stay. But only as long I can help.'

'Not much to whacking a lasagna in the oven, but sure.' Tom chuckled, making his way to the kitchen with the puppy following dutifully behind.

An hour later they had demolished the lasagna and a bottle of merlot Tom had found in the pantry.

'I can't believe your mum still has all that wine,' Laura said. 'Did she ever know you took any?'

'Doubt it. She did take some with her though. Think she figured she'd better drink it before it turns to vinegar.'

'Well this one went down very nicely.' Laura smiled.

In that moment, Tom felt the world was perfect. Dinner, good wine, Laura across the table, and a puppy curled up next to his feet. The gentle breeze rustled the fronds of the date palm against the roof, and the dull chirp of the crickets outside gave Tom an idea to make it even more perfect.

'Come on,' he said, getting to his feet and clearing their plates. He poured the dregs of the wine into their glasses and motioned for Laura to follow.

Once outside, it took a moment for his eyes to adjust, but he took Laura's hand and they made their way over to the old wooden swing his dad made when Tom was eight. It was a huge plank of hardwood big enough for three. The moon poked its head through the clouds, casting just enough light for Tom to grab an old gum branch and dust away any cobwebs. Then with the back of his sleeve, he wiped off the drops of rain water from the swing. Laura looked like she didn't think he expected her to hop on.

'It's okay. Smiddy's kids use it all the time. It's safe and spider free. I promise!'

Laura still didn't look too sure but followed his lead as he sat down on the swing and patted the wood next to him. She sat cautiously. Now, it was perfect.

They gently rocked back and forth, the wine casting a happy haze on Tom's thoughts. He watched Laura as she looked up into the night sky and wondered what she was thinking.

Her skin had a translucent milky glow under the moonlight, and her dark hair fell in brilliant contrast as it gently lapped against her cheek. He wanted so much to touch her. To softly tuck her hair behind her ear, like he'd noticed she always did. To lean in and kiss the small of her neck and feel how delicately soft her skin would be on his lips. To breathe in the scent of her. Tom felt himself fill with passion. If there was ever going to be a moment, it was now.

But what if she wasn't ready? What if she didn't feel the same way? Was it too soon? She was still grieving after all, for her mum, and again for Ryan. Especially after reading his journal. But surely she felt it too. She had to. There was so much more to them now. Every day since she had left, his heart had been aching for her. He'd never seriously looked at another girl. It was as if he was waiting, knowing she would return. He had never been in love, or so he'd always thought, though maybe he'd been in love all along.

'This is beautiful, Tom,' Laura said softly, startling him a little. She rested her hand on his knee, and it took all his patience and restraint not to passionately jump on top of her right then and there. But no, he had to take things slow.

'Laura,' he began, clearing his croaky throat as if starting an important speech.

She turned to face him, and he looked into her eyes, his heart pounding.

'I'm in love with you. I've always been in love with you.' As soon as he said it, he knew it came out wrong. Too full-on. Too fast. He was supposed to ease into it, not goddamned blurt it out like the answer on a quiz show.

'I ... I mean ...' He scrambled to recover the words.

Laura hung her head and avoided his gaze. He couldn't read her. He needed to see her eyes to know what she was thinking, to know if it was too much.

'Tom ... I ... I can't ...'

Tom felt the fire of passion inside creep up to his cheeks and turn into embarrassment. He rubbed his face with his hand.

'I'm sorry, Laura. I know it's too much. I just needed to tell you. You know, in case... In case you felt the same way. Or something, at least.'

Laura didn't say anything for a few moments, and Tom was lost for words. His whole body shrank in embarrassment.

'I was engaged, you know,' she said, stroking her ring finger. Tom felt the color drain from his face.

'You're engaged?' he said, hoping he had misheard her.

'Was.' She sighed. 'It's a long story.'

Tom's face flushed. The air suddenly felt thick and heavy. *Engaged*? 'Right,' was all he could muster.

'I wasn't in love with him. And I don't think he was in love with me either, to be honest. It was just sort of the progression of our relationship.' Laura's voice was a whisper.

'Have you told him?'

Laura shifted slightly on the swing. 'I broke it off before I came here, but he thinks it was all the emotion of everything talking. Mum's sickness, coming back here. All that.'

'Is it?'

'No. Well, yes ... but no. I've felt this way for a while. It's just ... urgh!' Laura plunged her face into her hands before throwing her head back and continuing. 'Do you ever feel like life is a never-ending road to nowhere? Like you hopped on a bus in the moment, even though you weren't sure of the direction, but you thought it would take you where you needed to go? And to begin with, it's fine. It's a smooth journey, fun even, but now you realize it's veered off course and there's no way of getting off? You've committed to the journey for too long, and now there's nothing you can do about it?'

Tom knew exactly what she meant. He'd been like that since Laura left. But his journey was much lonelier. Just him and the cows. Pushing through every day trying to make the most of it, hoping at the end of every day for an email in the inbox or a letter in the mail that would bring him happiness, or hope, at least. And although he loved the farm, he wasn't happy. And he knew what would make him happy. Laura. It had always been Laura. So why couldn't he bring himself to say it to her? Before he could muster the words, Laura broke the silence.

'I think I should go,' Laura said, maneuvering herself with a jump off the swing. But she mistimed her step and stumbled. Tom instinctively grabbed her arm, and she fell into his chest. Her warm body felt like the hot breeze of summer enveloping all around him. Tom stared into her eyes, his heart racing. Without giving himself time to talk himself out of it again, he bent down and kissed her.

Her lips were soft and tasted as sweet as sugar. She didn't pull away, but Tom could sense her apprehension as her back muscles tightened under his hands. Tom took every millisecond and implanted it into his memory. If this was the only time he would ever kiss her, he would cherish it for the rest of his life.

Laura finally pulled away. 'I'm sorry, Tom. I can't. I'd better go.' She turned her back to him.

Tom felt the giddiness of the kiss and the haziness of the wine combine. 'Laura, you can't drive yet. Not after half a bottle of wine. The cops are always on Turner Road.'

Laura ignored him and began walking back toward the house. Tom followed with a slight jog to catch up to her.

As they got to the back door, he stopped and reached his hand to Laura's shoulder. 'Lauz, just stay here. The spare bedroom's always made up.' He watched her eyes skip from side to side, avoiding his. 'Look, I know I shouldn't have kissed you, but stay. Please. It doesn't mean anything if you do. I know that. But just stay.'

Tom waited. He could almost see her thoughts fighting with each other as she contemplated his offer for the longest time. Finally, she nodded. She looked so sad and forlorn, and Tom was regretting everything he had said, almost even regretting the kiss. The last thing he wanted was to upset her. He just wanted to hold her in his arms and promise he'd look after her so she'd never be sad or lonely again. But he'd blown it. He'd come on too strong. A solitary cow bellowed in the distance, the lonely cry echoing around the farm.

In silence, Tom showed Laura to the spare room and gave her a clean towel out of the linen press. 'See you in the morning,' Tom said, hovering at the door. Laura simply nodded. Tom hung his head and began to close the door. Laura reached her hand out to catch the door, and Tom's eyes. 'I'm sorry,' she whispered.

'Me too,' he said.

· · ·

LYING IN BED, Tom wondered what was going through Laura's mind. She hadn't freaked out at his confession of undying love for her. Well, not totally. Maybe she did feel something. They had been through so much together, and there was so much they shared that nobody else could possibly understand. Surely, she had to feel something. But she had been engaged. Tom shivered at the thought that she'd loved someone enough to want to marry him. It felt like his heart shrank in pain at the thought of her ever loving someone . He'd never be enough. He'd never be Ryan. He'd never be the one she'd want to marry. Tom closed his eyes, his thoughts still swirling.

What did he have to give her anyway? The end of the month was approaching; the bank wouldn't hold off much longer. So, what was he offering her? He squeezed his wet eyes tight. Just a useless old farmer with no farm. And he still held close his secret about the night Ryan died. After her reaction to him not being upfront about Ryan and Rachel and now this, he knew there was no way he could ever tell her. No matter how much guilt he held inside.

25

LAURA WOKE TO the piercing screeches of the white cockatoos at sunrise. From her bed, she could see the pink sky as it began to lighten through the cracks in the curtains. The sun peeked its head over the easterly ranges, the colors rich and full of life. Laura watched as the sky changed quickly before her eyes, wondering how amazing it would be waking up to this each morning. To the farm. *To Tom.*

She'd spent the first hour in bed last night tossing and turning, trying to decipher the mixed emotions she was feeling. Something had sparked inside her, a warmth, a calmness when she thought of Tom. The possibilities of life with him, of seeing his Cheshire cat smile every day. Tom's admission of his own feelings wasn't entirely a shock to her, but her own response was, and she didn't know if she was ready to open herself up to a new love, or what was maybe even an old love.

She thought of Luke. Surely there'd been an attraction in the early days, but it was different to what she felt for Tom, and this new emotion scared her. It was both intense and calm at the same time, which didn't make any sense. And now she felt blanketed with feelings of guilt. It was too soon. Even though she'd been emotionally vacant from Luke for so long, she respected him too much to jump straight into another relationship, especially when she hadn't even properly finished things with him. She never thought she'd be the type to break someone's heart. She knew what it felt like. Knew it was something you never really got over.

As another group of cockatoos greeted the morning, Laura stared at the pressed metal ceiling, chasing her thoughts around in circles. She'd tried to convince herself coming back to Banyula was going to finally close the chapter of her life she had been hiding from, but she was fast discovering that 'the end' wasn't that easy. Her story felt more like one of those choose-your-own-adventure books she used to read as a kid, but this time she didn't have the opportunity to read through every possibility and select the one she liked. This time she had to make a choice, and it scared her; she had no idea which way to turn. When she thought about it, she'd never really made an adult decision without external influences. Every decision she'd made up until this point was like a tumbleweed racing down on her, gathering her up in the momentum and pushing her in one direction or another.

Laura yawned, her mouth sticky at the edges after sleep. She pulled back the blanket and tiptoed out of bed and peered out the window over the expanse of Tom's farm. The pink hopeful day was rapidly being taken over by rain clouds gathering from the south, gradually enveloping the pink sky. Downstairs she heard the familiar creek of the back door and watched as Tom, followed by the puppy bounding around his feet, made his way toward the shed. Tom threw on his hat and Driza-Bone and then lifted the excited puppy into his arms, scratching her under her neck, much to her delight. Her tail wagged madly.

She should leave now. Go home. Or maybe she could whip up

some pancakes ready for Tom when he returned. No, that would be too much. Leading him on to something she wasn't certain she was ready for. No, she had to go. Let her mind settle so she could think rationally and not just act on her knocking heart.

She padded down the staircase and pulled a piece of paper from Tom's desk in the living room. She scribbled a note thanking him for last night and apologizing for leaving without saying goodbye. She ended with a doodle of a smiley face, hoping that would lighten the words. Cover her guilt. Then she headed back into town.

LAURA PARKED her car in the supermarket parking lot. She planned on grabbing something for dinner before heading home to finish the house.

Standing in the freezer section, Laura was contemplating whether to choose the teriyaki chicken or shepherd's pie when she noticed a figure round the corner of the aisle and pause. The weight of the person's stare made her look up.

It was Rachel. But she wasn't alone. Hanging on to Rachel's hand was a boy dressed in a school uniform, staring straight at Laura. It took a moment to register, and then Laura inhaled sharply as she saw the speckled green eyes she knew so well. Ryan's green eyes.

'Laura. Um, hi,' Rachel said, her face flushed.

Laura couldn't stop staring at the miniature version of Ryan.

'Mitchell, this is ... um, Mummy's friend, Laura,' Rachel said, smiling down at the young boy.

'Hi.' The sweet little face beamed, a small dimple appearing in his cheek as he smiled.

Laura tried to regain her composure as her heart rate soared. 'Um, hi, Mitchell.' She looked at Rachel, whose face was awash with anxiety. 'Oh, god. Is that the time?' Laura feigned looking at the watch she wasn't wearing. 'Ah, I'm ... um, late. Sorry, Rachel, I have to run.' She turned on her heel and ran out of the supermarket, ditching the frozen dinners on a display of toilet paper at the end of the aisle as she went. When she made it back to the car, she collapsed on the steering wheel, unable to control the sobs escaping her chest.

LAURA SAT on the couch with her legs pulled up to her chest. She'd been that way since she got home. Outside, sheets of rain beat a steady drum against the window, but Laura barely noticed, all but lost in her thoughts.

She didn't know what hurt more, the fact that Rachel had slept with Ryan or the fact that Ryan had slept with Rachel. Although they were one and the same, each scenario was painful in its own way. The betrayal of a best friend. The betrayal of a boyfriend. And then there was Mitchell. An innocent child. A beautiful, innocent child the spitting image of the father he would never know. Laura's head ached. She knew coming back to Banyula would be hard. She knew saying goodbye to Ryan would be hard. But she had no idea it would be like this.

She tried to recall the memories of that year. Urging the neurons in her brain to fire them to life. She was looking for something. Something she had missed. Between Rachel and Ryan. A memory flickered to life. It must have been halfway through the year, as Ryan was still playing basketball then. She'd walked with him after school down to the basketball stadium where he had a practice match. Laura closed her eyes and dug deep into the memory.

· · ·

RYAN HAD PULLED Laura in for a kiss, and Laura wrapped her arms around his waist as she always did, secretly inhaling his boyish scent of soap and cola. She wished she could breathe him in all day long.

'I have to go,' Ryan said, pulling away slowly. 'You sure you can't come and watch?'

Laura peered into the basketball stadium. The harsh overhead lighting and neon scoreboard shone back at her through the open double doors. She wanted to, but the popular girls were sitting in the front row with their long, tanned legs on display from beneath their barely there cheerleading skirts. Laura turned back to Ryan, knowing she couldn't bear to set foot in there, no matter how much Ryan wanted her too.

'I know, I wish I could!' she lied.

'Hey Ry? Coach is looking for you,' came a voice from the doorway. Laura's eyes darted to see Stacey hanging out the door with her head tilted, one hand playing with her long blonde ponytail.

'Hi Laura,' she said with a cruel smile.

Laura's face burned.

'Gotta go,' Ryan said, jogging toward the stadium. 'I'll call you later, okay?'

'Sure.'

Laura watched as Stacey followed Ryan into the stadium, but not before turning to Laura and raising her eyebrow.

The pit of Laura's stomach churned as she turned for the walk home. Why was she so intimidated by those girls? She never used to be. She and Rachel usually kept to themselves. Off their radar was the best place to be. But now she was seeing Ryan, it was like she was a glowing beacon to them. Like she had something they wanted. But Ryan had never been interested in any of them as far as Laura knew.

Laura paced down the footpath toward her street, and her phone buzzed in her pocket. A message from a number she didn't recognize. She stopped and slid her finger across the screen to view the message. It was a picture of Ryan on the court surrounded by three of the cheerleaders, their heads tipped back in laughter. Laura's face felt as if it had caught fire. But that wasn't the thing that caught her attention: one of the girls was Rachel. Not in a cheer uniform, of course, but standing next to Ryan, laughing with them all.

She tapped her thumbs on the screen:

Who is this?

She waited for an answer with tears streaming down her face, turning her back to the passing cars. But there was no reply.

She tapped again, this time bringing up Rachel's number, and pressed the call button. It took an eternity for Rachel to answer.

'Oh, hey, Lauz. Where are you?' The thumping of the basketball on the court echoed through the phone.

'Where are you?'

'I'm at basketball. There's some practice game going on. I thought you'd be here.'

'Me? Why would I be there? Why are you even there?'

'Stacey asked if I was going. She said you'd be here to watch Ryan.'

Laura's chest tightened. She hadn't spoken to Stacey, apart from to apologize this morning at the lockers when she'd accidently dropped her psychology book on Stacey's foot. Stacey had just glared at her with icy blue eyes that could freeze the entire Pacific Ocean.

'I ... We ... we never go to basketball,' Laura replied.

'I know. I thought it was weird, but when I didn't see you at the end of school, I thought you must've come straight here. And you know, it's actually kind of fun,' Rachel said. A roar of cheering came down the line.

'I ...' Laura was lost for words.

'You should come down.' Another roar accompanied a cheer and thump of bass as music blared in the background.

'I can't. I have to babysit.'

'What? I can't hear you, Lauz. Come down. I'll see you soon, okay?'

Laura's legs felt like jelly. She wanted to go, but then Ryan would know she lied. And then there was Stacey and her gang. And what was with Rachel? Why would she believe Stacey and not check with her about it? Nothing was making any sense.

She brushed the tears from her face, threw her backpack on, and ran home.

LAURA OPENED HER EYES. Was that it? Was that the beginning of it? Laura remembered that later that night Ryan had called her like he'd promised. He'd sensed Laura's apprehension but had smoothed it over. Laura remembered not thinking of it again. She'd convinced herself it was nothing. But now, it felt like something. She was sure she could pull up another hundred memories and analyze them under a microscope and come up with more signs. But what good would it do? What happened, happened. Her embarrassment burned deep, but they were teenagers back then. Young, naïve, jealous, anxious, and pushing boundaries. That's what teenagers did. Laura knew now that the signs were there, she had just chosen to ignore them. It was easier that way. She had a boyfriend. Her *first* boyfriend. And it wasn't just any boy. It was Ryan Taylor. She didn't want to mess it up. A tear trickled down her face, stained with naivety. She had to let it go.

26

As Laura climbed into bed for the night, her phone echoed. Another text from Luke. He'd texted her three times already and she hadn't responded. What was the point? It was over. She couldn't keep stringing him along. And she also didn't trust herself not to take the easy way out and run back into his arms. Better the devil you know.

She placed her phone on the side table and made herself comfortable leaning against the pillow, the hum of the lamp the only noise until she opened up Ryan's journal.

She had promised herself, as she had her mum, to let it go. She berated herself for it taking so long. But this was it. This was the last thing she needed to take care of before she could leave it all in the past. She had to finish Ryan's journal. She knew that she owed it to Ryan and herself. Ryan deserved to be heard. And she needed to put it all behind her with full knowledge.

She slipped under the doona, propped herself against her pillow, and opened the journal.

6 November 2009

When you go looking for the truth, you expect finding it will change everything. That finally you will have answers for the endless mountain of questions that are floating around in your mind. What is it they say? The truth will set you free? Yeah, right. Today I found out the truth. And it didn't set me free. After what I found out today I feel like I can't keep my head above the water, like my legs are lead. The truth hasn't set me free; it's drowning me.

Gran tried to explain it all. She came home to find me in front of the computer Googling my father.

I hadn't meant to go snooping, but after she left for her nightly bridge game, I guess I got depressed. The two beers I downed probably didn't help. I shouldn't be drinking yet. We have that party tonight, but I couldn't move from the couch.

I stared at the frayed blue carpet. The carpet I used to play with my toy cars on when I was little. Where I used to lie next to Gran watching *Thomas the Tank Engine*.

A lump formed at the back of my throat that made me feel like throwing up. I swayed between self-hatred and anger at the world. My mood swings were worsening. I knew it.

There were days I didn't want to see anyone and days where I couldn't bear to be alone. And this restless feeling had buried itself right down in my core, asking me questions all the time.

Why doesn't Gran speak about your mum? Who really was your dad? What really happened the night of the car crash?

I don't know where the questions were coming from, but they kept getting louder and louder. I squeezed my eyes tight to shut them up, but they wouldn't quiet.

I went into the hallway, my chest feeling like it was being squeezed tight from the inside out. Light-headed, I grabbed the wall to steady myself and focus on my breathing and looked up toward the ceiling at the skylight.

For some reason, I knew I had to get into the attic. What I was looking for, I didn't really know. Anything to do with my mum or dad—photos, anything. I knew there had to be something up there, but I couldn't see any of the boxes that looked like they'd be helpful. I pushed aside the Christmas tree decorations, an old tent, until I came across a familiar box I knew had some old photographs and some of my early school stuff that Gran insisted on keeping.

I rummaged through the box, pulling out old black-and-white photos of people. Strangers I had no clue who they were. The only giveaway that they were relatives was Gran's dimpled-cheek smile in some of them. She was really pretty when she was younger. I flicked through the photos of my mother from when she was a young girl, but still nothing of Dad.

I gathered everything up and piled it back into the box, and out the corner of my eye, I saw another box that I'd never noticed before. It was a shoebox tucked behind an old sewing machine. I pulled it out and wiped the thick layer of dust off the top to see the word 'Private' scrawled across the lid in black marker in Gran's writing.

My stomach churned with a twinge of guilt, but I pulled at the brittle sticky tape, tearing it off in small slivers until I could poke a finger in and release the lid. Inside were a heap of old papers and documents that didn't really mean much to me. And then I saw it.

My birth certificate.

Ryan James Baxter. <u>Baxter</u>.

Not Taylor. *Baxter*.

I scanned the document, seeing my mother's name Jane Mary Baxter (nee Lincoln), and then my father's name: WILLIAM JAMES BAXTER.

It didn't make any sense. I was Ryan Taylor. My father's name was William James Taylor. Not Baxter. I flicked through the other documents and found another legal type document from the Department of Births, Deaths, and Marriages, Victoria, addressed to my grandmother, confirming the change of my name to Ryan James Taylor.

My head was spinning. I don't know if it was the beer, or what I had just found out, but I threw myself down the ladder and pulled open my laptop on the kitchen table and typed in the name William James Baxter.

It took a few minutes of scrolling before I found it. I clicked on the link and read the newspaper article. I don't know how long I sat there, staring at the screen, not feeling anything, But next thing I knew, Gran was standing behind me, her face ghost white and hand slapped across her mouth.

There was no accident. My father shot my mother and then killed himself. I was eighteen months old and custody was granted to Gran, and she moved us two thousand kilometers away to Banyula.

I felt bad when Gran started crying. I know she was only trying to protect me. She said she wanted to tell me the truth, but there never seemed to be a right time.

She told me my father was sick. Like sick in the head. He had a temper. Bipolar apparently, or something like that. It was then that everything started to sink in. It's not like an excuse, but a reason. Everything I've been feeling. There's a reason. I'm crazy. Just like my father.

I want to be okay with it. To just let it slide. But I can't. Everything I've done this year. To Laura. Rachel. I've lied, cheated. And if they all knew the truth—if Laura knew the truth, what I've done with Rachel—it would break her. I know Tom knows, but he hasn't said anything yet. I wish he would. Because I'm such a gutless pig and can't. Guess I really am like my father.

What if I end up like him? Violent. Abusive.
No.
I won't let it happen. I won't. I can't.

∾

27

LAURA STARED AT the words. Many were smudged and hard to read. She wondered if Ryan's tears had caused the smudging. She imagined him scribbling it all down on paper. How he felt. Was he in shock? Devastated? Or was he white hot with anger? Her own tears fell. Her heart breaking for Ryan. It wasn't his fault. It wasn't his father's fault. She ran her fingers over the bottom of the page where Ryan had dug the pen in as he carved deep patterns of black into the page, small rips and scribbles covered the adjoining one. She closed her eyes as goose bumps pricked at her arms, the chilling reality of Ryan's pain. *Oh, Ryan.*

Laura wiped her cheeks as her eyes once again scanned the page. She noticed the date this time—the day of the end-of-year exam party. The day before Ryan died. It all began to make sense. Ryan's mood that night. His drunken state. His words. She squeezed her eyes to bring back that night. The night she hadn't wanted to relive. She had to now, just to make sense of it.

. . .

SHE REMEMBERED HEARING Rachel and Tom's voices coming up the footpath as Laura lay sprawled out on her bed waiting for them to arrive. The excitement flitted through her like a thousand butterflies escaping their enclosure all at once.

'Laura, they're here,' her mum called out, tapping on her door.

'I'm coming.'

Laura looked at herself in the mirror again, standing there in her jeans, floral top, and Converse. She smiled, happy that she looked okay, and hoping now that exams were done and dusted, everything would be back to normal. Things been weird between her and Ryan. One moment he'd be all over her, the next distant and reclusive. Rachel had been the same. Whenever Laura brought it up with either of them, they brushed her aside. Rachel muttered something about exams, Ryan completely changing the subject. Lately, Tom hadn't been his usual jovial self either. Laura sighed and took a deep breath. Hopefully it was all in the past and everything would be like old times.

'See ya, Mum.' Laura gave her mum a kiss in the hallway. Her mum pulled her close, wrapping Laura in the fruity aroma of her perfume as she whispered, 'Have a good time. And stay safe.' Laura's shoulders caved with the hug.

'We will,' she whispered, breathing in the emotion so it wouldn't escape.

Laura walked out the front door where Ryan, Rachel and Tom were leaning on the front picket fence deep in conversation, looking up as she approached down the path.

'Hey.' Ryan gave her a quick kiss on the cheek, his breath already stale with beer. Rachel quickly linked her arm through Laura's and smiled. 'Let's go,' said Tom, unable to meet her eyes.

By eleven p.m. the backyard of Simon Duncan's house, a couple of blocks away from Laura's, was pumping with the excited bodies of over a hundred final year students. The Duncans' backyard was a large open space, fences lined with immaculately pruned hedges. Fairy lights were strung along the hedges, while colored disco lights stood tall near the jukebox, lighting a makeshift dance floor in flashes of rainbow. The crowd moved with a rhythmic sensation as Usher's silky voice rang out 'OMG' to the mosh pit of intoxicated bodies dancing like waves crashing on the sand.

Laura and Rachel were deep in the middle of the dance floor, bouncing up and down. Laura's scrambled emotions kept in check thanks to the five or six cans of scotch and Coke. She'd lost count as to exactly how many. All she knew was the stress had disintegrated from her mind and body, and all that mattered right in this very moment was singing—or yelling—as loud as possible with her best friend.

'I need to go to the toilet!' Rachel yelled in Laura's ear as the song changed to Katy Perry.

'But I love this song!'

Rachel grabbed Laura's hand and pulled her from the dance floor around to the side of the house where the porta-potties were set up.

'I really need to pee!' Rachel walked like a baby penguin pulling Laura, both of them stumbling over the trampled grass. Laura waited outside the toilets, trying hard to concentrate on staying still.

'Laura!'

She turned around to see Tom walking toward her, the frown on his face still intact, as it has been for most of the night.

'Tommmmmmmyyyy,' she yelled, throwing her arms around his neck.

Tom slowly peeled her away.

'Lauz, I think you've had enough to drink. Just slow it down, okay?'

'Oh Tom, you're such a party pooper sometimes, you know? You need to relax a little,' she blabbered before deciding she really needed to sit down. The fairy lights were spinning.

'I'm just gonna sit here, okay?' she said, planting her backside on the grass, the wetness of the dew off the ground or god knows what soaking through her jeans, not that she cared.

Tom sat next down next to her, which was the perfect opportunity for Laura to rest her head on his shoulder, just for a moment. She inhaled the musky scent of his usual aftershave, wondering what it was. Hugo Boss or something. Probably not, more like Cool Water. That would be more Tom.

'Lauz,' Tom said. He was sitting cross-legged, pulling at the laces on his boots.

'Yup,' she replied, staring blankly at the sky above, trying to count the million stars blanketed above them, but they kept moving out of focus. *One, two, three ...*

'I can't do this anymore,' he said.

'Can't do what?'

'This,' he said, throwing his hands up, causing Laura to lift her head. *Damn, where was I ... One, two ...* 'Us. You. Ryan. Rachel.'

'What are you talking about?'

'There's just so much you don't know, and I know I shouldn't tell you, but I have to. It's gone on too long. I have to tell you. I know Ryan hasn't got the balls to.'

Tom's voice was blending into the noise of the party and becoming one big thump in Laura's head. She tried hard to decipher his deep tones from the heavy beat of the music, the screaming of the girls, and the raucous laughter of the boys, but it was no use. It was one big, heavy mess, tossing from side to side in her head.

'Okay,' she said, searching for what would be a good response, she hoped.

'It's about Ryan ...' Tom continued.

'Tom, what the fuck are you doing?'

Laura looked up, startled. She tipped backwards to see Rachel standing behind them, hands on hips. 'Rach!'

Rachel pulled up Laura violently, so hard it felt like her arm was about to be ripped out of its socket.

'What the hell?' Laura yelled, holding her shoulder.

'Come on Laura, we're getting out of here,' Rachel said, pulling Laura again.

'No you're not!' Tom said, grabbing Laura's other arm by the elbow. She felt like a rag doll being pulled in all directions. A very sick rag doll with a spinning head.

'It's not up to you to say anything, Tom, so just fuck off, okay?' Rachel yelled into Tom's face.

'How about you fuck off, Rachel! I hear you're pretty good at it.' Tom's voice was rough and edgy, a tone Laura didn't recognize.

'Just leave it. It's none of your business.' Rachel pulled Laura out of Tom's grip, and she tumbled to the ground, trying to focus her eyes, her stomach churning, and beads of sweat forming on the back of her neck. Suddenly all those drinks didn't seem like such a good idea.

'Hey! Hey! What the fuck is going on?' Ryan appeared by Laura's side, wrapping his arm around her waist and pulling her to her feet.

'I don't feel so good, Ry,' she mumbled.

'You make me sick. You can all go to hell,' Tom yelled before storming off.

Poor Tom. Laura wished she knew why he was so on edge lately. Refocusing, the nausea slowly disappeared, and Laura wrapped her arms around Ryan and went to kiss him, but her weight forced them to stumble onto the nearby picnic table.

'Lauz, Lauz, hang on,' he said, unwrapping her hands from his neck.

'Tom's right.' Rachel's shaky voice seeped into Laura's ears. 'You need to tell her. We need to tell her!'

Laura frowned. What was it everyone needed to tell her? Whatever it was, surely it could wait. She was having the best time she'd had all year. This was their final party, and she didn't want it to end. She jumped to her feet. 'Hey! You two! Settle!' she announced, holding both her hands in the air. 'Let's not fight. Let's dance!' And with that, she swallowed the acidic taste in her mouth and stumbled off toward the dance floor again, swept into the current by a group of girls. In the background, Laura could hear Rachel's high-pitched voice and Ryan yelling back at her, but it was all a blur of white noise. All she wanted to think about was keeping her feet moving and her arm hanging on to the girl next to her to support herself as she let the rhythm of the dance take over.

Laura had no idea how much time had passed, but the next thing she remembered was dry-retching after eliminating the entirety of her stomach contents onto an oily pizza box. Her throat burned and her eyes leaked, but at least the heaviness of her stomach had begun to ease.

Wiping her mouth, she wandered out into the front yard where a few remaining partygoers were lingering. Red and blue lights illuminated the driveway as the police stood around waiting for everyone to disperse orderly. Laura watched as a couple of her classmates were loaded into the back of the police car. She scoured the yard and street for Ryan but couldn't see him anywhere. She didn't see Rachel or Tom either. Her head began to pound as the fresh air hit her. She just wanted to go home. As the police walked down the driveway toward the back-yard, Laura stepped out from behind the house and made a run for it, slowing to a walk once she knew she was far enough out of sight.

It was only a five-minute walk home, and the fresh air would help clear her head. At least the alcohol had worn off sufficiently for her to be able to walk in a straight line. One foot in front of the other, Laura looked down, staring at her bare feet. She had no idea where her shoes were, vaguely recalling flinging them from her feet during the Macarena. It didn't matter, they'd no doubt be ruined just like her jeans were—covered in things she didn't want to try and identify.

Hearing the pounding of footsteps behind her, Laura's heart raced as she spun around.

'Hey! I've been looking for you everywhere!' Ryan said, grabbing her from behind.

'Geez, Ryan!' she yelled, peeling his arms off her. 'You scared the shit out of me.'

Under the glare of the streetlight, Laura noticed his eyes were glassy and bloodshot and his hair was wet. His T-shirt was covered in a pungent stench of beer.

'Where have you been?' he asked, slurring his words, grabbing her shoulder to stop himself stumbling.

'Me? I've been at the party. Where have you been?' Laura smelled the sweet scent of pot on his breath. 'Have you been smoking weed?'

Ryan laughed, his voice echoing in the stillness of the night.

'Ryan. You can be such a tosser sometimes,' Laura said, shaking her head and turning for home.

'Rachel! Wait!'

'Rachel? I'm Laura, you idiot.' She turned back to see his mouth drop and color run from his face. As it did, a cold realization washed over her.

Rachel?

'You and *Rachel*?' She frowned as the acid crept up from her throat again. It all made sense now. All the signs rushed back to her, playing hastily in rewind. Ryan being distant, Rachel acting weird. The looks between them. She felt as if she'd been punched in the gut.

'Laura, wait! Let me explain.'

But Laura didn't want to hear an explanation. She turned and started to run, the soles of her feet slapping the pavement as she did.

At the railway line junction Ryan grabbed her by the arm. She stumbled onto the rough ground near the edge of the embankment to the tracks.

'Ow!' she yelled. 'Let me go.'

'You don't understand!' he yelled. 'I never wanted any of this to happen.'

Laura squirmed under his weight as he pinned her arms down to the ground, something sharp piercing into her back.

'Get off me, Ryan,' she cried. 'You're hurting me!'

'I wanted to tell you. Tell you everything. About Rachel. About me, but ...' Ryan was crying now too, his words frantically falling out of his mouth. 'I never wanted to hurt you. I never wanted it to happen, but it did. You deserve someone so much better.'

None of what he was saying made any sense. All Laura could see were visions of the two of them in her mind. Dirty visions. Visions that made her physically recoil.

'How long, Ryan? How long?' she screamed into his face.

'It was only one time. We both felt so bad. I just ...' Ryan rolled off her and slumped to the ground, holding his hands over his face. The wind of rage disappeared from him.

'You deserve better than me. I can't give you what you want. I'll hurt you. Even more than I've hurt you now. And I never wanted to hurt you. You've got to believe me. I don't want to hurt anyone.

You or Rachel. But you don't know. You don't know.' Ryan was ranting now, stumbling to his feet. 'I'm nothing but a piece of shit! Just like my father,' he said, floundering one foot in front of another up the embankment toward the rocky edge of the train line.

Laura's breath was fast, and she was shaking with anger. 'No, Ryan. You don't get to do that.'

'Do what?'

'Pretend. You can't pretend that you couldn't help it. That you never wanted it to happen. That you never wanted to hurt me.' She doubled over, yelling as loud as she could, aiming her words at him sharply so they'd cut. So they'd hurt him as much as she hurt right now.

'Is that how you want to play this?' His words were acidic, his eyes blank and soulless under the milky light of the full moon.

Laura stared at him, at this stranger. She didn't know him. She barely recognized him.

'Fine. It's your fault,' he said, throwing his hands in the air, then pointing at her. 'You're always little miss perfect. You had our whole fucking lives planned out. You never even asked me what I wanted. You just assumed what we'd do. You practically had us walking down the aisle without a second thought to me! What about what I wanted? Did you ever listen to me? I never felt like I could really tell you how I feel. Your life is so perfect.' He spat his words at Laura like venom from a snake's fangs.

Laura clapped her hands over her ears. She didn't want to hear it. She wanted to throw up. Scream. Every bone, every sinew of her body hurt. Her insides, her feet, her head, her throat. Her heart. Her shoulders slumped, weakened as Ryan sat down in the middle of the train tracks, staring down the vacant line. It was like all his anger had disappeared into the blackness of the night as quickly as their vicious words had.

Laura sucked in her sobs. 'Get off the tracks, Ryan,' she said. Ryan continued to stare straight ahead.

'Get up!' This time she spoke louder, trying to walk toward him, but the sharp bluestone rocks pierced her already tender feet.

'Just leave me alone,' Ryan said, his voice low. The air was still, the night silent. It was as if time had paused.

'Fine,' she said, staring toward the lights that glared along her street. Still, Ryan didn't move, didn't speak. He simply stared zombie like into the distance. Laura's frustration simmered to the surface again as she yelled in despair.

'Fine! Get hit by a train, Ryan Taylor. See if I care!' she screamed in one last vent of anger toward him before turning and running down the darkened path under the railway line and toward home.

She ran as fast as her exhausted legs would take her, refusing to look back. She couldn't. Everything had ended here tonight. Her boyfriend had cheated on her. Her best friend had betrayed her.

They'd lied.

As Laura reached her front porch, she paused to catch her breath before gently opening the front door and creeping down the hallway, careful to miss the creaky floorboard. Once in her bedroom, she silently clicked the door shut and hopped into bed. Her lungs searched for air between the deep sobs she tried to suppress with her pillow. Her body pulsated with a sickening mix of hurt, anger, lethargy, and hopelessness. She felt like a piece of glass, shattered into tiny shards.

She squeezed her eyes shut as her body shook. She just wanted to sleep. To have her brain switch off so it couldn't think anymore, couldn't hurt. Her breathing slowed as she let the last remnants of alcohol drift her towards the blackness. In the distance, she thought she heard a scream, but it was just the whistle of a freight train. She let the sound that rattled her window lull her toward sleep.

LAURA FOUND herself in a ball on her bed as she peeled herself away from the memory. Her head throbbed and her eyes were wet.

Ryan *had* tried to tell her. Even in his last moments he'd tried, but she didn't listen—wouldn't listen. Her hurt in that moment had been all-consuming. Anyone her age would have done the same thing. Hindsight and wisdom were no use to her teenage emotions. All that was left to do now was to forgive herself and forgive Ryan. They had both been young and afraid. Fears compounded by hormones and emotions they couldn't under-stand. She didn't feel sorry for Ryan, but she finally understood.

28

TOM WOKE WITH a start as a crack of thunder shook the house. He glanced at the clock which glowed just after five a.m., and he pulled himself out of his warm bed. Dawn was still at least half an hour away, but Tom knew he couldn't wait any longer. It was raining again—or hadn't stopped—Tom wasn't sure, but he knew he had to check the gauge and move the cattle.

After pulling on his boots and heading over to the rain gauge, his heart sank. Even without good light he could see it wasn't good. It must have rained nonstop all night. He pulled his phone out of his pocket and dialed his farmhand's number. Yeah, it was early, but Tom needed help. As the line rang out, Tom cursed. 'Shit.' Not even a message bank to leave a message. He tried calling his neighbor but again, no answer. He was probably out checking his own stock. With the rain pooling on the lip of his hat, Tom decided he had no choice but to head out alone.

The horizon was beginning to lighten, but it only reflected the grayness of the sky, and Tom's heart pounded. The slow dawn shed a veil of light on just how much rain had fallen overnight.

Paddocks now looked more like swamps, and Tom could see in the distance the eucalyptus trees that usually bordered the river were now surrounded by water. The river was unleashing a torrent toward Tom's lower lying paddocks. He saw a herd of cattle clambering on the only high spot and to the right in the distance, a handful of cows struggling in the water and mud, their painful bellows haunting.

The squelch of the tires in the mud caused the Ute to come to an abrupt halt. 'Shit!' he cursed again, unable to find any other words that fit the moment. He pushed his foot on the accelerator, but the engine squealed as the tires spun uselessly. Tom slammed his hands on the steering wheel, his heart pounding in his ears. He'd have to go on foot. He grabbed a couple of lengths of rope from the Ute and jumped out. The gate wasn't budging either, so Tom had to jump the fence, catching his leg on some wire jutting out from the post. He didn't even feel the pain as he pulled his leg free, just the warmth of a trickle of blood on the inside of his leg.

Tom sloshed through the paddock toward the struggling cows, his thoughts ticking over at a rate of knots. The realization sunk into his heart like his boots in the mud, drowning him in despair. This was bad. Bloody bad. He rounded the back of the six cows and they lurched forward. 'Heah-ya!' he yelled, waving his arms. The cows stumbled and bellowed, but they moved forward into the direction of the high ground. Tom continued yelling and prodding them for another hundred meters until their hooves gripped onto the drier ground and they bounded up to the top, huddling together under the canopy of an old oak tree.

Catching his breath, Tom turned back toward a lone cow a little further back who hadn't managed to move. With his legs heavy, he made his way back to her. As he edged closer, the cow snorted. 'It's okay, girl. It's okay,' Tom whispered. He attempted to loop the rope he was carrying around her neck, but she threw her head back, her eyes white with fear.

'Hey, hey,' Tom said. 'Let's get you out, okay?'

He swung the rope again, this time catching it around the cow's neck. The slip knot tightened and Tom began to gently pull her toward him. 'C'mon, help me out. You can do it,' he eased. The cow struggled, but instinct seemed to tell her Tom was her only hope. As the rain continued to fall, Tom pulled again, and this time the cow's back legs loosened, as she leaned forward. But her back legs were stuck. It was only then that Tom noticed the body of her six-month old calf in the muddy water.

Tom's chest tightened and tears stung at the back of his eyes. They'd had no chance. Tom had failed them. The cow again heaved forward, but it was no use—Tom couldn't budge her. She bellowed as Tom let out a raw, primal scream from deep inside. Emotion clogged in his throat as salty tears mixed with the rain on his face. *This couldn't be happening.*

The water seemed to be rising at a rate of knots, now up to Tom's groin. If he didn't move now, he would suffer the same fate as his herd. The cut on his leg had begun to sting and he fingered the hole, covering his fingers in blood. He stared blankly at the devastation before him. Too much rain. Ground too hard. Nowhere to go.

His thoughts tangled into knots, and in that moment, he felt like giving up. He was a failure. He'd failed his father. Disappointed his mother. Failed his farm, the cows. Failed himself. What was the point? Tom looked toward the sky, and even though the rain had finally stopped, the drab skies were like a blanket of lead hanging over him. His chest heaved and he hung his head.

29

WITH HER EYES thick with dried salt and grainy sleep, Laura fumbled her hand on the bedside table looking for her buzzing phone. She turned over and squinted to read the number of the caller. It was a local number, and although it seemed familiar, she didn't recognize it. She cleared her throat and answered,

'Hello, Laura speaking.'

'Laura, hi! It's Mick. I hope I haven't called too early, but I have some exciting news for you.'

Laura glanced at her watch, which read 8:08 a.m. It did seem a bit early, but if he had good news, it would be worth it.

'Hey Mick. Ah, no, not too early at all,' she said, shuffling herself upright. 'What's the news? I could sure do with some.'

'I have an offer on your mum's house.'

Laura sucked in a deep breath. 'Oh wow! Really? But you haven't even started showing people yet.'

'Well, that's the thing. I haven't. But I've been ringing around a few contacts on my books, and one of them in particular is an investor. He's a local but lives in Sydney at the moment. Anyway, I told him about the house, and he said he knew the one and that he could be interested. Long story short, I shot him through some photos, and he rang me first thing. He loves it! Wants to do it up. You know, restore it to its *original splendor*, I think were his exact words.'

'You mean he wants to buy it? Sight unseen?' Laura was glad she was sitting down. Although she was hoping for a quick sale, she wasn't expecting this.

'Yep. He's put an offer to me. Full price, thirty days, unconditional. So not subject to finance. Doesn't even want a building or pest inspection.'

'Wow! I ... I don't know what to say.'

'Say yes!' Mick laughed down the line.

Laura hesitated.

'Laura, it really is the perfect offer. It doesn't get any better than this,' Mick continued. 'But, I get it. It's a big decision. What if you get back to me by tomorrow? That'll give you some thinking time. Maybe discuss it with your solicitor?'

Laura swallowed. 'Yeah. Okay. I'll do that. I'll let you know by tomorrow.'

'No problem. I'll speak to you then.'

'Okay. Great. Thanks, Mick.'

Laura ended the call and stared blankly at the screen. This was it. Her chance to finalize everything and move on. Mick was right, it was an offer way too good to refuse. All she had to do was say yes, sign the paperwork, and that was it. She could go back to the city and leave Banyula, and all it held, behind her.

But as much as she wanted that knowledge to make her feel better, it did just the opposite. A deep ache formed in the pit of her stomach. And as her racing thoughts collected, Laura felt farther from a decision than she had before the phone call. She had to talk to someone. Her mind wandered to Tom. He'd know what to do. But then she remembered how she had left without saying goodbye. Tom hadn't even called to find out why, not that she expected him to. He was probably still so embarrassed about what happened. Laura felt queasy. She hadn't been fair to him at all. The least she could have done was listen to him.

She swiped at her phone and began to compose a message.

Tom, I'm really sorry I didn't say goodbye when I left yesterday. I can explain. Please call me. x

There. Now the ball was in his court. If he had forgiven her, he'd ring and then she could explain everything. For now though, she still had the issue of the offer. Laura thought about calling her solicitor, but she knew he would simply advise her to take the offer. She decided to go and see Stella. Of course Stella would know what to do. She always did.

After a quick breakfast and shower, Laura closed the front door behind her and headed to her car. Although it wasn't raining, the clouds were still as thick as smog smothering whatever sunshine was trying to break through. She saw Mrs. Hatfield across the road sweeping her footpath, the slow swish of the broom grating over the concrete.

'Morning, Mrs. Hatfield.' Laura waved.

Mrs. Hatfield looked up. 'You off to help out too, are you, love?'

Laura crinkled her nose. 'Help out who?'

Mrs. Hatfield stopped sweeping and walked toward Laura, using the broom as a makeshift walking stick. Laura met her on the footpath.

'You haven't heard?'

'Heard what?'

'The river's broken its banks. I told you it would. All this bloody rain.' She shook her head.

'Oh, right.'

'Yeah, out on the flats road—you know, Turner Road, out that way? It's pretty bad apparently, though they expect it's not the worst of it. Anyway, that's what Deborah said when I saw her at the store just before. Can't always go on her word though. She gets a bit muddled these days,' Mrs. Hatfield said, tapping her temple. 'You know.'

Laura's thoughts rushed to Tom's farm. 'You mean out near the Gordons' property?'

'Yeah, out that way. The Moores have had to leave their place, she said, and the State Emergency Services are closing the road. I'm sure she said something about a search party.'

'A search party? For who?'

Mrs. Hatfield twisted her mouth and looked to the sky as if trying to jog her memory. She didn't say anything for the longest moment, and Laura began to get impatient, her heart knocking inside her. 'Tom. Tom Gordon. Did she say anything about him, about his place?' Laura thought it was strange she hadn't heard from him, and he still hadn't replied to her text. It wasn't like him, but then again, it was still early, or he might be ignoring her.

'Ah yes. Tom Gordon. Something about saving his cows, and they couldn't find him.'

Laura gasped for breath as she felt her airways struggle for oxygen.

'Oh, I'm sure he's all right, love. He's a smart one, that Tom Gordon. Like his dad. Although I thought he would have been smart enough to have moved his cows by now.'

Laura didn't hang around to listen to the rest of Mrs. Hatfield's commentary. She ran to her car and slammed it in reverse.

'Where are you going?' she heard Mrs. Hatfield call out to her, but all she could think of was Tom. Where was he? Was he okay? She tried to close her mind to the worst-case scenarios.

Laura sped toward the Gordon farm. The rain had started again, just a slight drizzle, enough to wet the windshield. The sky looked like it even might be breaking up, with the sun straining through the edge of the lighter cloud. But all Laura could think about was Tom. What if something happened to him? They hadn't even had a chance to talk more about everything. Her heart raced in her chest, and tears sprang to her eyes with the thoughts of never seeing Tom again. She hit redial on her dashboard, but it went straight to voice mail.

As she approached the Clear Springs Creek Bridge, the orange lights of the SES trucks flashed in front of her as workers put out yellow-and-black roadblock signs across the road. As far as Laura could see, the street was still clear, but the water was lapping at the road's edge. It wouldn't be long before it was inundated. As she got closer, a man in a high-visibility vest waved his arms at her, indicating for her to stop. She wound down her window.

'Can't go through. Sorry, love. This road's gonna be cut in no time,' he said, leaning through the car window.

'But I have to get out to the Gordons' property. Tom's in trouble,' she pleaded.

The man shook his head. 'The Gordons? There's a unit out there already, and another one about to head out there now. Sorry, love, I can't let you through.'

Laura pounded her hands on the steering wheel. She couldn't just sit and wait. Then her face lit up. 'I'm a volunteer,' she said defiantly. 'I'm here to help.'

The man furrowed his brow, his eyes questioning. Laura opened her door and stepped out of the car, thankful she'd decided to wear her gumboots instead of her flats this morning. 'Where's the team?' she said, hands on hips. 'I'll need a suit.'

'You're Judy's daughter, aren't you?' He shook his head. 'Same determination! But I'm sorry. I can't let you through. Leave me your number and I'll call you once I know something. Sorry, love.'

Laura reluctantly gave the man her number and returned to her vehicle, slowly pulling her car from the side of the road and doing a U-turn back toward town. With her head racing and gut churning, she wracked her brains for another solution. It was then she noticed a dirt track off the side of the road. *That's it!* she thought, spinning the car back around. It was an old track that curved through a handful of unfenced paddocks and led to the west side of the Gordons' property. Tom had taken her down there as a shortcut a few times on their bikes when they were younger. Although, she didn't really think it was a shortcut. It always seemed to take them longer over the barely worn track and through the long grass.

Laura turned into the track and pulled up at the gate, hoping it wasn't padlocked. She almost jumped for joy when it wasn't. She pushed it open and looked down the track, her initial glee disappearing as she noticed the edges of the track slowly being swallowed by the rising water. Her spine tingled as nerves crept up to her neck. What if she got bogged herself?

She shook the thought from her head. She had to try. She couldn't bear to think of Tom out there stranded and waiting for help. Although her memory was sketchy at best, she knew if she tried she could make her way back to the farm. Without thinking any further, Laura climbed back into her car and shoved it into gear, heart racing frantically as the vehicle sloshed through the mud. 'Come on, ol' girl, you can do it.'

Sitting close to the steering wheel so she could see the track ahead, Laura began driving, not slow enough to get bogged, but not fast either. The last thing she needed was to get stuck out here. She felt the wheels slipping on the muddy ground but focused ahead. Visibility was becoming increasingly difficult as the rain began to fall harder. The windshield wipers whipped the rain from the screen with a whooshing sound and Laura revved the engine to make it through a particularly soggy part, the wheels skidding and slightly sliding the rear end of the car out. She pulled it back to the track and continued forward, her heart in her throat.

A few minutes later, she found herself at the gate to the Gordons' property. She jumped out to open it. But this one was padlocked.

'No! This can't be!' she screamed into the sky. She glanced back at the vehicle. Could she possibly? Her little Mazda? She didn't think twice. She had to. She had no choice. She jumped back in and aimed the vehicle toward the gate. Then, squeezing her eyes tight and biting her lip, she lurched forward on the accelerator. The wheels spun and then, all of a sudden, gripped, plowing her through the gate with a crash as it snapped open to let her through. Laura tried not to think about the damage to her bumper and front panels, but instead she kept driving, hoping she'd remembered to renew her insurance last month.

Laura looked from side to side around the waterlogged paddocks, trying to get her bearings. With so much of the paddocks underwater, it was hard to work out where she was on the farm. The only thing recognizable was the line of trees along what was once the riverbank, now just a sea of water steadily encroaching on the higher paddocks. She could see a cluster of trees on a slightly higher mound in the distance, the paddock wet but still not engulfed.

She continued down the track a little more, but it was soon obvious she wouldn't be able to go any farther. The track was now hardly wide enough to walk through. She came to a halt and jumped out. The water was only just covering her feet; she'd have to hike it on foot. The high ground in the distance was only about two hundred meters away. She could make it. At least then she'd have a higher vantage point from which to survey the paddocks. As she neared the high spot, she noticed a group of waterlogged cows, gathered behind a large gum tree, their eyes wide. One had a nasty gash in its leg, and they were all covered in sloshy black mud up to their bellies. *Tom must have saved them*, she thought. *He must be here somewhere.*

She felt so helpless. She tried Tom's phone again, but still nothing. She squatted down on her haunches, staring at the cows. They glared at her with their wide eyes, as if pleading for her to keep her distance. Poor Tom. Everything he'd worked so hard for. She wondered if he would shrug it off. 'Life on the land,' he might say. But, looking around her, Laura knew this wasn't something he could shrug off so easily. Her heart caught in her throat as she realized she loved this place as much as Tom did. Seeing it engulfed in water, the understanding of how much Tom meant to her broke her heart.

'Oh, Tom. Where are you?' Laura whispered to herself, scanning the surrounding paddocks. She'd never seen so much water. Her heart panged for Tom and his beloved farm. A boom of thunder cracked above, making Laura jump. And then, out of the corner of her eye, she noticed a movement in the distance. A figure slowly coming into view.

'Tom?' she said quietly, and then as the figure grew closer, she realized it was him.

'Tom!' Laura ran toward him, her legs heavy as her boots pooled with water. Tom was soaked head to toe. His coat hung heavily off his slumped shoulders, his jeans and boots covered in the same thick black mud as the cows. His face, too, was streaked with mud and a smearing of bright red blood down his right cheek. He staggered slowly, feet heaving across the soggy ground.

'Oh my God, Tom,' Laura said, throwing herself toward him once he reached the higher ground. 'Thank god you're okay.'

Tom caught her in his arms. 'Laura. What are you doing here? You shouldn't be here.'

Laura shook her head, ignoring Tom's concerns, simply thankful he was okay. 'Look at you. Are you okay?' she said, peeling herself away from him to look him in the eye. His eyes were filled with exhaustion and despair.

'I couldn't save them,' he said, his face breaking.

'Oh, Tom.'

He closed his eyes. 'She was my best cow. Her calf had no chance.'

Laura's heart tightened. 'I'm so sorry. But you saved most of them, right? And I'm sure the SES and volunteers have saved some too.'

Tom nodded weakly.

In the distance, a bright yellow dingy pulled up toward the edge of the embankment. A couple of SES volunteers waded out toward them.

'Jesus, mate! You bloody scared us,' one of them said. Laura realized it was the man who'd turned her around at the bridge. He looked at her and shook his head with a wry smile. 'I'm not even going to ask. Come on, let's get you both back to safety.'

Laura felt the relief engulf her like a river. Tom was safe. He was going to be okay.

The ride back to the farmhouse was eerily quiet. The desperation and sadness on Tom's face broke Laura's heart. She just wanted to hold him. Be there for him.

When they arrived back at the farmhouse, Tom was checked over by the paramedics and now sat on the back porch covered in a blanket. The yard was buzzing with farmhands and SES volunteers, the atmosphere less frantic since the skies had broken through with rays of sun. Word had it that the latest issue from the weather station said the rain was gone. And there was nothing in sight for the next five days at least. The river had peaked and tensions had eased, but there was still work to be done. For now, they had to wait for the water to subside before cleaning up and assessing the extent of the damage.

Laura, now wearing some dry clothes Tom had told her to borrow from his mother's closet, approached Tom and sat down next to him.

'Hey,' she said quietly, wrapping her arms across her chest.

'Thanks. You shouldn't have come out here, you know. It was dangerous.'

Laura swallowed. 'I had to come, Tom,' she said, turning to him. His eyes were almost empty, the usual lightheartedness vanished and replaced by hopelessness. 'Tom, I ...'

Tom lifted a thick finger and placed it gently on her lips. Laura's pulse raced. Then Tom cradled her face in his hands and kissed her. Every pore of her body responded to his kiss, and Laura allowed herself to be swept up in his embrace and lose herself in the tenderness.

'I'm sorry I left without saying goodbye,' Laura managed as they broke from the kiss.

Tom shook his head. 'It doesn't matter. You're here now.'

Laura smiled as Tom reached in again and stroked her face.

LAURA DIDN'T THINK there was ever a more perfect moment than lying there in Tom's arms. After dark had fallen, the SES volunteers, farmhands, and helpers disappeared, leaving the house still and quiet. The aftermath of the flood left a dank smell of mud and water in the air. There was so much that had to be done. So much damage to be assessed. But neither Laura nor Tom wanted to think about tomorrow. All that mattered was they were safe. They were here. Together.

And now, with her head nestled in the crook of Tom's neck, lying in the aftermath of messy sheets and tossed clothing, Laura smiled. She inhaled his smell, warm and manly, and watched as his soft snoring fluttered his lips, his face tired but peaceful. His five-o'clock shadow lined the curves of his strong jaw. Laura felt an overwhelming surge of emotion. A peace that she hadn't experienced for so long. As if she were home. Somehow, after all these years, it felt like she was in a place she was meant to be. She wondered if the feeling would last or if morning would bring the truth, and leave her once again unsure. She closed her eyes; she didn't want to know. Not yet.

30

THE NEXT MORNING, Tom sat at the kitchen table sipping his coffee to the sound of bacon and eggs sizzling in the pan as Laura busied herself over the stove. Outside, rays of yellow sun bounced off the hay shed, and crisp blue sky surrounded the farm. Tom had to squint at the brightness. He swore he could almost see the water evaporating. Not soon enough though.

'Thank god for the sun,' Laura said, popping down a plate of crispy bacon, fried tomato, and farm eggs. Tom's stomach rumbled. 'You can say that again,' he said, taking in a mouthful.

'So, the cleanup begins.'

Tom sighed. 'Yep. Not looking forward to assessing the damage.'

Laura walked over to Tom and put her hands on his shoulders. 'It'll be okay. I'm here to help,' she whispered in his ear.

Last night had been close to perfect. Laura had told him about Ryan and how he found out about his parents. Tom had no idea. None of them had. He couldn't imagine how he'd deal with something like that and was glad he didn't have to. He was still processing the guilt that he'd not given Ryan a chance. Not been there for him. But that was all in the past. All he could do was hold Laura. He'd told her again how much he loved her. And how he couldn't remember a time where he didn't. Laura responded by kissing him and leading him upstairs. Tom was completely overwhelmed, as if it weren't real. Last night, with the haze of lovemaking still hanging in the air, the moment was perfect. The taste of her lips, the softness of the skin on her stomach, the immense feeling of love as he'd taken her into his arms and lain her on the bed.

Tom swallowed, wishing the feeling he'd experienced last night would return. It wasn't that it was gone, just that it had been pushed aside by the return of his guilt. He'd only ever wanted Laura. And now, it seemed she was on the same page, but the light of day brought a stark reality with it as it bounced off the receding water and into Tom's heart. He had nothing left.

There was no way his insurance would go even halfway to covering the damage and loss of stock. And then there was the bank. As he once said to Ryan, *Laura deserves better.* Someone who could look after her. Not a broke and broken farmer.

'When will everyone arrive?' Laura asked as she cleared the plates and broke into Tom's thoughts.

'Any moment, I guess. There's another SES crew coming out and a few farmhands from Jim's property to lend a hand.' Tom rubbed his forehead. There was so much to do. 'Then, I guess the insurance assessor will be here. Around lunchtime, he said. I've gotta head into town and arrange some feed first thing, though.'

'Would you mind giving me a lift? I don't think I'll be getting my car out for a few days. Oh god, I don't even want to think about that.'

'I think the SES towed it in last night, but I don't reckon it's going anywhere right now. I'll take a look at it for you, but sure, I'll take you back in.'

'Thanks, I've got the op-shop guys coming to collect the furniture at eleven.'

'No worries.'

Laura slipped her arms around Tom's waist. She fit so perfectly in his embrace.

Half an hour later, Tom drove his Ute toward Laura's house, aware of the thick air between them.

'You okay?' Laura said, sliding her hand across to his leg.

'Yeah.'

'You've just been really quiet this morning.'

Tom shrugged. 'A lot on my mind, I guess.'

'Of course. Hey, do you mind just finishing off that last cupboard door for me in the kitchen? It'll only take a minute,' Laura asked as they pulled into the driveway.

'Yeah, sure.'

Tom followed Laura into the house. 'Leave the door open,' she called. 'Let the sunshine in. The house could do with a good airing after all that rain.'

After Tom had fixed the door, Laura turned him to face her. 'Tom, what is it? I know you've got a lot on your mind, but something tells me it's more than that.'

'It's nothing. Really,' Tom lied.

Laura smiled. 'Did I tell you I've sold the house?'

Tom raised his eyebrows. 'Wow! That was fast.' He didn't even realize she had formally put it on the market. 'So, now what?'

'Well.' She smiled. Tom loved how the freckle under her right eye seemed to dance when she smiled. 'I have some stuff to work out, but...' She paused, twisting her fingers. 'What I'm trying to say is, if you're wanting to ...'

Tom's heart both leaped and thumped. This was what he'd wanted since he first understood his feelings for her. But it all seemed wrong now. He could barely look at her. How was he supposed to tell her he was going to lose the farm? How even with the insurance—if it came through—there was no way he could meet the bank payments now he'd lost so much stock, especially his prize heifer. And she still didn't know the truth about Ryan. It was wrong. He had to come clean. If he had any chance to make things right, it was now.

'Laura,' he started, reaching for her hands. Her palms were butter-soft against his calloused fingers.

'I can't do this,' he said, staring at the floor.

'You can't do what?'

'This. Us.'

'What?' Laura's face fell. 'But, I … we …'

'It's not that I don't love you. I do. I've loved you forever, it seems. But …' Tom's brow furrowed, then he shook his head. 'It's not that simple.'

'I know it's not going to be easy, Tom. I know we've been through a lot. And I know I have to earn your trust. I promise I'm not going to run off again. And I have to deal with Luke.' She paused, and Tom felt her tension. 'I know there's going to be some tough times on the farm. But, I want to be there with you for it. I want to invest in the farm with the money from mum's house. Invest in us. I've loved that farm since I can remember. It's every childhood memory for me. I didn't realize how much it felt like home until … well, until I thought you'd lost it all. A piece of me felt lost too. And then … then I realized I love you. I think maybe I always have.'

Tom couldn't look into her eyes; he knew he would lose his nerve. He turned away, trying to hide the emotion that was building. 'I can't, Laura. I'm sorry.'

'Tom! Please, listen to me, listen to what I'm saying. We can do this together,' Laura said, reaching for his shoulder.

'No, Laura. I can't take your money. Your mum's money. I've got to take responsibility. That's just how it is. I'm a Gordon. It's what we do. And you know, maybe the farming life isn't for me anyway.' His voice broke with the words.

'Don't you ever say that!' Laura said, turning him around to face her.

A hopeless expression was etched into the fine lines on Tom's face. 'I want you, Laura, but you don't need to buy me. I would take you if I had nothing else in this world and we had to live on the streets. But you deserve so much more than that.'

Laura shook her head in frustration. 'If it was because I felt sorry for you or just wanted to help you out, that would be different. But I'm standing here telling you I love you, telling you I want to spend the rest of my life with you. This is the only thing I've ever been sure about in my whole life,' Laura said. 'For once, I know what I want. And it's you.' Tom watched Laura as she blinked, and tears trickled down her face and onto her neck. He reached to her and wiped them away with his thumb, and she grabbed his hand. 'I love you, Tom.'

He looked her deep in the eyes, summoning the courage. 'Laura, I'm going to lose the farm.'

'What do you mean you're going to lose the farm?'

'I've missed too many loan payments; they're going to foreclose on me. And now with all the flood damage,' his voice broke, 'I'm nothing, Laura.'

He watched her, expecting her expression to change to one of disgust, pity even, but it didn't. Instead, she pulled him close, and whispered, 'I don't care. We'll figure it out.'

But there was one more thing he had to come clean with. One

last thing would need to be laid bare in front of them if they were ever going to have a chance together. He knew this would break her, but he had no choice.

'And there's something else,' he said, pulling away from her. 'I was the last person to see Ryan alive.'

31

LAURA FELT HER face flush as the words lingered between them, hanging in the silence as if suspended by time. The words slowly seeped into the part of her brain where she could decipher them. But even then, she didn't understand. How could Tom have been the last to see Ryan alive? She was. She left him on the tracks. She heard the whistle of the train only minutes later. It couldn't be true.

'That's not true. You can't have been,' she whispered, confusion blanketing her face.

Tom turned toward her. 'I saw you and Ryan on the tracks. I'd been looking for you. I wanted to tell you everything. About Ryan and Rachel. And then I saw you both.'

'How? Where were you?'

'I was hiding behind the bushes near the walkway. I don't know what made me hide. I was a coward. I know. But you guys were arguing. And I thought that maybe he'd come clean on his own. Man up about it, you know?'

Laura's eyes searched Tom's for answers. For anything that made sense. What he was saying didn't make sense.

'But I couldn't really hear much, and then I saw you storm off. I wanted to follow you, but I couldn't take my eyes off Ryan. He just sat there. I was so angry, Laura. So angry at him. But I knew if I approached him I'd beat the shit out of him. I didn't know what he was going through then. If I'd known ... I dunno, I'd have gone for help or something. I should have gone to him. Maybe, if I had ...' Tom shrugged. The weight of his confession pressed down his shoulders so much that they only twitched. 'But, I just left him there. I turned away and walked back toward town, then I heard the train coming. But I didn't think anything of it. I didn't put two and two together. I left him there to die.' Tom's face crumpled. He turned his back to Laura and leaned his head on the kitchen cupboards. His shoulders shuddered.

Laura was frozen to the ground, her feet unable to move. She wasn't even sure she was breathing. All this time she had blamed herself. Thinking she could have saved him—should have saved him—when all along Tom had been carrying this weight too. The awful heaviness that no matter how hard she tried, couldn't be shaken. Suddenly, this wasn't just Laura's pain. This was their pain. She felt sick to her stomach at her selfishness. At the way she had run away, turned her back on everyone. So young, so naïve, so self-centered. She could barely bear to be in her own flesh. And there was Tom, broken, just as she was, although worse. He felt he'd let her down. Let Ryan down. And he'd said nothing. She reached over to Tom and put her hand on his back.

He spun around, his eyes holding a hopeless expression. 'I should have beaten the crap out of him, Laura. At least then he wouldn't have been on the tracks. At least then he'd still be alive!' He turned away again.

'Tom, no. You don't know that!'

Wrapping her arms around him from behind, Laura cradled his shaking body, wondering how things got to this point. A mess of confusion, heavy secrets, and tear-soaked memories. An anger began to bubble inside her. Anger laden in guilt. She'd turned her back on her friends when they needed each other. She'd acted as if she were the only one hurt in the aftermath, that her emotions were the only ones too fragile to deal with the tragedy. She'd walked away from her own mother! Laura squeezed her eyes tight, trying to stop the clashing emotions. How could Tom keep this from her? Why did Rachel and Ryan betray her, betray Tom—the friendship? Why didn't her mother try harder for Laura? Make her come back. Face her friends? Face Banyula? Why didn't she make her listen? Laura's body was stiff with all these colliding thoughts and emotions. She couldn't identify the feeling as it surged inside her, gripping at her throat, clawing at her stomach. She tried to breathe through it, but her breaths were shaky and short. Tom mumbled almost inaudibly, 'I'm so sorry, Laura.'

She pulled away, visibly shaking, the tightening in her throat making her breaths short. 'I know, Tom. I know.' She rubbed her temples. 'I just need some time to process all of this.' She walked to the kitchen window and stared into the empty backyard, still trying to focus on her breathing.

'Okay, I'll go. I don't blame you for not being able to look at me.'

It took all of Laura's strength not to turn around. She didn't know what emotion would emerge first, the overwhelming need to forgive Tom or the crushing force to scream at him. She couldn't risk it. It was only when she heard the front door close behind him that she let herself erupt into sobs over the sink.

Laura wasn't sure how long she sat in the kitchen. The sunshine through the kitchen window had changed the shadows on the carpet, and Laura felt cold. Her mind was blank and numb.

Her limbs were heavy, and her eyes grated against the lids when she blinked. Then she remembered. *The removalists!*

Half an hour later, she emerged from the bathroom with fresh makeup, including a thick layer of concealer to cover her blotchy face. Although her thoughts were still murky, clarity was beginning to form. Her anger now dissolved along with her tears. She couldn't cry anymore. She had nothing left. While blackening her lashes, she'd looked at herself in the mirror and told herself it was over. There was nothing else that could break her further.

A rap on the front door broke her thoughts, and she spent the next half hour directing the removalists to what furniture and boxes were to be loaded onto the truck. Just as they were pulling away from the curb, and Laura was unclipping the front door from its propped-open position, she noticed a car pull up. Her eyes widened.

Luke jumped out of the car, his clothes creased and stuck to his back from the long drive. His beard was longer than she remembered, and his eyes were surrounded by a grayish tinge, as if he hadn't slept in a while. He walked toward Laura, scooping her in his arms before she knew what was happening.

'Laura! You don't know how good it is to see you,' he said, rubbing her back. Laura wiggled out of the embrace to be greeted with the force of his lips on hers. The familiar lips, which she realized she hadn't missed.

'I've missed you so much. I've been a jerk, I'm sorry. I should have been here for you.' He didn't wait for her to respond. Rather, he stepped back and surveyed the weatherboard cottage. 'Wow! So, this is where you grew up?'

Luke's raised eyebrows told Laura everything she needed to know. He didn't know her. He didn't understand. She knew that it was her own fault. She'd never been forthcoming. She knew he, who grew up in the affluence of Toorak, wouldn't get it even if she had have explained things to him. They were worlds apart, but it was only now she allowed herself to see the chasm clearly for the first time. She sucked in a deep breath, willing her courage to not let her down this time.

'Luke,' Laura paused, 'we need to talk.'

Laura led Luke into the kitchen. 'Sorry, there's nowhere to sit right now. Pull up a bench, I guess.'

Luke did just that and hoisted himself onto the bench. 'I really am sorry, Laura. I shouldn't have chosen work over you.'

'Luke, I ... meant what I said. It's over,' she said as matter-of-factly as she could.

'C'mon, let's not do this now. I'll help you finish up here, and we'll deal with things when we get back to the city.'

'I'm not coming back with you, Luke. I can't,' Laura responded, taken aback by her own abruptness.

'What do you mean? Look, if you don't want to get married, it's okay. If you want to wait, we'll wait. It's no big deal. And I know it doesn't feel right now after your mum and everything. We'll know when the time is right.'

Laura looked at Luke, seeing him in a completely different light than she had a few weeks ago. He was a good person. She knew that. He just wasn't *her* person. He deserved someone who wanted the same things out of life: success, money, notoriety. Someone whom he made feel right, like pulling on a well-worn pair of lamb's wool slippers. Now that Laura was being completely honest, it had never been like that for her. Not with Luke. And that wasn't fair to either of them.

'I meant what I said. I'm not in love with you, Luke.'

The words stilled in the silence, and Laura watched as Luke's face crunched into confusion.

He jumped down off the bench and paced the kitchen. 'I don't get it, Laura. When I asked you to marry me, you said yes. What, you didn't mean it? You didn't love me then? You fell out of love with me? What is it? You don't feel it?' he said, his hand slapping his chest.

'I don't know. I was trying. I thought I'd get there, but ...' This wasn't going how she had planned. Her initial confidence was now shaky.

Luke walked to Laura and took her hands. 'Okay, I know you're hurting. I know that coming back here must have brought back so many memories. You just need to grieve. Everything will be fine. I know it will.'

Laura sucked in a deep breath. She wanted so much to give in. To end his hurt. But she couldn't. For the first time in her life, she had to be honest about her feelings. She couldn't run away from herself any longer; she had to tell the truth.

'I'm sorry, Luke. I'm not coming back with you.'

Luke dropped her hands and fell silent. His face held an expression Laura couldn't decipher, but she knew he finally understood. Laura was suddenly aware of the kitchen clock, its loud rhythmic ticking the only sound, as there was nothing left to say.

32

THE NEXT MORNING, Laura woke to the sun sneaking around the corner of the blinds. Although yesterday was emotional, to say the least, Laura felt lighter. Open. As if the hard casing protecting her heart was beginning to crack and crumble away. But she still had no idea where her future lay. Was it here with Tom? And what about Rachel? And Ryan and Rachel's son Mitchell? Her thoughts confused her. If only her mum was here. She'd know what to do.

The thought of her mum made her throat snag. How she longed for a warm hug. She closed her eyes and imagined snuggling into her mother like they used to on the couch. A ball of love, her mum called it. They'd snuggle for what felt like hours, and everything, no matter how bad, would feel right with the world.

Laura contemplated what life would look like without her mum in it. She wished she'd come back sooner and faced everything. But there was no use in wishful thinking or trying to reinvent the past. Laura knew much better than that.

Over the past few weeks, Laura had been hanging off the dark end of the emotional spectrum. All the grief and loss for her mother. The pining for the past and days long gone. Then the apprehension, hurt, and heartbreak for Ryan, Tom, and Rachel, as she tried to make peace with the secrets and misunderstandings that had stood between them. The regret for teenage stupidity and naivety and her own stubbornness that had consumed her over the past years. The despair she felt saying goodbye to Luke, not wanting to hurt him, but knowing it was the only thing she could do. He would find someone, someone perfect for him. It just wasn't Laura.

Now she felt ready to say goodbye. Not to Banyula, not even to the past, but to her old self. The old Laura who would have kept running. Not now. Now the only place she wanted to run to was Tom.

Laura felt a warmth course through her. As much as she'd felt exhausted from the dark emotions, she couldn't deny she was feeling something good inside. Something had sparked inside her. She wasn't lying when she told Tom she loved him. It felt right. She wondered if her feelings for Tom had been there all along, simply buried under the weight of teenage bullshit. Of self-importance. It was cool being Ryan's girlfriend back then, but when she really thought about it, her best times had always been with Tom. Those innocent moments of pure fun when nothing else mattered. Like netting yabbies in the dam. Building treehouses by the river. Watching Tom's wide grin as he ran through the fields after being dared to enter the bull paddock. Those moments were etched deep in her heart, and up until now, she'd thought they were just fond childhood memories. But now, she understood they were so much more. She could see herself on the farm. With Tom. She could see a future she hadn't been able to envision with Luke. A life. Love. Kids. A future that made her heart skip and body twitch with anticipation.

Laura had never wanted to look to the future before, held back by hurt and betrayal. It was as if, if she looked forward to something, it would break and shatter to pieces as it had with Ryan. But now, it was different. Her heart was thawing. Who knew if those feelings were always there for Tom, or if it was simply meant to be? Laura was over agonizing about the past. She had to move forward. And even though it pained her to see Rachel, and now Mitchell, it also brought hope. Hope that Ryan would live on. Not only in her memory, but in the face of that little boy who knew nothing but innocence. Who didn't yet know of the tragedy and heartache. Who should only know about the good in Ryan's soul.

But still, even though she knew she had to move forward, had to look to the future, what did that future look like? And what steps did she need to take? Would Tom even want her anymore? These were questions she didn't have answers to. But she had to find them.

As she arrived at the cemetery, Laura let Mick's call go through to voice mail for the second time that morning. She was surprised at his persistence on a Sunday. *The buyer must be keen*, she thought, stepping out of the car.

Laura tightened the belt of her coat around her. The autumn wind felt more like a winter southerly as it whisked away the clouds and delivered a clean blue sky. *A fresh slate*, thought Laura. She weaved her way through the headstones, nodding at an elderly woman praying at a large grave flourished with roses. When she arrived at her mother's grave, she noticed another bunch of white carnations, still fresh, had been laid in front of the new headstone. She picked them up and pushed their stems into the florists' foam of her own pink arrangement, then placed them down again before squatting on her haunches.

She sighed. She didn't think she'd ever be the type of person to talk to a gravestone, but that was before.

'Well, Mum.' She paused to bite the inside of her cheek before continuing. 'I wish you were still here. So I could properly apologize to you for everything. But, I kind of want to know why you didn't push me earlier. Why you let me run away? I know you thought that maybe I'd come around once I'd grieved. But didn't you see? I didn't let myself grieve. I moved straight on with life. A life I thought would fix everything so I wouldn't have to face the past. Why didn't you tell me I was wrong?'

A single sparrow fluttered down, landing on the headstone next to Judy's. It cocked its head to Laura and flew away.

'I know what you'd say right now if you were here. That I wouldn't have listened to you. And you're probably right. But maybe I wanted you to try?' Laura's eyes welled, and she sat down on the damp ground, feeling it seep through her coat and jeans onto her legs, but she didn't care.

'What do I do now? I wish someone would tell me.' Laura looked into the vacant sky, as if Judy would send the answer floating toward her from heaven. The pale sun warmed her face, and she closed her eyes, listening to the quiet that surrounded her. The chirping of nearby birds, the gentle hum of the odd passing car, the whisper of prayer from the elderly woman, the rhythmic tick of her watch. She sighed and opened her eyes. That's when she noticed the single white feather, the color of fresh snow, lying next to the headstone. Laura was sure it hadn't been there before. She reached out and picked it up, gently stroking the outer vanes. It was so delicate and fine beneath her fingers. And then, all of a sudden, her eyes flew open, a warm rush surging inside her.

That was it. She knew what she had to do. She jumped to her feet, brushing off a few crumpled leaves from her coat. She wished she could reach out and hug her mother, but instead she smiled and whispered, 'Thank you, Mum. I love you more than ice cream.' And with that, she wiped away the tears and tucked the feather into her pocket. She had plans to make.

33

THE MAIN STREET hummed with Monday morning shoppers and shopkeepers sweeping their footpaths as Laura pulled into a parking lot outside Wood & Lewis Solicitors. As she gathered her handbag off the passenger seat, Laura's phone rang. It was Mick, but this time she was keen to answer and put the car in park quickly. 'Hey, Mick,' she said.

'Laura. I thought you'd gone rogue on me,' he laughed, his voice echoing. He must have had her on speakerphone.

'Yeah, I'm sorry I didn't return your calls yesterday. I've just ... had a lot going on. But yes, I'll take the offer.'

She heard his hands clap together. 'Fantastic! That's great news. I'll get onto my buyer and get the ball rolling. Want me to get in touch with your solicitor, or do you want to handle that?'

'I'm already one step ahead of you, Mick.' Laura smiled.

AFTER COLLECTING the documents from her solicitor and delivering them to Mick to sign, Laura drove to the library. She didn't know if Shea would be there, but it was worth a shot. She had to talk through these plans with someone objective. And she liked Shea. She was easy to talk to. She'd mentioned how she wanted to find a hobby since moving to the area but hadn't found anything. Although it wasn't technically a hobby, she was hoping Shea would jump at the chance to somehow help Laura with her plans.

Laura bounded through the double doors, seeing Shea's face light up with a smile when Laura entered. Shea rounded the counter and greeted her with a warm hug.

'Hey, I hadn't seen you for a few days. Thought maybe you'd already left town,' Shea said, gathering up a stack of books from the returns counter.

'You didn't think I'd leave without saying goodbye, did you?'

Shea laughed. 'Glad you didn't. Hey, want to help me put these away?' she asked with a grin.

'Sure.'

Shea handed half the books to Laura, who followed Shea to the shelves, talking as Shea filed away the books and straightened the shelves as she went.

'I have some news,' Laura said, shifting the weight of the books to her other hip.

'Good news, I hope?'

'Well, yes. I think so. Looks like I'll be sticking around.' Laura felt an amazing sense of relief as the words floated past her lips. It felt right. Like every broken road she'd had to travel over the past years was to direct her back here, back home.

'Really?' Shea stopped and turned to Laura. 'That's awesome!' She pulled her into another embrace around the books.

'Yep. And I need your help.'

'My help? Of course. Anything.' Shea looked at her watch. 'It's break time, come with me and I'll make you one of my awesome double soy lattes with caramel.'

Sitting down in the library café, Laura sipped on the latte Shea had just made her, the foam bubbling at her lips as she drank. 'Wow! This is good,' Laura said.

'I know, isn't it? Anyway,' Shea replied after taking another sip herself, 'how can I help you?'

Laura took a deep breath. This was it. She'd come too far to curl back up into herself and hide. That was the old Laura. The new Laura—the real Laura—wasn't going to pretend the world wasn't happening around her. She was going to make it happen. Laura pulled a large notebook from her bag and began explaining to Shea the idea that had appeared in her head at her mum's grave the day before. An idea so wild, that for the first time in an eternity it excited Laura to no end.

During her unfinished counseling training, Laura had studied how farm stays had helped troubled youths find purpose again. There were particular farms that helped city youth deal with drug and alcohol addiction, but also a handful that concentrated on country youth exhibiting initial signs of struggle.

'The idea is to get to these teens before they reach the point where they're considering drugs and alcohol as a way to deal with their issues, or even the boredom and the hopelessness of being stuck in a country town,' Laura said.

Shea was listening intently, nodding throughout.

'Getting them out onto the farms—and not just in the boring jobs, but actually working on the farm, knowing they are making a difference, shows them the value of hard work. Rewarding work. Doing something that's appreciated and valued reinstalls a sense of hope and responsibility for them. And it helps the farmers as it's—hopefully, I haven't got that far yet—partly funded by government initiatives. Tom tells me farmhands are hard to come by these days.'

Laura knew her plan wasn't without its flaws. There was a lot of legwork to be done. She'd of course have to finish her counseling course and get through the red tape of dealing with government departments. Grants would need to be applied for. And then there was the farm. Tom's farm to begin with. He'd of course have to agree to it. But, with the sale of the house, Laura was sure she could convince Tom that they could make it work—together. And from there, she hoped that other local farmers would be willing to join the program too.

Laura leaned back against her chair and twisted her mouth. 'Well?' she said to Shea with hopeful eyes.

'Laura, this is such a brilliant plan. I can't believe you pulled all this together in one afternoon! Of course I'll help you.'

'Really? That would be so great. You seem to be in touch with the community, and you are so amazingly organized, from what I can tell. I'd love you to help me set it up. If, of course, you have time.'

Laura noticed Shea's eyes becoming glassy as she listened to her. 'You have no idea how much this town needs this.'

Laura buzzed inside. 'I wish it didn't. But, if I can help even one young person get back on track, I think it will be worth it.'

'Of course it will. This is amazing!'

'I just wish someone could have done something for Ryan,' Laura said, sucking in her bottom lip.

Shea nodded. 'I wish I could have been more helpful finding out what happened.'

Laura looked down at her hands and began flicking her fingernails. 'I know what happened now.'

'You do?'

'Tom told me.'

Laura explained the developments of the past few days.

'Oh Laura,' Shea gasped before cupping her mouth. 'I'm so sorry. I just can't believe it. And you, you're so calm.'

'I don't know. Maybe it hasn't really hit me yet. Or maybe, I'm just—which sounds awful—relieved to know what really happened.'

'True. At least you know now,' Shea said. 'And, you can write your own ending.'

Laura tilted her head. 'What do you mean?'

'Make Ryan's life count for something. Sure, he may have been depressed, and he really stuffed up, but from what you tell me, he was a good person. Wasn't he?'

Laura stared into the distance, past the other tables and the shelves of books, and into space, thinking. Of course he was. Deep down, despite the depression, despite his confusion, his mistakes, his family, he was a good person.

'What would Ryan want you to do?'

Laura turned back to Shea, her eyes misty again. 'He'd want me to do this.'

Shea pushed her glasses back up the bridge of her nose and smiled, patting Laura's hand. 'Well, that's all you need to know.'

34

THE AFTERMATH OF the flood wasn't pretty. Tom had been out surveying more damage in the lower paddocks. Fences compromised, two of his pumps ruined, and more stock losses than initially thought. And although the water was receding, it was doing so at a snail's pace, stalling the cleanup process. Thankfully the steps in the flood management plan he had taken to protect the sheds and machinery had worked. Small mercies.

Tom checked on the couple of new calves that had survived, pleased they were okay. Then, he made his way back to the house to order fencing supplies and feed. As he pulled the farm Ute to a bumpy halt behind the house, Tom noticed an unfamiliar vehicle making its way down the long gravel driveway. The midday sun reflected off the windshield, making it difficult to see who was behind the wheel. Tom jumped out of the Ute and jogged over to the front porch, his socks squelching inside his soaked boots, while his visitor climbed out of the car. It wasn't until she stepped onto the porch and pushed her sunglasses up into her blonde hair that he recognised who it was; Rachel.

Tom took a deep breath.

'Hey, Tom!' she said with a soft smile, as if her rocking up on his doorstep were a casual occurrence, and not a ten-year time lapse. Tom noticed she had aged. Her once long blonde mane was now cut into a short bob that framed her face. Her eyes were flanked by small wrinkles as she squinted in the sunlight.

'Geez, Rachel.' Tom tried to hide his shock at her impromptu visit. 'Long time no see.'

She walked over to him and gave him an awkward hug. They had never been close enough to hang out much on their own. Laura had always been the glue between them. In fact, Tom and Rachel had an almost love-hate relationship, always taunting each other, but it was always in good spirits. She was fun, and they'd all shared some great times, but unfortunately the good memories were all too hard to recall. It was the bad ones that lingered closer to the surface, raising Tom's hackles.

'I heard the flood was pretty bad out here,' Rachel said, surveying the farm.

'Yeah, not great. A lot of work to be done, that's for sure.' Tom sighed. There was an awkward pause. 'You coming in for a minute?' Tom said, motioning toward the verandah. Rachel nodded, and Tom led her around to the back door.

When they were inside the kitchen, Rachel hung her bag off the back of the kitchen chair and took a seat at the small, worn timber table.

'Coffee?' Tom asked, hoping she would say yes so he'd have something to do.

'Yeah, thanks. Black, two sugars.'

Tom switched on the kettle and busied himself with the cups and sugar.

'Wow this place hasn't changed much,' Rachel said. 'Still as I remembered.'

'Yeah, nah, nothin's changed much around here,' Tom replied, attempting small talk. 'Except the water.' The unspoken hung between them like a thick fog. He stirred in the sugar and brought the cups to the table, breaking the silence with the question he really wanted answered. Subtlety and patience never was his thing.

'So, why are you here, Rachel?' Tom said, turning his cup around in circles on the table.

Rachel took a long sip of the coffee, drawing the liquid in with a small slurp. She swallowed and kept staring at her mug, lost for words. Tom waited, his knee jiggling impatiently or nervously, he wasn't sure which, under the table.

'I want to make amends,' she finally said with a shaky voice, staring into her cup.

'With me?' said Tom, frowning.

'With you. With Laura. With what happened.'

Tom sighed. He didn't want to be the go-between. He had his own issues he needed to sort out with Laura and knew Rachel's complications wouldn't be helpful in the least.

'Just let it go, Rach. Laura's had a rough few months, what with Judy's death and coming back here. I think it's best to let sleeping dogs lie, you know?' He shrugged.

'I know. It's just …' Tom could see the frustration creep across her face and strain the small creases at the corners of her mouth.

'Look, Rach,' he said. 'You need to leave it. Too much happened back then. There's too much water under the bridge.' He cringed at the ironic metaphor.

Next thing he knew, tears had welled in Rachel's eyes and spilled over the edge, slowly making their way down her flushed cheeks. The events of the past were still obviously raw and close to the surface for her as well.

'I'm sorry,' he said. 'I didn't mean to upset you. But don't you see? It's just all too much. We need to move on. Let Laura finally move on.'

He'd messed up with Laura. Thinking over the past few days, he wished he'd done it differently, maybe even stayed quiet. Then maybe she'd be here with him, rather than him having no idea what she was thinking. And if Rachel were to come and stir things up again ... Man, that could only make things worse. No. If he'd learned anything over the past few days, it was that the truth wasn't worth it.

Rachel broke into his thoughts. 'But maybe we do need to deal with it, Tom. We never did. No one knows the truth. There is so much you both don't know that I've been carrying around for so long. I never had the chance to explain. To apologize.' The tears continued to trickle down Rachel's face, and Tom almost felt sorry for her. Well, he did feel sorry for her, but each time, a wave of nausea would take over as he remembered how Ryan and Rachel had hurt Laura. The anger reared up like a provoked bull. But it was no use. None of it mattered anymore. Tom propped his elbows on the table. Now it was his turn to stare into the coffee for the answers. They weren't there. 'I don't know, Rachel.'

'Please, Tom, you have to make Laura see me. I need the chance to explain. I've been living with these feelings, and I just can't move on. I know that if you both knew the truth you could move on too.'

'You know I didn't speak to Laura the whole time she was in Melbourne?' Tom said, running his finger over the small scratches on the table.

Rachel's eyes widened in shock. 'Oh my God,' she whispered. 'I thought ... You two were always so close.'

Tom breathed out heavily. 'I thought so too. But after she left, I never heard from her again. I'd begged Judy to get her to talk to me, and I know she would have tried, but nothing. I guess it was Laura's way of dealing with it. We were all so young back then.'

'I'm sorry, Tom. I had no idea.'

'You took off too, not long after.'

Rachel went to speak, but Tom waved his hands and pushed himself out from the table, the chair scraping on the boards and echoing around the kitchen. 'This isn't going to help, Rach; it's no use. And I don't want to see her hurt again. Any of us, for that matter. We're all adults now. We all have our own lives to get on with. That's just what we need to do. End of story.'

He picked up the two mugs, both unfinished, and put them in the sink. 'We need to let her go,' he said, staring out the window into the stagnant water lying in the low areas, a tightness in his heart.

Tom heard Rachel move toward him, then felt her warm hand on his back. 'We need to do this, Tom. And we need to do it together,' she said. 'I know how you felt about her.'

Tom huffed and shook his head. 'Yeah, well it's too late for all that now. None of it matters.' He walked toward the back door and held it open for Rachel, hoping she'd get the message that this conversation, which was going nowhere, was over. She twisted her mouth, grabbed her bag, and walked outside.

'I know you don't want to hear this, Tom,' Rachel said as they walked around to the front porch. 'But I'm going to make it work. I'm going to go and see Laura. Make it right. I have to tell her the truth.'

Tom rubbed his hand across his forehead and sighed, losing patience. 'The truth? You keep going on about the *truth*, Rachel, and it's the truth that caused all this pain for Laura. She knows about you and Ryan. That's the truth. How on earth is it going to help her now?' He kicked a stone off the porch in a fit of anger. Rachel was still as stubborn as ever.

'I was there, Tom. I was there when it happened.' Her tears were back, her face stricken with sadness.

Tom frowned, trying to comprehend what she had said. 'When what happened?'

'Ryan ...' Rachel's voice broke and she steadied herself on the verandah post, her small frame shaking as she sobbed. Tom's heart stopped as he tried to process what he'd just heard. It didn't make any sense. 'You were there?'

Tom listened while Rachel told her story, not sure if he could actually believe it. All along he'd thought he was the one who could have saved Ryan, but Rachel had been there too. She could have ... He stopped his thoughts there. There was no use in that line of thought. But, the one thing Rachel was right about was that they had to tell Laura. As much as it would hurt her, it was the only way he could possibly get her back. If she knew Tom wasn't the last one to see Ryan, she couldn't blame him. It was his only chance. Yes, it was self-serving, but he had to be. He couldn't let another opportunity slip through his grasp.

'You have to tell her, Rachel,' Tom said. They both sat on the back porch steps, staring out into the sodden paddocks, the breeze rippling the water and rattling a loose bit of tin on the nearby windmill.

'I know. You have to help me. I can't do it alone.'

Tom nodded. She was right. He had to be there. He had to be the one to pick up the pieces as Laura's heart and soul shattered yet again. He pulled his phone out of his pocket.

'What are you doing?'

'I'm texting Laura. We need to go and see her. Now.'

35

LAURA AND SHEA pulled up outside Stella's as a message pinged on Laura's phone. It was Tom.

Where are you?

An odd question, Laura thought. She tapped out a reply.

I'm at Stella's. Why?

I need to see you. It's important.

Okay. I need to see you too. I'll be home in about an hour.

It can't wait. I'm coming to Stella's. Stay there.

Laura bit her lip. That was all a bit strange. She startled as Shea tapped on the outside of the car door, her head tilted in question.

'Sorry,' Laura said, opening the door and hopping out.

'Everything okay?'

Laura waved her hand. 'Yeah, it's nothing. Just nerves, I guess.'

Shea smiled. 'Okay. You ready to do this?'

'Ready as I'll ever be.' Laura tried to settle the butterflies in her chest as they walked to Stella's front door. 'I really value Stella's opinion, so if she thinks it's a good idea, it's on! And, Shea?' She paused and looked at her new friend. 'Thanks for being here. It means a lot to have someone's support.'

'No problem. I'm just as excited as you!'

Laura knocked on Stella's front door. 'I hope she's home. She said she had today off for report writing.'

Laura had spent the last couple of hours researching at the library and had pulled together a rough plan for her idea. There were lots of grants she could apply for, and if she could get in with the right government department, she could even receive proper funding and backing. She'd filled Shea in with all the details and insisted she come along for moral support. Laura's skin prickled with excitement. She'd even thought of a name for the program. The Ryan Taylor Project. She smiled to herself.

'Laura,' Stella said, wrapping her thick arms around Laura. 'And who do we have here?'

'Stella, this is Shea. Shea, this is Stella. Shea works at the library.'

'Of course. Yes, now I recognize you,' Stella said, reaching out her hand to Shea.

'Hi, Stella, lovely to meet you.'

Laura and Shea followed Stella into the kitchen, where breakfast dishes were piled neatly beside the sink and the newspaper lay open on the bench. The smell of coffee lingered, and the oven door gently rattled.

'What's in the oven?' Laura asked before turning to Shea. 'Stella here is an amazing cook.'

'Chocolate brownie.' Stella smiled. 'It'll be ready soon.'

'Perfect timing!' Laura grinned.

'You haven't changed, Miss Laura.' Stella laughed. 'Coffee, girls? It's freshly brewed.' She motioned to the coffee machine.

Laura and Shea had taken up the stools at the breakfast bar and placed their paperwork on the bench, both nodding at the offer of a coffee.

Stella folded the newspaper and busied herself with the coffee mugs. 'Now, what can I do you ladies for?' she asked.

'Well, I'm here for some advice,' Laura began. 'Oh, gosh, where do I start?'

'Best place is at the beginning, I always find,' Stella said, sliding mugs of coffee across the bench to Laura and Shea.

Laura took a mouthful of the hot coffee, the bitterness making her suck in her cheeks as she swallowed, but it calmed her as it slid down her throat.

'Well,' Laura began, 'I've got an offer on the house.'

'Wow! That's great!' Stella said, raising her eyebrows. 'Isn't it?'

'I think so, but I've decided I'm not going back to the city. I think I might want to stay here.'

Stella tilted her head. 'What about your fiancé? What's his name? Liam. No, Luke, isn't it?'

'Luke. We broke up.'

'Oh, darling. I'm sorry. Are you okay?'

Laura nodded. 'It's for the best. Coming back made me realize I was chasing something I thought would make me happy. I thought he would make me happy, but ...' Laura tipped her head back and stared at the yellowed ceiling.

'What will make you happy, Laura?' Stella asked matter-of-factly.

Laura sighed. Stella always knew how to ask the hard questions. 'I think this will,' she said, pushing her notes forward.

Laura watched as Stella's eyes scanned the pages, her head nodding, mouth twisting.

'If you'd told me even a month ago that I'd be sitting here discussing my future in Banyula, I'd have called you crazy! It's the last thing I ever wanted,' Laura continued.

'You know, your mum always said she thought you'd come back one day.' Stella smiled.

'She did?'

Stella nodded, swallowing the last of her own coffee. 'Yep. Said she knew you would have to stop running one day. That you'd come back to make peace with what happened.'

'She was always a lot wiser than me. Pity I didn't inherit her foresight.'

'But you did, Laura. Look at you. You're here.'

'Only because I promised.'

'Promised who?'

'Mum. She made me promise to say goodbye to Ryan.' Her eyes began to cloud again.

'And have you?'

Laura nodded as Shea rubbed her back.

'Well, good,' Stella said, reaching her hand across to Laura's. 'And this sounds like a fantastic idea.'

'I think so too. I really think it can work,' Shea added.

'Absolutely. God knows we need it around here,' Stella replied. 'The kids need something, and I love that you want to catch them before it's too late.'

Laura saw the worry creep over Stella's face. 'How's Gem been?'

Stella shook her head. 'No different. I'm trying a new tactic. Doing nothing.' She forced a small laugh.

'Oh, Stel. Maybe I could try and talk to her again?'

'I don't think so. I don't know why, but every time I mention your name, she switches right off.' Stella put on the oven mitts and took the brownie out of the oven. Laura's and Shea's eyes lit up.

There was a knock at the door, and Stella frowned. 'Don't know who that would be?'

'Oh, that will be Tom. Sorry, he said he needed to see me urgently. I hope that's okay.'

'Of course, love. There's enough brownie to go round,' Stella said, walking down the hall to open the door.

Laura and Shea gathered the paperwork, both smiling proudly at each other before Stella returned.

'I think I might put the washing on the line and leave you to it,' she said, leaving the room.

Laura spun her seat around to be faced with not only Tom, but also Rachel. She swallowed.

'Hi, Laura,' Tom said. 'I'm sorry to turn up here, but ...' He glanced at Shea and furrowed his brow.

Shea turned a bright shade of red. 'Um, I can wait outside,' she said, starting to get up.

'No, stay. This is Shea,' Laura said. 'Shea, this is Tom. And Rachel.'

The three made quiet and polite hellos before Rachel began talking.

'I'm sorry, Laura, but I really need to speak to you.'

'I don't have anything to say to you, Rachel. What's in the past needs to stay there. I need to move on. We all do.'

'Lauz, you really need to hear what she has to say,' Tom interrupted.

'What? That she's sorry? That she didn't mean to sleep with my boyfriend, and then fall pregnant?'

Tom frowned. 'Pregnant?'

'Oh, hasn't she told you either? Why am I not surprised?' Laura tried unsuccessfully to fight the anger that had risen from inside again. She may have thought she could make amends with Rachel, but thinking and the reality of doing so were two different things.

Rachel shifted nervously on her feet, her head hanging low.

'You had Ryan's child?' Tom asked.

'That's why I went away after the accident. Mum and Dad thought it would be for the best. And of course, "for the best" meant so they weren't involved in any scandal. You know, can't bring shame on the local doctor.'

'Look, I'm fine to wait outside, Laura, really,' Shea interjected, shifting uncomfortably.

'No, it's fine. Whatever Rachel has to tell me she can tell me right here, right now.' Laura looked Rachel directly in the eye, her heart twisting with emotion. Rachel looked tired, as if she was carrying the weight of the world, but she deserved it. Laura fought with her clashing emotions. 'Well?'

Rachel took a deep breath before speaking. 'I was the last to see Ryan. Before he died.'

Laura flinched, then gathered her composure and rolled her eyes. 'More lies, Rachel? I can't deal with more lies from you.'

'I don't think she's lying,' Tom said.

'I'm not lying. It's true,' Rachel said, slumping down at the kitchen table.

'Tell her,' Tom said, his voice barely a whisper. Laura tightened her arms across her chest and stared at Rachel.

'I saw Ryan on the track when he was talking to Tom. Then I saw Tom walk away,' she began. 'I didn't know what had happened, and I didn't know where you were. But I knew Ryan wasn't in a good place. I just wanted to talk to him. He'd told me about his parents earlier that day. I knew he was upset, but he shrugged it off. He'd been drinking all afternoon. That's why he was already drunk when the party started. And then, halfway through the party when Tom started to confront Laura, I tried to speak to Ryan, but he stormed off.

'I saw Joel and he told me they'd gone down the river to smoke some pot, but Ryan had stayed there after they'd left. I was worried about him, so I left the party to find him. When I came back, everyone was gone, so I began walking home. That's when I saw him on the tracks. I just wanted to make sure he was okay. I was going to tell him I couldn't do it anymore. Behind your back.' Rachel's eyes caught Laura's, and she quickly looked up at the ceiling. Tears spilled down onto her lightly freckled cheeks.

'He was just sitting there. So sad. So broken. I'd never seen him like that.' Rachel's voice broke and she blinked more tears. 'I'm so sorry, Laura. I know it doesn't mean anything now. But ...'

Laura swallowed back her own tears. What did it matter what Rachel was saying? It didn't change anything. 'Just tell me what happened.' Laura sighed. As much as she didn't want to hear it, as much as she still didn't believe it, Laura knew she had to hear the full story.

'He kept saying that it was over. Everything was over. You and him. Him and I. Rambling that he was no good and we both deserved better. I tried to talk to him. Tried to tell him everything would be okay if we just sat down and talked about it.' Rachel was visibly shaking now. She gripped both her hands tightly as she spoke to try and stop the movement.

'I reached over for him, but he stumbled to his feet, pushing me away, saying he was dangerous. He was just like his father and couldn't be trusted. That he needed to get away from everyone. It was like he was someone else, Laura. It wasn't Ryan. He was talking crazy. I know he was drunk, stoned, whatever, but it was more than that. I was so upset, and then I told him ...'

'Told him what?' Laura furrowed her brow, looking from Rachel to Tom. Tom shifted on his feet.

Rachel hung her head. 'I told him I was pregnant.'

'You told him then?' Tom said.

Rachel nodded.

'I'm so sorry, Laura,' Rachel said. 'For everything that happened. What we did. That's not what friends do. And then, after he died, knowing it was my fault ...' She drifted off for a moment. 'I need to know that you can forgive me.'

'Hang on.' Tom held his hands up. 'I'm lost. You didn't tell me this part of the story.'

Rachel stayed silent.

Laura furrowed her brow, trying to make sense of what Rachel was saying, 'But that still doesn't explain why you think you were the last one to see him.'

Rachel peered into the distance between Laura and Tom, her eyes vague and glassy. 'When I told him I was pregnant, he turned toward me, in shock I guess, and he started breathing heavy. He was really angry. He said he didn't believe me.' Rachel began sobbing, her shoulders shaking as she pushed the words out. 'Then, then he stumbled backwards, and I don't know, lost his footing or got his foot caught on the rail and he fell back onto the track. I don't know exactly what happened.' Rachel's voice went quiet, her eyes staring as if back in the moment. 'I can still hear the thud of his head,' she said, squeezing her eyes tight. 'He didn't move. I tried to wake him up. I pulled at him, yelled his name...'

'Was he breathing?' Shea asked.

'Yes, I think so. I tried to pull him off the tracks, but god, he was so heavy. There was blood seeping out of his head, and I didn't know what to do. So, I went to get help. I was going to run to your house, Laura, but I ... I got really scared. I didn't know what to do.'

Laura covered her face with her hands.

'Laura?' Tom looked at Laura, his face awash with confusion.

'No, you didn't come to my house. You didn't. Mum would have told me!' Laura said, confused. Swirling black-and-white images began to flicker through Laura's mind again.

'I panicked. I ... I ran ... I ran down to the river. I was so scared. I didn't want ... I didn't ...' Rachel shook violently, spluttering through her fingers across her mouth.

'You left him there?' Laura's voice quivered as the reality of what Rachel said began to sink in. She felt like the oxygen had been sucked out of the room, and the walls began closing in around her.

'No. I don't believe it. That can't be right,' Laura breathed. This was all too much. So many different versions of events. None of them making sense. There was no answer. No one really knew what happened. Tom, her, Rachel.

'I'm sorry, Laura,' Rachel whispered. Laura stared ahead blankly.

The back door opened, and Stella entered, carrying a washing basket. 'Everything okay in here?' she asked, placing the basket on the bench.

No one replied.

'What's going on?' Stella asked again, her face tight with concern.

Tom was first to speak. 'Rachel was the last to see Ryan alive.'

'She left him on the tracks,' Laura said. Shea sat wide-eyed, unmoving. Rachel sobbed into her hands.

Stella pulled back sharply, as if shocked, and then let out a heavy sigh. 'Oh, god.' She shook her head.

'What is it?' Laura asked, frightened by the look on Stella's face.

'Judy told me not to, but this has got to end.' All eyes turned to

Stella. 'Laura, that's not what happened. Well, whatever she said may have happened, but that's not the full story.'

At that moment, Gemma entered the kitchen, slamming her hands on the benchtop, staring at Laura, who jumped to her feet. 'You need to tell her, Mum,' she said, her lips pursed.

'Tell me what?' Laura said.

A look crossed over Stella's face that Laura couldn't place. Shock? Fear? Stella's brow furrowed and the whites of her eyes glowed.

'Gemma, stop.'

Gemma scowled at Stella. 'Maybe if this town stopped keeping so many secrets, things would be better!' she blurted out.

'Now isn't the time or the place,' said Stella, rounding the bench toward Gemma.

'You don't remember, do you?' Gemma turned to Laura again. Her stance was wide, her face flushed red.

'Remember what?' Laura stammered.

Gemma rolled her eyes. 'Well, I remember as plain as day. Mum crying, whispering to Dad what had happened. I might have only been a kid, but I knew what I was hearing.'

'Gemma. Enough. This isn't yours to tell.'

But Gemma ignored her and glared at Laura. 'You killed Ryan.'

The rush of blood to Laura's head was like a jet plane. She tried to gasp for air, but it was as if her lungs had frozen.

'What?' she finally managed.

'Gemma!' Stella yelled. 'That isn't true! That's not what happened.'

'I heard you say it!' Gemma yelled back. 'That's why she ran away. That's why she left me here.' Gemma was crying now as she looked at Laura. 'You were like my big sister,' she said, her voice now almost a whisper. 'I looked up to you. And then you ...' Her voice trailed off.

Laura felt like she was out of her body, floating above the kitchen, witnessing a movie scene in a movie. She was trying to speak, but she was unable to make a sound; the noise in her head was too loud. She blinked, trying to focus, but everything began whirling around then faded to black.

36

'LAURA? LAURA?'

Laura opened her eyes to see Stella's face close to hers. Her head was cold, and she reached up to feel a wet towel across her forehead, a dull ache knocking behind her eyes.

'Ah, there you are. You fainted, love. You're okay,' Stella said, adjusting the knitted throw across Laura's chest. Laura's eyes began to focus, and she remembered she was in Stella's living room, lying on the couch. She could hear a few hushed voices in the room. And then she remembered what Gemma had said.

'I didn't kill Ryan!' Laura said, sitting up, panic thickening her throat.

'Shh. I know. I know. Of course you didn't. It was an accident. A tragic accident.' Stella gently eased her back down.

'But it wasn't an accident. He, he killed himself. I read his journal. Gemma read part of it too. Why? Why would she say I killed him? Why would she say it, Stella?' Nothing was making sense to Laura, and her head began pounding louder. She squeezed her eyes to try and stop it.

'It doesn't matter. It's all okay,' Stella was saying.

'But it's not okay!' Laura demanded. Why wasn't Stella listening to her?!

'Lauz, it's all right.' Tom appeared beside her, stroking her arm.

'Tom?' Laura said. 'What happened? Tell me.' Laura's eyes glanced around. Rachel and Shea were sitting beside each other on the couch, their faces pale, while Gemma sat cross-legged on the floor, picking at the carpet.

'I'm so sorry about everything, Laura,' Tom said.

'I didn't know any of it either,' Rachel said. 'If I had, if we had,' she looked at Tom, 'we would have never let you turn away from us. You needed us.'

Laura sat up. Now she was angry. Her head throbbed, but it was nothing compared to the confusion that clouded her mind. 'What are you all talking about?'

'You still don't remember, do you?' Stella said gently.

'Remember what?'

Stella shook her head. 'It was such a shock. Your mum, she didn't know what to do. She thought sending you away to your aunt's would be for the best. You refused to go to the doctor, then refused the counseling. You shut yourself off, and that's how you dealt with it. A type of dissociative amnesia, I think Judy said the doctor thought it could have been. It was hard to know without a proper diagnosis, but that's what was most likely.'

Laura knew what that term meant. 'What? Me?'

'From ... from that night, love.'

'But I remember everything that happened that night. I remember the next morning. Mum telling me about Ryan. Running out to the train tracks. Telling Mum I wanted to go away. It was my idea to go to Melbourne, not hers.'

'Our memories play tricks on us, love. Especially when things are too painful. The only way your brain knew how to deal with such a shocking thing was to forget the painful details. Make new memories, even,' Stella was saying.

Laura's shoulders felt heavy, her head like it was on fire. 'I don't under—' and then suddenly, mid-sentence, she stopped. A memory flashed out of nowhere. Ryan. Sticky, congealed blood matted the hair on the side of his head. He was standing outside her bedroom window.

Laura threw her hands up to her face and began shaking her head. 'No ... no.'

'Laura?' Tom knelt and put his hand on her knee. 'I had no idea, Lauz. Neither did Rachel.'

'I'm so sorry, Laura. I have nightmares. I can't ...' Rachel's voice began to crack.

'No, that's not right. It can't be right,' Laura said, squeezing her eyes tight, trying desperately to bring the faded memory back to life.

Laura opened her eyes and looked at Stella, her brows knitted and eyes as large as dinner plates. 'No? Oh my god.' Then Laura froze as the memory came fully into focus.

'Neither of you were the last to see Ryan alive,' she whispered. 'I saw him! I saw it happen!' Her hand flew to her mouth.

'Laura, it's okay.' Stella sat next to her, trying to pull her into her arms, but Laura jumped to her feet, the wet towel slapping on the floor.

Laura was pacing now as the memory picked up speed. 'It must have been after you saw him, Rachel, because his head,' she put her hand to her own forehead, 'was all bloody. The blood. It ran down the side of his face. He was there at my window. I remember.' Nausea filled Laura's stomach.

Rachel's face paled.

'I remember,' Laura said.

Laura sat down in the middle of the couch as the memory now

fully formed replayed to her as clear as day. 'He knocked on my window. I wasn't asleep.' Laura shook her head. 'It wasn't long after I'd got into bed. I remember hearing the train whistle, and then a few minutes later, I heard my window rattle.'

Laura looked at pale-faced Tom. He was on his feet now, beads of sweat forming on his brow.

'Laura, don't. It doesn't matter. It won't change anything.' He turned toward her.

She shrugged him away.

'Let her go on, Tom,' Stella added. 'Remembering might be the best thing for her.'

Laura squeezed her eyes closed, watching the memory as if it were an old black-and-white movie. 'I opened the window and saw the blood and asked him what happened. He said he couldn't remember. I wanted to get Mum, but he didn't want me to. He said he'd have to go to hospital and that he didn't want to upset his gran. Then ... then I told him to go away. That I didn't want to see him.' Laura gasped, trembling. 'I was angry with him. I wanted him to leave me alone.'

'You didn't let him in?' Rachel said slowly.

'No, but he kept tapping on the window and I, I ...' She began to sob. She continued recalling the memory.

'Go away, Ryan. Please. I don't want to see you,' Laura cried, pressing her hands over her ears. Her stomach churned with acid. And then her mum knocked on the door and entered in her dressing gown. 'Laura? What is it?'

Ryan tapped on the window again.

'Who's there?' Judy said, entering the room and peeking out from behind the blind.

'No. Mum. Don't,' Laura cried, trying to pull her mum's arm.

Tears were streaming down her face now. She didn't want her mum to know.

'Oh my god! Ryan!'

Laura chased after her mum as she ran down the hall, out the front door, and around the side of the house. Ryan had already started clambering over the front fence.

'I'm sorry, Mrs. Murphy. I'm going. I'm going.'

'Mum! Let him go!' Laura screamed, pulling at her sleeve. 'It doesn't matter.'

'Laura. Stop it! He's hurt.'

'I'm okay, really,' Ryan said as he climbed over the knee-high wire gate. 'I'm going to make things right, Laura. I promise.'

'Ryan! Come back here. You're hurt. You need a doctor,' Judy said, standing in the middle of the path. 'What on earth happened?' she called before she turned to Laura and grabbed her by the arm. 'What happened? Are you okay?'

Laura shrugged, watching as Ryan stumbled down the middle of the road. 'I'm fine, Mum. Ryan's fine. It's nothing. Please, please. I just want to go to sleep,' Laura cried, pulling at her mum.

'I'm going to ring the ambulance.'

'Mum! No!' Laura looked toward Ryan as his dark figure began to disappear toward the railway line. Then she heard the screen door slam as her mum went inside.

Laura panicked. She had to get Ryan back here and make him tell her mum he was okay. Otherwise everyone would know. Everyone would know he cheated on her. That she wasn't a good girlfriend. She ran down the road toward Ryan.

'Ryan! Wait! Please,' she screamed at him, but he didn't stop. He'd reached the railway line, but instead of going under the pedestrian tunnel, he climbed up the embankment.

'Ryan! Please come back,' she yelled in a hushed voice, trying not to disturb any of the sleeping houses.

He turned toward her, and she saw his white teeth catch in the streetlamp. He was smiling. Laura reached the ridge, her breathing heavy. 'Ryan, just come back. Tell Mum you're okay,' she panted. 'Please. She's going to call an ambulance.'

'It's okay, Laura. Everything's going to be okay. I'm not going to be like my father. I have to be a man. I have to be a father now. I'll marry Rachel. I'll make it okay. I can't fix us. I broke us. I know it now. I know it was my fault. But I won't fuck up anymore. I promise. I'll make you proud. I'll be there for Rachel. For our child. I don't care if we're too young. We'll make it work. Everything will work out.' He let out a laugh as he almost lost his footing on the loose stones, stumbling back to his feet. 'We'll look back on this in ten years and laugh about it. We will.'

Laura rubbed her face with her hands. He was crazy. He'd gone mad. He did need a doctor. 'Ryan, what are you talking about? Come back!'

Laura heard the whistle first, not the rumble. She was used to the rumble of the train, but the whistle caught her off guard, so close, so piercing. A light grew closer, shining off the rails of the track. Ryan continued down the middle of the tracks, the light shining on his back. 'I'm okay, Laura. I'm going to find Rachel. Tell her it's all going to be okay.'

Laura's heart stopped. The train. It was going too fast. Ryan wasn't looking. He hadn't seen. How did he not see it? Not hear it?

'Ryan! Get off!' Laura's throat hurt with the strain of her scream.

At the last moment, Ryan turned his head toward the train. The screeching of the brakes cut through Laura's own scream. She ran toward the track, but the gust of wind from the train pushed her back. 'Ryan!' she screamed. Then another voice from behind her, her mum's voice. 'Ryan! Oh my god, Laura.' The last thing

Laura felt was the biting of the asphalt into her knees as she fell to the ground and into her mother's arms.

LAURA SAT on the couch dazed after telling the story, the tick of Stella's grandfather clock the only sound in the room. Tom, Rachel, Shea, Stella, and Gemma sat silently.

'It was an accident,' Laura whispered, all the energy knocked out of her.

The grandfather clock chimed out and echoed around the room, but it took a moment for anyone to move, as if the truth had frozen them in time as they processed it.

Tom was the first to move.

'Lauz, I ...' he began, slumping next to her on the couch.

Laura nodded. She felt herself shaking. Shivering. It was an accident. Ryan didn't kill himself. It was an accident. An unfortunate series of events no one could have ever foreseen. Laura thought back to Ryan's diary. His darkest thoughts, harrowing, filled with utter hopelessness. He masked himself so well. Kept everything so well hidden while Laura carried on blissfully with her rose-colored glasses. Laura's thoughts ducked and wove around each other, tangling themselves in knots. There were no clear answers. No one was to blame. Just an indecipherable, black inkblot that had permanently stained her—stained all of them —forever.

37

THE FLORESCENT LIGHT over Stella's kitchen table flickered. After Tom, Rachel, and Shea had left, Stella insisted Laura stay and had promptly sat her down at the kitchen table with a bowl of leftover spaghetti. 'You need to eat, Laura. I know it's all a shock, but you need to eat,' she'd said. Laura sat pushing spaghetti around the bowl, her appetite nonexistent.

Despite all the revelations and regaining her memory, Laura felt surprisingly numb. Almost at peace.

'I'm sorry I blurted it out before. Sometimes I don't think before I speak.' Laura looked up to see Gemma standing in the doorway, picking off the black polish on her fingernails.

'It's okay, Gem,' Laura said. 'I guess you helped me remember.'

'I s'pose. I was just angry. I didn't mean you killed him. Well, I thought that's what happened until you remembered it.'

'Why were you angry? At me?'

'I dunno. I just thought you were mocking me. Telling me I was like Ryan, when all along you were to blame for it, at least I thought. I guess I just felt like I was getting all the bad attention and you got off again.'

'I'm sorry, Gem, I wasn't trying to interfere. I truly just wanted to help you.'

Gemma shrugged, and Laura pushed herself from the table.

'I do see a lot of Ryan in you. But only in that I think you feel like you've got nowhere to turn. Like Ryan.'

'I don't need to be saved, you know.'

Laura looked at Gemma. Behind her scowl, beyond the black eye makeup, Laura could see her determination, but also her fear. Fear of needing someone. Fear of not knowing what choices to make. Fearing she'd make, or already had made, the wrong ones. Laura bit her lip, contemplating what to say next without upsetting her.

'I know you don't, Gem. I can see how strong you are. So much stronger than me. You know, I always wanted a sister. Someone to count on, someone to fight with.' She smiled and saw Gemma's mouth twitch as well. 'I let you down, running away like that. But if you let me, I'm here for you now. I know I'm a bit messed up, but maybe we could work through stuff together.'

Laura watched as Gemma shifted on her feet, considering what Laura had said. No eye rolls. Not yet anyway. Gemma tilted her head. 'You're not going home to the city?'

The back door creaked open, and Stella manoeuvred a large load of dry washing through the space, pausing to pick up a sock that fell off the stack. 'You two okay?' she asked, plonking the basket on the table.

Laura took a deep breath. 'I was just telling Gemma I'm planning on sticking around.'

Stella's eyes rose, the lines on her forehead thickening. 'Good news, hey, Gem?' It was more of a statement than a question.

Gemma smiled.

. . .

LAURA WAITED on the front porch for Tom and Rachel to arrive. They'd arranged to meet and say goodbye to Ryan. All three of them together. And although Laura's stomach flipped with apprehension, she knew it was the right—the only—thing to do.

Tom and Rachel arrived within minutes of each other, Rachel holding a gorgeous bouquet of purple and white orchids. Laura grabbed her own bunch of white lilies off the front verandah and stood up, sucking in a deep breath of courage.

Rachel leaned in and wrapped her arms around her, the brokenness between them slowly knitting their friendship back together. Laura inhaled the soft, vanilla scent of Rachel, remembering what a kind and beautiful person she still was. One teenage mistake couldn't change that. Laura saw how Ryan could have opened up to her. Mitchell was lucky.

'You sure about this?' Tom asked, his hands shoved deep in his blue jean pockets.

Laura nodded, 'Yep.' She exhaled. 'Phones off, everyone. This is just for us.'

They walked silently toward the railway line. A couple of teens on bikes screeched by, and an elderly couple walking their Jack Russell nodded politely as they passed. Once they'd reached the walkway under the tracks, they turned off and made their way through the scraggly bush.

Not long after Ryan's death, the track was lined with a ten-foot chain fence, stretching fifty meters on either side of the walkway. A deterrent, a protective barrier.

Approaching the tracks, Laura wondered what went through Ryan's mind the moment he turned into the train. Did he really not see it? How was that possible? Was he really planning on making things right? Being there for Rachel? As much as Laura wanted to understand the hopelessness and the frustration that crippled Ryan, she wanted to know how it manifested inside and built into something bigger, something that seemed unsurmountable.

She smiled. Hindsight brought such clarity. As much as she thought she loved Ryan, she loved the *idea* of Ryan more. The teenage vision of perfect, young love. Handsome, vibrant, exciting, and full of anticipation. It ignited a current through her that made her feel more alive than she ever had. Real love, on the other hand; real love was plain and simple. It may not always spark adrenaline or passion, yet it was deep under many layers of meaning. Real love was often right there in front of you, overlooked for the shiny gem of young love sparkling in the sunlight. It was only now she understood.

As the sun slowly sank in the distance, the sky changed to a deep midnight blue. The shadows of houses and trees darkened and lengthened. The low-lying clouds offset by the twilight were a perfect backdrop to say goodbye to Ryan. A shiver ran up Laura's spine as they stepped out onto the tracks, checking up and down to make sure no one was there and nothing was coming. Laura had checked the timetable, and the next train wasn't due until 8:45. They had half an hour.

Tom encased Laura's hand, helping her to balance on the sharp blue rocks shifting under her feet. Rachel hung her head, face glistening with silent tears. Laura took hold of Rachel's hand and they stood, heads down, the gentle hum of life surrounding them but the finality of death uniting them.

Laura could feel the emotion building. It raced through her veins, grabbed at her chest, and clawed at her throat. When she finally let out a gasp of sobs, the relief of letting go overwhelmed her. Tom stared silently, his eyes heavy, mouth tight. Rachel squeezed Laura's hand. Laura wanted to say something, but the emotion-filled silence said it more eloquently than any words could.

Bending down, Laura placed the lilies at the side of the rail, her fingers lingering on the smooth iron, as if she were once again touching Ryan's soft, tanned skin. Rachel placed her flowers beside them and gulped back her own tears. Tom squatted down and pulled out his phone to play the song they had chosen. The haunting introduction of INXS's 'Never Tear Us Apart' settled in the air as Michael's velvet voice filled the void. Laura's tears fell fast, washing away the grief and hurt and bringing forgiveness in its wake. Goose bumps pricked at her arms, making her shiver as she thought of Ryan, of the four of them in simpler times. She allowed the good memories she'd hidden to flow into her consciousness. The love, the fun, the freedom of their youth. It may have been only for a few months, but she remembered those moments with a full heart, no longer allowing them to be tainted by the loss of innocence from the event that had torn them apart. For a brief moment, the four were reunited.

LAURA AND TOM waved Rachel off outside the front gate. They planned to catch up that weekend at the park, so Laura could officially meet Mitchell. They would take things slowly, but eventually Rachel wanted Mitchell to learn more about Ryan. About the good person he was. Rachel wanted Laura to be her son's godparent.

'Guess I'd best be off too,' Tom said, placing his Akubra back on his head.

Laura caught his hand in hers, 'Tom. Wait,' she said. 'I know a lot has happened over the past few weeks since I got back.'

Tom raised his eyebrows. 'You're telling me.' He smiled.

'I meant everything I said.' Laura looked up at Tom, his dark curls flicking in the slight breeze, his eyes dark in the night. 'I love you.'

He reached out to Laura and gently stroked her cheek with the back of his thumb, causing a warmth to flood through her entire body. 'Are you sure?'

'I'm sure.'

'I don't need your money, Laura. I don't need help. I just want someone to love me. Like I love them. Like I love you.'

Laura's heart felt like it was about grow arms and jump out of her chest and embrace Tom all on its own. The feeling encompassed her whole body. She wanted to dive into his eyes and get lost in them forever. 'I can't keep running, Tom. And even if I did, every road leads back here to you. So much in the past has tried to keep us apart, but I won't let anything come between us again.'

Laura lifted herself onto her tiptoes and kissed him. A kiss strong and passionate. A kiss of a new love, but a love with a past. A kiss for the future. Tom lifted her up in his arms and pulled away enough so he could speak. 'I love you, Laura.'

EPILOGUE

Spring 2019

Laura swung gently on the old wooden swing, sipping on a steaming cup of English Breakfast, her feet dangling below her. In the distance under the canopy of the peppercorn tree, she watched Tom teasing Rosie with treats. Rosie's tail was wagging way too fast for her to sit in any controlled manner. The late afternoon sun poked its way through the branches, casting shadows on Tom's face. Her Tom. The Tom she had finally let into her heart, which had since been filled with an overwhelming sense of contentment. Things were good.

The insurance money covered the flood damage, Tom's genetics contract had come through, and the bank was happy again, and they'd been spending time with Rachel and Mitchell. Mitchell was a ball of energy and loved visiting Tom and Laura on the farm. He'd help Tom with the calves and then they'd all sit around the bonfire, toasting marshmallows. Tom had planned on checking the swimming hole and affixing a new rope to teach Mitchell to swing off it now that he could swim properly.

Laura had completed her counseling course and set up an office on the main street. Although there were still a lot of plans to finalize, the farm sessions were coming together too. Laura hoped to begin them early the following year. Gemma had already begun working on the farm with Tom and the other farmhands, and her outlook on life had done a complete turnaround. She still had moments where she slipped back toward depression, but Laura had taught her skills on how to deal with those times. Gemma also made a bunch of friends through volunteering with Greening Australia, an environmental organization that focused on restoring natural habitats and environments. She also had her eye on one of Tom's farmhands, which Laura was constantly jibing her about.

Laura smiled to herself. She never would have believed this would be her life. But she was home. And the contentment it brought her made her realize how grateful she was to have found it again. Not only was she happy, but she was also making a difference. For her hometown. For Ryan. This was the first time in so long she felt she was where she was meant to be.

She blew on her tea before taking another sip and exhaling. The breeze rustled the long grass across the paddocks as the Angus lingered peacefully, enjoying the last few rays of sunshine. She took in another deep breath of country air, filled with eucalyptus and wild rosemary. The air was different out here. So familiar, so full of life, peace, and warmth. To Laura, it was as if they were, in that very moment, the only things that mattered. Everything, everyone, she loved was here. She smiled. It had been right here under her nose for so long.

Thinking back now, she could see her love for Tom had been there all along. She'd just been attracted to the shiny object she thought was out of her reach. For some reason, she had to take the long way around, but it had brought her back home.

The past year had taught her to trust her instincts and delivered her closer to forgiveness and understanding. She'd learned to open up the box of hidden memories and sit with them. But to also remember the good memories. The bad memories were only meant to color her life experience, not taint it. Her safe place to fall was where she always ended up—with Tom.

Tom threw his hands in the air in bewilderment as Rosie slobbered all over his face, before running in circles trying to sniff out the treats in the back pocket of his jeans. Even eighteen months later, she was still a puppy at heart and most definitely Tom's shadow. Laura felt as if her heart was going to explode in her chest, as if the birds and wildlife would begin singing to her like in *Snow White.* She felt complete. No longer running from someone or to someone. She was just being. And it felt good. She subconsciously rubbed her hand over her belly, ready for the new experiences life was going to bring.

She finished the last of her tea and put the cup down on the ground beside her. As she looked down, she noticed a single white feather. She smiled, picked it up, and ran it along the side of her cheek. It was so beautifully soft.

A glimpse of Ryan's dimpled smile flickered through her mind, resulting in a tear pricking at the corner of her eye. He would always be with them, an intrinsic part woven into their past and forever binding them all together. The tear slowly fell down her cheek, but she didn't brush it away. Instead, she let it soak into her skin, absorbing it back into her body. A memory to hold forever.

If you enjoyed *The Memories We Hide*, I'd love for you to leave a review or Goodreads. Reviews are the easiest way to share the love and help an author, so thank you for taking the time.

You can also stay up to date with my new books by signing up to my VIP list. By signing up, you'll also receive a free ebook *The Collection* – handpicked fragments and short stories that I've written which are perfect for diving into with your next cuppa and maybe one of Stella's chocolate brownies! (Recipe at the back of this book!)

And if you want to say hi, please drop me an email through my website contact page or you can catch me on social media
Facebook
Instagram
Twitter

ABOUT THE AUTHOR

JODI GIBSON is an Australian women's fiction author, or as she likes to call it: *fiction with all the feels*. Her debut novel, *The Memories We Hide* was published in August 2019. Her next novel, *The Five Year Plan*, a lighter romantic women's fiction combining travel, food and romance will be published by Brio Books in September 2021 and is now available for pre-order.

Pre-order THE FIVE YEAR PLAN here

Jodi lives with her husband, daughters, and fur babies on a mini-farm in regional Victoria. She spends her spare time baking up sweet treats in her kitchen, reading and recommending her favourite books, and dreaming of her next travelling adventure. Sign up here for her monthly newsletter (& free short story)

Website: https://jfgibson.com.au/

ACKNOWLEDGMENTS

I'd always been excited by the prospect of writing my acknowledgements when I dreamed of becoming a published author. But, now that it's here, I don't know where to start!

Writing a book is initially a very solitary undertaking, but to take that messy first draft and turn it into a novel takes a village. I'm fortunate to have a wonderful village.

First props need to go to my amazing editor Nicola O'Shea, for without Nicola there would be no book. Her ability to 'get' my vision and help direct it into something of a publishable quality, is beyond brilliant and I am so grateful to have her by my side.

As an indie publisher I have so many people to thank who've helped me create a real book. Cover designer Stuart Bache who floored me with the very first concept. Jessica Holland and Stephanie Parent who helped me fine tune the final manuscript. And of course, the team at Polgarus Studios who were responsible for formatting. I can't thank you all enough.

To my writing mentors Fiona McIntosh, Natasha Lester, Allison Tait and Fiona Lowe, who have helped me transform from aspiring writer to published author. Each of you have helped and inspired me in different ways, but all of you have given me the confidence to believe in myself and my stories.

A huge thank you to my writing community. How grateful I am to be a part of a vibrant online community of inspiring, talented and wonderfully awesome women. I would not be here without your support and I must name each and every one of you. Vanessa Carnevale, Joanne Tracey, Natasha Lester, Pamela Cook, Louise Allen, Cassie Hamer, Kylie Orr, Cat Blessing, Kylie Hough, Melanie Strangio, Annabelle McInness, Claudine Tinellis, Kirsty Dummin, Leah Vevke, Michelle Barraclough, and Alyssa Mackay. Thank you. Thank you. Thank you!

To my Super Reader Team who have been instrumental in shaping this book and supporting me every step of the way. You guys are super special and I couldn't have done it without you.

It seems odd to acknowledge things such as podcasts and courses, but I would not have reached this point without them. To Valerie Khoo and Allison Tait and the *So you want to be a writer* podcast and Australian Writers Centre, you helped me begin my journey all those years ago, and you continue to make it a fun and informative ride. To Joanna Penn of *The Creative Penn*, and Mark Dawson of *The Self-Publishing Show*, who have taught me almost everything I know about the indie publishing world. And thankfully so. To Adam Croft's *Indie Author Checklist* who helped me get my head around the whole process, and to Sarah Painter's *The Worried Writer* podcast who continually helps me remember I'm not the only 'worried writer' out there.

And finally, the biggest thanks of all goes to Shane and our girls for putting up with me trying (mostly unsuccessfully) to juggle writing with life. Thank you for allowing to me to make writing a huge part of my life and supporting me following my dreams. And yes girls, they do come true.

STELLA'S CHOCOLATE BROWNIES

185 grams dark chocolate
125 grams butter
3/4 cup sugar
2 free range eggs
1 cup plain flour

Grease a deep 20cm square cake pan, and line the base with baking paper.

Melt chocolate and butter together in a saucepan over low heat, and stir in sugar and eggs, one at a time. Beat well with wooden spoon, then stir in sifted flour.

Pour into prepared tin and bake in moderate 180 degree Celsius oven for approx. 25 minutes. Cool in pan.

Remove slice from pan and sprinkle with icing sugar before cutting into squares.

Best enjoyed with a cup of tea.

Printed in Australia
Ingram Content Group Australia Pty Ltd
AUHW021025081123
386168AU00001B/3